"Do you have t̶

Liz questioned, thinking what beau̶... ... for a lunatic.

Garrett met her penetrating gaze. "Only the ones I've made love with."

Liz's breath caught in her throat. She might as well be honest with herself, she decided. To her dismay, an undeniable chemistry existed between them, regardless of the fact that history branded Garrett a murderer.

Garrett's words interrupted her thoughts. "I admit the consummation of our marriage wasn't the most fulfilling encounter either of us has ever experienced, but we agreed it was necessary so that the marriage couldn't be annulled on a technicality."

The present situation was inconceivable to Liz. Not only did he think she was married to him and carrying his brother's child, Garrett Rowland actually believed they'd been intimate!

This whole thing was too bizarre, even if she believed in the possibility of time travel....

Dear Reader,

They're spooky and they're creepy—but they'll never make you sleepy! They're our newest Shadows titles, guaranteed to keep you awake, reading—and shivering—long after you should have turned out the lights.

First up is the newest from Jane Toombs. *The Volan Curse* has it all: a sexy hero with just a touch of amnesia, and an innocent heroine who believes in the power of love and the hero's innocence—she hopes! There's also an evil family curse and a couple of villains who'll scare you out of your wits and make you glad you're safe at home, not roaming the grounds of Fenn Volan's familial estate.

Then travel back in time with Vivian Knight Jenkins in *By Love Possessed*. The post-Civil War past is only a lightning storm away for Liz Hayden. And so is a passionate affair with Garrett Rowland, the most sensual man she's ever met. But is he also the murderer history has branded him?

Next month, expect another shiveringly good time here at Shadows. And until then, be careful where you look for love. You never know what might be waiting for you . . . in the dark.

Yours,

Leslie J. Wainger
Senior Editor and Editorial Coordinator

Please address questions and book requests to:
Reader Service
U.S.: P.O. Box 1325, Buffalo, NY 14269
Canadian: P.O. Box 1050, Niagara Falls, Ont. L2E 7G7

VIVIAN KNIGHT JENKINS

BY LOVE POSSESSED

Published by Silhouette Books
America's Publisher of Contemporary Romance

 SILHOUETTE BOOKS

ISBN 0-373-27036-4

BY LOVE POSSESSED

Copyright © 1994 by Vivian Knight Jenkins

Printed in U.S.A.

VIVIAN KNIGHT JENKINS

is a native North Carolinian and lives in a rural community three hours from both the mountains and the coastline. She works in the academic advising center of a local college.

A creature of habit, she nonetheless delights in the changing seasons—spring cherry blossoms, summer storms, autumn leaves and crisp winter nights. Author of numerous romances, she's happiest when developing characters and plots, or researching through books and travel.

As a child she feared the dark and knows firsthand what makes the heart palpitate and the imagination soar. Now the mother of two teenagers, she says night has become a friend that allows her quiet writing time. Drawing from her intimate knowledge of both the darkness and romance, she explores the darker side of love in *By Love Possessed*.

In keeping with promises, this book is dedicated to Dawn, Ellores, Jean B., Jean H., Karen, Lois, Rebecca and Vickie

PROLOGUE

Odd, Liz Hayden mused. The early-evening thunderstorms that frequented the metropolitan New Orleans area during the waning summer months never frightened her. Ordinarily she'd hardly bat an eyelash at the gathering wind tugging at her striped muslin day dress. Or at the drumlike roll of thunder and the darkening sky. Or even the first fine mist of a sure-to-be-pelting downpour blowing in across the Mississippi River.

But today, for some inexplicable reason, the encroaching storm sent a shiver shimmying down her spine. The air felt abnormally static, hotter and heavier, like a human hand reaching out from the grave to caress her. It held the almost tangible promise of something more than simple, life-giving moisture. Of something powerful and disturbing—something formulated especially for her, and her alone.

Now she was really being fanciful! What had happened to the levelheaded composure so necessary to a librarian? If she could keep her cool with a horde of anxiety-ridden students with term papers due hugging her desk, she could weather a little ol' thunderboomer without turning to jelly, Liz told herself, clutching her nylon umbrella in one hand and a padlock key so tightly in the other that it left a toothy impression in her palm.

Liz frowned at the brooding sky. Apprehension getting the best of her, she added a healthy dose of zip to her already lengthening stride.

Today made the fifth time since she'd won the Elizabeth Rowland look-alike contest last month and volunteered as a tour guide at the historic homesite that she'd lost the coin toss and been forced to lock up the back gates. And never had the job spooked her.

Until now.

Liz eyed the second major contributor to her present state of uneasiness. Built of red brick showing through a veneer of cracking whitewashed plaster, the Rowland family vault appeared forlorn, ravaged by time and the steady decline of the estate following the Civil War. The codicil to the parish grant that had placed the estate in the local restoration society's competent hands required that the tomb, like the plantation house, be restored to its original beauty. Sadly enough, economics deemed it the last item on an endless list.

Like a strained whisper from the past, the wisteria-shadowed inscription arching across the tomb's warped doorway seemed to call to Liz. She paused, squinting up at the words—"Never To Be Forgotten"—carved above a rampant garland of roses. The blossoms appeared to undulate, then solidify once again before her eyes.

Liz gasped, scurrying past the tomb to glance uneasily down the quarter-mile oak alley leading back toward the rear entrance of Rowland Plantation. Wait until she returned to the house and told the other tour guides she'd fallen prey to an overactive imagination. They'd laugh themselves silly, she thought, unable to dispel the creepy sensation causing her scalp to prickle and her hands to tremble as she swung the creaky wrought iron-gate shut.

Unable to stop herself, Liz recalled reading that during a similar thunderstorm the plantation's mistress had vanished without a trace, blackening the already tarnished reputation of the estate's nineteenth-century owner—the legendary Garrett Rowland. Though Garrett had been acquited of his wife's murder due to lack of evidence, the stigma of guilt had dogged him the remainder of his life.

Intrigued by the unsolved disappearance, Liz had devised all sorts of possible scenarios. Each and everyone revolved around the fascinating and mysterious Garrett Rowland. Had he been man or monster? Insane, or simply cruelly calculating? Had he, as history suggested, been . . . capable of cold-blooded murder?

Peering over her shoulder as if invisible eyes might be watching her every move, she hastily ran the chain through the rusty, jaillike bars. Unlocking the padlock, she secured the shackle through the links and snapped it into place, pocketing the key.

"There. Done," she said with infinite satisfaction. Brushing her hands together, she pivoted, gathering the ankle-length skirts of her period costume to make a mad, if somewhat unladylike, dash for the house.

As if to dispute her statement, lightning brightened the bleak sky with jagged flashes of high-voltage electricity. Liz started as a particularly brilliant bolt split the heavens. It illuminated the sky with an almost spectral incandescence before touching down outside the gate to scorch a circular patch of crisp green grass into a smoking black hole.

The next violent discharge hit far too close for comfort, striking the top of an ancient, Spanish-moss-draped oak on the estate side of the fence. With a shudder and a wooden groan, the crown of the tree cracked, toppling over to crush the gate into a distorted heap of moisture-laden branches and mangled iron. At the same moment, almost as if the elements were singling her out, the wind surged, tearing the umbrella from Liz's grasp. Like a lost kite, it cartwheeled over the damaged gate, snagging on the power lines bordering the asphalt service road.

The rain started all at once, cascading from the sky in gray sheets, stinging her face and hands and deepening her honey-blond chignon to chestnut as it plastered the heavy knot to her head. Eyes widening, Liz frantically searched for someplace she could take shelter until the savagery of the storm abated. Her gaze fell on the only building between her and the antebellum plantation house—the tomb. Clear of the trees, still internally sound, it sported the added allure of a lightning rod. The gaping doorway beckoned like an open invitation.

Following a basic instinct for survival, Liz made a beeline for the Rowland family vault.

Loath to actually step inside the musty tomb, Liz huddled beneath the arch. Rain clinging like crystalline teardrops to her eyelashes, she slid her hands up and down her arms, breathing deeply to control her rising panic—panic made more acute by the eerie scent of roses wafting from the tomb's pitch-black interior.

The relentless storm stalked her. With an angry pop, a lightning bolt zigzagged directly above the tomb, hitting the metallic lightning rod as if targeting a bull's-eye. The walls of the vault trembled threateningly.

Horrified, Liz flung her arms over her head, only to be rocked by a powerful jolt of current shooting up through her canvas tennis shoes. The fiery sensation reminded her of stepping barefoot on broken glass.

Surging along her slender legs, the current traveled up her trunk to bombard her brain with splinters of white-hot light.

For a split second, Liz heard a woman sobbing as if her heart would break. Then the mournful keening subsided, swallowed by a moment of dead silence—a moment enhanced by the acrid aroma of singed hair blending with the subtle fragrance of roses.

CHAPTER ONE

Momentarily blinded, Liz sagged, throwing her arms wide, groping for the tomb's doorjamb to steady herself. Instead of wood, her hands met with soft, damp linen and hard, corded muscle. She retreated a step only to discover a cool marble panel pressing solidly against her spine.

"My God, Elizabeth!" a masculine voice growled impatiently, reaching her ears as if from a distance, though the man stood only inches away. "This is madness! At some point, this obsession of yours must cease. Michael wouldn't expect you to place fresh flowers on his coffin each and every day, regardless of the weather."

Liz wanted to correct the stranger, to explain that there were no remains in the vault. That over the years, the insufferable subtropical heat of the Louisiana summer had cremated the wooden coffins and their grisly contents as efficiently as a brick oven would have. That only rusty metal coffin hardware remained as a memorial to past Rowland generations. But her throat seemed paralyzed.

"Look at you! Your skin is as pallid as bleached cotton. And you've become so painfully thin, I could span your waist with my hands. Can't you see that you're making yourself ill with mourning?"

The rain was easing now, the thunder was receding and the somber clouds were shifting to cast mottled patterns of light and shadow across the rain-drenched landscape. Stunned and bewildered, Liz Hayden blinked, once...twice...three times. When that didn't work, she squeezed her eyes shut and slowly counted to ten. Like the spots produced by a camera's flash, she fully expected this man who smelled of spiced brandy and ginger tobacco to disappear when she reopened them.

He didn't. Not by a long shot.

"Damn it all, Elizabeth," he said, his voice growing stronger by the second, like a plane zeroing in for a pinpoint landing, Liz thought. "You're making me ill, as well. I haven't had a decent night's sleep since we married."

Married?

Liz opened her mouth to speak. But her lips refused to form the denial trapped in her larynx. Shaking her head, she placed both palms flat against the stranger's sternum and shoved, attempting to physically remove him from her path though inside she quaked with fear.

Expression darkening, he braced himself against her. "I must insist you accompany me back to the house."

Liz's tongue felt like putty. Had he been lurking along the oak alley, lying in wait for her? she wondered. And how did he know her name—her full name, rather than the nickname she preferred? She wasn't wearing her name tag, and she would certainly remember someone like him if he'd taken one of her tours during the day.

Teetering on the narrow borderline between calm authority and abject hysteria, Liz finally managed to whisper, "How...did you...

get onto the grounds? We don't . . . allow visitors in after four o'clock on Sundays. You're trespassing," she added accusingly, unable to keep the tremor from her voice.

As if accustomed to humoring such outlandish statements from her, the man said, in a deep, somber voice, "You're not yourself. You don't know what you're saying."

Liz responded defensively, "Yes, I most certainly do. The house . . . is officially closed for the day. I locked the back gate myself only a few moments ago. But then, that was before the tree fell and smashed it to smithereens."

Together they turned their heads and stared toward the spiked wrought iron-gate. It stood perfectly intact.

"But I saw the tree fall," Liz insisted in a hushed tone. "The lightning blasted the crown out of the oak, and it took a nosedive across the gate," she elaborated, experiencing the sinking feeling that something was terribly wrong. Beyond the undamaged gate, the service road had disappeared, taking the power lines and her umbrella with it!

"You're distraught, Elizabeth," the man assured her.

"I'm telling you it happened. A streak of lightning started a grass fire. I was more afraid of the flames than the storm. I was backing away from them, and the next thing I knew, a bolt hit the tree and—"

"I'll send the cook for Dr. Breninger. He'll bring you something to help you sleep."

Her hands fluttered from his chest to her sides, inadvertently brushing the ivory-handled knife riding jauntily in a sheath attached to his belted waist. Liz felt as if a leaden ball had settled in the pit of her stomach. He was armed!

"I . . . I don't need anything to sleep," she protested, her mind running a mile a minute. Maybe she was asleep. Perhaps she was already at home in her cozy little shotgun duplex in the Garden District, buoyed by her snug waterbed mattress, caught in the throes of a nightmare.

But the man felt so real. So solid. Seemed so virile, rationality argued. And, with the knife at his hip, far too menacing to be a dream-induced hallucination.

The man raked his fingertips roughly through his curling, sable hair—hair drenched from the same rain that dampened her own. "You're on the verge of causing me to lose patience with you," he ground out ominously.

Liz glanced at the knife, feeling as if her vertebrae were making fossil-style impressions in the tomb's door. "No. I have to...", she began, contemplating the question of the door. It hadn't existed moments earlier. Of that, if nothing else, she was absolutely certain.

Cursing beneath his breath, the man captured her clenched fists in his own strong grasp, pressing them almost painfully against his broad chest. Liz could actually feel the steady rhythm of his heartbeat through the gauzy material of his aubergine shirt.

Heart skipping in her chest, Liz studied his linen shirt in fascination. It tied at the throat with a drawstring instead of buttoning. And the black broadcloth pants that hugged his muscular thighs, tapering to tuck into leather riding boots, seemed a rather unusual choice of dress when denim and running shoes were all the rage.

"You have to what, Elizabeth?" he said, dragging her attention to his face. "You have to stand sentinel by the vault day and night and hope that by some miracle, if you stay out here long enough, if you pray hard enough,

if you suffer more than you already have, you'll somehow bring Michael back from the dead? You won't."
He frowned. "But I guarantee that if you continue at
this rate, you might well join him."

"I don't...understand," Liz managed to say, her
voice wavering with uncertainty. The man was invading her space, threatening her, and she could do nothing about it. How foolish to have left her cayenne
pepper spray on the homesite's kitchen counter with her
pocketbook and car keys.

Capturing her shoulders in his hard grip, the man
shook her.

"Listen to me, damn you! Think of your delicate situation. I refuse to allow you to do this to yourself and
the child you carry. Yellow fever stole my brother's life
from him, and there's nothing on this earth you can do
to change it."

Liz shook her head from side to side in earnest, not
knowing what else to do. There was no mistaking the
bitterness and resentment in his voice. It was as if he had
some personal vendetta against her.

Either the man was crazy, or her own near electro-
cution had catapulted her off the deep end. Because Liz
didn't have the faintest idea how he'd materialized, or
what child he was talking about, even though she sensed
something strangely familiar in the arresting quality of
his hypnotic cerulean eyes and the aura of danger emanating from his muscular six-foot frame.

Eyes narrowing, Liz concentrated on his face through
a debilitating haze of confusion. The way his dark hair
fell over his arrogant brow. The sensual fullness of his
lips. The faded scar that marred his beard-shadowed
cheekbone, making him appear all that much more intimidating.

She knew that face! But from where? Television? The library where she worked? An FBI poster at the local post office? She simply wasn't sure!

He bent slightly at the knees so that their faces were level. His demeanor was relentless. "I intend to force you to go on, just as you've forced *me* into this preposterous alliance."

Liz surveyed her own reflection in his turquoise-flecked eyes as he traced a callused fingertip across her ice-cold cheek and down along the side column of her throat. His touch seemed more warning than caress.

"Don't," Liz said haltingly, thinking that he'd been right. She did look as if she'd just been through an extended illness. Not at all like the conservative, athletic-minded, healthy person that she was in reality. And not at all like the fearless woman she liked to think herself.

"I know you're not dim-witted," he said. He slowly withdrew his hand. "You comprehend what I've said. I think it's more a matter of my allowing you to drift beyond caring." As he squared his shoulders, a grim look settled over his ruggedly handsome countenance. "In which case, I'm prepared to fight you right up to the end," he said, with a finality that frightened Liz far more than the recent thunderstorm.

"You've made a terrible mistake. I—"

Frustration clearly gaining the upper hand, he quickly interrupted her. "I can't condone you harming the child. I've sacrificed too much to see it safely birthed," he growled, his voice filled with scorn.

"What have you sacrificed?" Liz asked, fearing that her immediate safety required that she keep him talking.

He smiled sardonically, his expression suddenly ruthless and purposely intimidating. "Why, the thing I prized most highly—my freedom. But we need not re-hash this. I know you despise me. My sins are many. But that is neither here nor there, for we have a private understanding between us," he hissed. "You made me a promise, and I mean to hold you to your end of the bargain. That's the least you can do in exchange for my protection and the family name that goes with it."

Protection? Since when did she need protection, es-pecially that of a man's name? She'd done pretty well on her own . . . up until now.

"There's been some kind of a mistake," she said, her voice faltering. *A dilly of a mistake!*

He responded bluntly, his tone forebidding. "Have a care, Elizabeth. It's far too late for second thoughts. Your fate is sealed." His eyes glittered dangerously. "*I* make the rules, not Calvin Trexler."

Calvin Trexler. Now there was a name she recog-nized! He'd been a prominent New Orleans entrepre-neur around the time of the Civil War. Much of the glass and jewelry exhibited in the plantation's histori-cal museum was attributed to him—gifts through the years to his favorite cousin, Elizabeth.

Wide-eyed, Liz asked incredulously, "Who *are* you?" What insane asylum have you escaped from? she felt tempted to add, but refrained.

He chuckled without humor. "Why, the one and only Garrett Rowland."

Her own voice unnaturally high, Liz exclaimed, "Garrett Rowland!"

It was obvious the man was suffering from delu-sions. She'd heard of people with fixations like this. People who believed they were historical figures rein-carnated. But if he wanted to pretend he was Garrett Rowland, she wasn't going to argue with him.

"Garrett Rowland," he reiterated. "Remember me? Your husband, your legal guardian, your savior." His voice rose. "And your two-faced cousin can say or do anything he wants. I'm not the least bit impressed by his wealth. Calvin can go to hell, for all I care! If it comes down to it, I might send him there myself." The last sentence flowed from Garrett's lips in a snakelike hiss.

Liz cringed at the suppressed fury visible on his face. There was no doubt he hated Calvin Trexler, though she wasn't certain why. History had painted Elizabeth's cousin as a fine upstanding citizen.

Swallowing her fear, she said, "But I can't—"

"You've got to!" he exploded, cutting her off again. "We've had this argument before. Seven months from now, when you hold my brother's child in your arms, you'll see I was your only option."

Obviously this man was determined to coerce her into something by the sheer force of his will, Liz decided. She didn't like it one bit, but her saner side whispered incessantly, *Humor him.* If only she could reach the house, telephone the local police and explain that an armed kook was running loose on the grounds—an incredibly handsome kook, but a kook all the same— maybe they could make sense of the situation. Clear up all this nonsense about brothers and cousins, husbands and babies, promises and protection.

Liz cleared her throat, forcing herself to remain reasonably calm. In her self-defense classes, she'd learned that during a crisis it was mandatory to keep cool. That calmness represented the best chance for survival when battling an assailant.

Liz breathed deeply, mentally reaching down to her toes to tap a pocket of courage she hadn't even known she possessed. To her relief, her voice sounded relatively normal as she said, "Perhaps you're right. Maybe I can...I can wait a few months and...finish out the terms of our agreement...make it until the...the baby is born. I mean, if you think that's best, then it probably is. Right?"

The man relaxed perceptibly, though when he spoke again, a hint of sarcasm tinged his voice. "I can't tell you how pleased I am to finally hear you say those words. There was a point this evening when I thought we might never come to satisfactory terms."

She didn't have to humor him long before his grip slackened sufficiently to afford her the opportunity she sought. Making the most of the moment, Liz yanked free, darting past him. Skirts bunched up to her knees, she raced in the direction of the plantation house. But for some reason, the alley didn't look quite right. And the farther she went, the worse her disorientation became.

The spreading water oak lining the narrow avenue didn't seem as mature as she remembered them. Liz could even see the overcast sky peeping through where before the limbs had formed a continuous canopy. To compound her growing perplexity, unmarked forks splintered off to the right and the left of what she remembered as the main path. What a horrid time for her mind to be playing tricks on her. There was only one path leading from the house to the back gate—wasn't there?

Where had she gone wrong? This *had* to be some incredibly vivid daymare. She'd read about those waking fantasies which had all the qualities of a nightmare. She'd just never experienced one.

Of course, if it wasn't a daymare...

Liz paused and glanced furtively over her shoulder. Good, she'd lost him—but she didn't dare backtrack for fear of running into him again.

Liz forged ahead.

Several minutes later, she stumbled onto a kind of careless, overgrown garden. A plant enthusiast, Liz readily identified the magnolia, chinaberry and aromatic camphor trees overshadowing the gargoyled birdbath, the prickly holly and Spanish daggers, the disorderly Cherokee roses reaching out to entwine the concrete bench squatting within a rampant border of wild jasmine bushes. It was reigned over by a latticed gazebo in dire need of fresh paint. The garden might have been a pleasant place, if not for the neglect that lent it the creepiness of an abandoned cemetery, Liz mused fleetingly.

Disturbed that she'd never run across the garden before, she made a mental note to speak to the new plantation curator concerning her discovery. He was due to arrive any day. Perhaps he could shed some light on all this confusion. But for now, although she was winded, necessity dictated she continue on.

Liz sniffed the breeze, her senses telling her the river flowed nearby. Since the plantation rested near the banks of the Mississippi, it should be simple enough to follow it until she reached the security of the house.

Continuing on for what seemed like forever, Liz slowed to a jog as a levee rose into sight. *Wait one minute!* She might have overlooked a garden, but she'd be darned if she could miss something as big as a river levee, she thought. The hairs on the back of her neck rose to attention.

Thoroughly disoriented, Liz decreased her pace to an uncertain crawl. Then she realized that the stranger from the tomb was stalking her like a predatory animal, yelling passionately, "Don't run from me, Elizabeth!" She could hear his words clearly over the roar of the swollen Mississippi. And judging by the increasing volume of his voice, accompanied by the pounding of his footsteps, he was gaining on her.

Her muscles tensed as she fought down panic. Glancing from side to side like a cornered doe seeking a hidden thicket, Liz bounded down the levee, across the cypress landing and out onto the dock.

The man who called himself Garrett burst from the garden, stopping just short of the unrailed floating boat dock.

"You've led me a merry chase, but I'm in no mood for games. Come down off the dock before you're sorry," he demanded.

Secured with a coiled hemp line to one of the cleats ringing the dock, a small launch thumped against a pylon. Her back to the river, Liz glanced over her shoulder at the muddy water churning below.

"There's not supposed to be a dock here," she rasped, deeply troubled. *Nor an earthen levee. Nor a garden. Nor a darkly compelling man harboring an imaginary grievance against me and challenging my sanity.*

The stranger raised an eyebrow. "We've had a dock for as long as I can remember, Elizabeth. My grandfather built it years before the war. According to the account ledgers, you've caught the *J. M. White* from here for shopping in Natchez more times than I can count on both hands." As if to emphasize his statement, the haunting shriek of a steamboat whistle resounded in the distance.

Liz backed away, shaking her head. "No. I'm afraid you're mistaken. I can't be that disoriented. You see, there hasn't been a dock here since a hurricane washed it away at the turn of the century. That's another thing on the restoration society's list—replacing the dock."

Cautiously he stepped onto the dock. It swayed, dipping with his added weight. Eight feet separated him from her.

Liz's inner struggle to remain calm must have shown on her face, for he extended a hand toward her. "Come back to the house with me." His voice sounded soothing, yet she had the distinct impression that he held it tightly under control. Though it was obvious she faced a man accustomed to issuing orders and having them obeyed, she defied him.

"I want to go back to the house. But I don't want to go with you," she said. She retreated another step, realizing little by little that this was no dream. It was as real as the man standing before her.

He scowled, looking toward the heavens as if for strength. Then his lips tipped into a cunning smile.

"I'll have the cook make you a nice hot cup of rose-hip tea. You love rose-hip tea," he said cajolingly.

He wasn't fooling her. His tone was intentionally disarming, but his hooded eyes told her a story of their own.

"You're trying to manipulate me, and it won't work. Besides which, I don't drink hot tea," Liz responded, thinking how extraordinary it was to be carrying on a conversation about rose-hip tea, with a stranger who thought he was Garrett Rowland, on a levee that didn't exist any more than the marble door to the Rowland family tomb did.

"Why are you doing this to me? What kind of morbid game are you playing? Did someone pay you to confuse me like this, or is it a fraternity prank. Do you have a hidden camera somewhere?"

Liz watched his control break. "God's blood, Elizabeth! What are you talking about? Sometimes I could strangle you with my bare hands," he ground out between clenched teeth, flexing his hands against his muscular thighs.

Liz could almost feel his tapered fingers splayed around her throat, squeezing.

"This isn't funny. You're really scaring the heck out of me," Liz murmured, sidestepping to dodge past him once again. To her consternation, her foot tangled in the rope linking the launch to the dock cleat, and she stumbled backward instead.

With a surprised exclamation, Liz tumbled off the dock. Following a muffled splash, she slipped beneath the murky water, strangling as silt-tinged liquid rushed into her nose and mouth, stinging her eyes, loosening her hair from its pins so that the tendrils swirled around her head like a wavering halo.

A strong swimmer, Liz fought the current, attempting to kick to the surface of the churning river. She bobbed once, spitting out water and sucking in a great gulp of air. But the yards of saturated material fashioning her tour guide's costume quickly weighed her down, anchoring her to the river's slippery bottom like a cement suit.

Blood pressure skyrocketing, Liz fumbled frantically with the glass-beaded covered buttons on the bodice of the muslin day dress. Wet on wet, the buttonholes acted as if they'd been stitched closed against the buttons.

Damn! Double damn! An authentic reproduction,
her ensemble tipped the scales at fifteen pounds when
it was dry. Liz dreaded to think what it would register
now.

One way or another, the costume must go! Grabbing
the gown's pristine lace collar in both hands, Liz ripped
the bodice apart.

*Be cool. Stay calm now. You're a survivor. It'll be
okay. It's going to be all right,* Liz coached herself as
she wiggled the dress over her hips. Free of her body,
the stripped gown ballooned like a misshapen jellyfish,
the vigorous current instantly washing it out of sight.

Seconds lapsed into several minutes as Liz unzipped
the more deadly petticoats, peeling them off one by one,
until all that remained was her eyelet camisole, gossa-
mer silk underskirt, and lace-edged pantalets. *Ah, sweet
freedom,* she thought triumphantly. But by then it was
too late. Near exhaustion, ears ringing from the hydro-
static pressure underwater, lungs afire and head spinning dizzily, she let her natural reflexes take over and
began inhaling water.

CHAPTER TWO

Semiconscious, Liz sensed a presence nearby even before searching hands brushed against her, long before a muscular arm snaked around her waist, crushing her against a lean, hard flank. She was limp as a rag doll, and would gratefully have allowed Satan himself to ferry her to safety.

Trembling with exertion, slipping and sliding, the man who called himself Garrett roughly dragged Liz up the red clay bank of the muddy levee.

"Don't you stop breathing on me, Elizabeth! Don't you *dare* stop breathing!" she heard him exclaim in short gasps. She opened her eyes, only to discover a dark scowl distorting his handsome face.

"Say something, damn you!" he demanded.

Liz half attempted to respond, but instead of words, discolored water spewed from her lips.

Dropping to his knees, the man rolled Liz onto her side, holding her head steady as she coughed up the river water. Then, as if dissatisfied with her progress, he flipped her on her back. Clearing her passageway with his forefinger, he pinched her nose closed and pressed his lips to hers, breathing for her, demanding through the pressure of his mouth that she accept and respond to the puffs of air inflating her traumatized lungs.

Time ticked backward for Liz Hayden as she struggled to refocus on the world around her, as, slowly but surely, he brought her back to life. And when she'd had enough of his warm, insistent breath inside her, the electrifying sensation of his body pressed against hers, when she could once again function under her own steam, she reached up and placed a fingertip against his rigid cheek.

Almost fiercely, he captured her hand. Their eyes met and held, and for a split second she imagined he might kiss her palm. Until his eyes shadowed and he forced her hand away, saying in a harsh voice, "Well, I daresay it's about time!"

Liz slowly propped herself up on one elbow. Only inches separated her nose from his. "You look like a...mud wrestler," she slurred, her mind rambling aloud.

"A what?" Garrett rose abruptly to his feet. Hands on his hips, water running in rivulets down his taut jaw, he scrutinized Liz from head to toe. "God, if you aren't a handful!" he exclaimed, not allowing her time to respond to his question. "I must have been demented to—"

Whirling, he stomped down the bank of the levee, swore, then turned and marched back to tower over her.

"If I didn't know better, I'd swear you just did that to get back at me," he said accusingly. "Keep this nonsense up, and I'll lock you in your bed chamber and throw away the key," he continued, shrugging out of his shirt. Wringing the water from it, he shook it out and offered it to her.

Liz stared at the man's naked chest, with its mat of dark, curling hair. Then her gaze shifted back to the shirt.

"What am I supposed to do with that?" she asked, throat sore from his rough ministrations.

Garrett's lips twitched. "Put it on, Elizabeth, for modesty's sake. I can see the outline of your breasts through your camisole. And I'm not sure you're prepared to be ravished, to top everything else that's happened today."

"Oh," Liz squeaked. Deciding it was in her best interests to appease him, she accepted the shirt, still warm from his body heat. She quickly tugged it over her head, thinking that it was more difficult to get into wet clothes than out of them.

He must have read her mind, for, as if he couldn't help himself, he bent to assist her. His fingers felt hot against her tepid skin. Hot, and slightly cruel.

Liz hurriedly waved him away. Because he swept away her control, made her heart perform triple somersaults. Because he was drop-dead gorgeous. Because he threatened and yet intrigued her. Because there was something heady about his touch, something that moved her both emotionally and physically.

And because she was appalled by her reaction to him, even though, for his own twisted reasons, he'd saved her life.

No man had ever affected her the way he did, Liz admitted to herself. He made her blow hot one minute, cold the next. The trick was that he moved her at all. Quite a monstrous feat, she decided. She'd come to think of men in general as nothing more than business associates. Solid, yet dull, and as unappetizing as dry toast. This one caused the foundation beneath her feet to tremble. Her imagination to soar. Her mouth to water. Her adrenaline to flow, in fear . . . as well as desire.

"Would you really lock me in a—in my room?" Liz asked, gazing at her bare feet. Not only had the river devoured her gown and petticoats, it had sucked off her tennis shoes and footie socks, as well. Hungry thing, the mighty Mississippi, Liz mused, realizing the cuffs of his shirt fell well below her fingertips. Scrunching up one sleeve, she began to roll the other over her hand.

"I wouldn't try my patience right now," Garrett warned. "I'm teetering on the edge as it is." Resentment darkened his voice.

Liz stopped rolling to stare up at him. *He* was on the edge? Where did he think she was? She hadn't asked for this insanity... or whatever it was. All she had wanted to do was lock up the back gate and go home. Eat dinner. Read the newspaper. Perhaps take a hot bubble bath. And the next thing she knew...

Liz's chest heaved sob-like.

He swallowed, his gaze swinging to her breasts.

"The shirt doesn't help," he informed her.

"What do you mean?" she asked, tears puddling in her eyes.

"I *mean,* if anything, it makes matters worse, molding to your skin as it does."

Determined to armor herself against the stranger's penetrating perusal, Liz crossed her arms over her breasts. "Well, then, don't look."

To Liz's surprise, a sardonic half smile appeared on his lips as his eyes lifted to lock on the pulse beating erratically at her throat. "How refreshing. I never realized you could be such a spitfire."

He was mocking her, and she knew it.

"There's a lot you apparently don't realize," she muttered under her breath.

Expression hooded, he seemed to latch on to her statement like a bloodhound on a scent.

"Such as?" he asked, stepping even closer.

A tremor coursed through Liz; she could have bitten her tongue for speaking without thinking first.

Garrett waited expectantly, his gaze unwavering.

Liz fumbled for the words to express her fears without giving too much of herself away. She was already treading on dangerous territory. The last thing she needed was added complications.

Finally, she said, "Like what's at stake here."

"I'm well aware that the hazards couldn't be higher," he said evenly.

Liz could only assume this man was referring to the welfare of his brother's unborn child.

He continued, "The only way to decrease them seems to be to actively quell your resistance."

Dumbfounded, she croaked, "Is that what you think I'm doing? Resisting you?" Defensively, she dabbed away the tears with her forefinger.

Liz watched as a dark frown gathered like a thundercloud across his brow. "I'm not entirely sure what you're doing. But as I live and breathe, I certainly intend to find out!"

Liz's mouth dropped open as the man grudgingly reached out to assist her to her feet. She ignored his extended hand, a golden spark flashing in her eyes. "I'll be all right from here on out."

His half smile transformed into a stern line reflecting his doubt. "I wish I could believe that."

Lips trembling despite her best efforts to control them, Liz said, "So do I."

His gaze intensified, probing, searing her with its cerulean flame.

"How did I miss it before? I thought your eyes were brown, but they're not. When you take a moment to really look at them, to drink them in, they become liquid fire, like fine whiskey on a warm day. I swear, even in your present disheveled state, I can see why Michael found you so distracting. You're actually a most disarming piece of fluff."

Slack-jawed, pupils dilated in acute astonishment, Liz could only stare up at him as he hovered above her.

It wasn't the words that chilled her, but rather the way he said them, as if they left a sour taste in his mouth. History recounted that Garrett's relationship with his wife had been rocky from the start, growing more so up until the point when she disappeared under mysterious circumstances.

"What do you want from me?" she managed finally.

His dark brow arched in momentary surprise before his expression hardened. "Cooperation. Now, if you don't mind, we've dallied long enough. I'd like to be getting back to the house now," Garrett commented curtly. Without asking her permission, as if she weighed no more than a bedraggled kitten, he scooped Liz up into his arms. Rising in one fluid motion, he pivoted toward the neglected garden path she had so recently descended, the knife at his waist pressing into her hip.

"Please, put me down," Liz rasped, anxiety warring with the wild rush of desire hurtling through her overtaxed nervous system.

"I'm afraid not. I've no doubt Calvin is in the parlor, consuming my finest bottle of bourbon while awaiting our return. No telling what the snoop has gotten into while I was away," he said, his breath fanning her face as he navigated the garden with her riding securely in his arms.

Somehow she had to overcome her fear, make him understand that he'd made a horrible mistake. "But don't you see? I want to go home. I really have to get back somehow. There's no one to water my plants or pick up my mail," Liz babbled lamely, unsure of herself, of Garrett, of exactly what was happening to her. Knowing only that she was suddenly weary enough to sleep for a hundred years.

Without a break in stride, Garrett directed solemnly, "For better or for worse, Rowland Plantation is your home, Elizabeth. You're going to have to learn to accept that, no matter how much you hate the idea of sharing it with me. Now, if you know what's good for you, I suggest you hold on tightly."

It seemed, at twenty-six years of age, Liz had suddenly lost control of her well-ordered life. With a weak sigh, she momentarily gave up the battle, resting her cold cheek against Garrett's warm chest. As if of their own accord, her arms crept around his neck, and she clung to a man whose unshakable strength of purpose might well be lethal.

From what Liz could discern through the violet-hued twilight, the exterior of the plantation house appeared much as she remembered it. Sheltered by a hipped cypress roof, the two-story structure appeared to possess a luminescent aura, due to the linseed-oil-based paint that adorned it. Dove gray, with pale blue shutters, colonnaded galleries, a brick *garçonniere* on one wing, which she'd learned as a tour guide was built to accommodate unwed male guests, and a conservatoire on the other to balance it out, the enduring beauty of Rowland Plantation never failed to coax a sigh of appreciation from her.

The interior, however, was quite a different story.

Instead of contemporary recessed lighting fixtures, a tarnished brass chandelier fitted with oil lamps illuminated the foyer, casting grotesque shapes across the dusty rosewood furniture. The peppy aroma of lemon-scented polish and beeswax that Liz associated with the house had been replaced by a decided fustiness, as if the four rooms off the gloomy central hall had been shut up for a period of time and only recently reopened. And instead of a gaggle of smiling tour guides to greet her upon her return, yet another stranger awaited Liz's attention.

Fair-haired and ashen-faced, with fine hazel eyes that seemed about to pop out of their sockets, the dapperly dressed young man stared at her as if he'd just seen a ghost.

Lips curling over even white teeth, he exclaimed, "Merciful heavens, Garrett! What have you done to my cousin this time?"

His cousin! Liz thought, fighting down the hysterical giggle that bubbled in her throat. How absurd! She had no family to speak of. Raised by her grandmother after her parents' death in a house fire, she'd been on her own for years.

"This latest escapade is your fault, Trexler. I know I never should have left you two alone. What in blue blazes did you say to her at dinner to cause her to react this way?" Garrett demanded fiercely.

"Nothing, really..." Calvin replied, his voice faltering. "She wanted to talk about Michael, and I obliged her by listening. You know, Garrett, you Rowlands always have had a talent for placing the blame at another man's feet."

Garrett glowered at Calvin. "Get out of my way. And while you're at it, get the hell out of my house, as well!"

"Elizabeth's house."

"*Out,* you pompous, snoot-nosed little charlatan. I should never have allowed you to come to dinner in the first place."

Calvin trailed them to the foot of the balustraded staircase rising to the second-floor landing and the bedrooms. "I demand leave to speak with Elizabeth."

"The lady is indisposed," Garrett stated flatly.

"You can put me down now. I'm perfectly capable of standing on my own two feet," Liz said faintly. Her tone of voice belied her words.

Garrett's embrace only tightened more possessively as he gazed down at Calvin Trexler from his superior vantage point.

"You know, Trexler, for a man standing on the outside looking in, you do an awful lot of demanding," Garrett spat out.

"*The outside looking in?* Everyone knows your brother and I served in the same company during the war. We were great friends. Why, I introduced Michael and Elizabeth. I was best man at their wedding."

"There never was any accounting for my brother's taste in companionship," Garret commented dryly.

"You can't fool me with that high-handed attitude. I know why you married my cousin. You covet the dowry she brought to Michael, and well you know it," Calvin countered. "You can't even pay this year's taxes on the plantation without her inheritance."

"I married her because I didn't want to see my brother's child under the tutelage of the likes of you," Garrett snarled, a lethal note in his voice.

Calvin casually inspected his fingernails. "Better, I should think, a Confederate who knows the meaning of honor than a Union sympathizer and a traitor to his country. You're a fallen angel, Garrett. Of that there's no denying."

"We should have remained in Baton Rouge, where Elizabeth was less susceptible to your disruptive influence," Garrett growled under his breath.

"Elizabeth never would have stood for it," Calvin said, hand dropping to his side. "Without someone here to manage the land, Michael's beloved plantation would have been lost."

"I'm beginning to think you delight in filling Elizabeth's head with nonsense."

"You're jealous of my relationship with Michael."

"Of all the preposterous—"

"It's also common knowledge that you were livid with your brother for marrying a tradesman's daughter instead of the Louisiana blue blood he'd contracted with before the war. And now you're stuck with his—"

"Enough! I'll not be baited. Get out, before I thrash you and throw you out," Garrett said.

Calvin shifted uncomfortably, tugging at his starched collar. "Did I hear you correctly, cousin? Are you threatening me?"

Liz watched the exchange between the two men in mute fascination.

"You'd best remember that I'm your cousin by law—not by choice. And I don't make idle threats," Garrett stated, eyes glittering dangerously.

"But Michael's last wish was that I care for Elizabeth."

"That was before I arrived on the scene. She no longer needs you. She has me."

Calvin blanched. "You have no conscience."

"A conscience is a troublesome liability."

Digging into the pocket of his embroidered waist-coat, Calvin extracted an ornate pocket watch. Fidgeting with the catch, he flipped open the cover, quickly checking the time before closing and shoving it back into his pocket. Smoothing his lapels, he buttoned his frock coat to his throat. "I'm going. But you'll rue the day—"

Garrett stopped the younger man dead in his tracks. "I already do," he stated coldly.

Calvin shook his clenched fist at Garrett. "You allow harm to come to my cousin, and I'll enjoy seeing you hang," he said as Garrett stiffly presented his back to him, climbing the mahogany staircase with his soggy burden.

"Do you hear me, Garrett?" Calvin called after them, adding, "I swear I won't allow him to make a bloody invalid out of you, Elizabeth. Damned laudanum, or arsenic, or whatever it is he's feeding you. Never fear. I'll be back to see you again soon. He can't keep you a prisoner, away from polite society, forever."

Garrett deigned no reply. Nonplussed, Liz couldn't have mustered a coherent response if she'd tried.

In turmoil, Liz watched over Garrett's shoulder as Calvin collected his gold-knobbed cane and straight-sided top hat off the hall table. Settling the hat at a jaunty angle on his fair head, he sauntered to the front entrance in rather superb style, considering his lame leg, Liz thought to herself. Leaning heavily on his cane, he paused a moment to stare up at her, gallantly touched the brim of his hat, then turned his thin back on her and exited through the fan-lit enhanced front entrance.

As they ascended the stairs, Liz could see Calvin through the window above the door, limping across the front lawn. With difficulty, he levered himself into a horse-drawn buggy. Releasing the brake, he clucked to the horse, turning the vehicle around in the yard. Liz watched helplessly as her potential savior disappeared down the graveled drive.

"He's gone," she stated softly.

"For now," he said harshly.

"He wouldn't risk coming here again, after what you said to him. No one would."

"I wish I could believe that. But I can't. Calvin Trexler reminds me of the yellow fever that took Michael—grasping, terminally hungry, absorbing into itself everything and everyone it touches," Garrett muttered.

"Why, you miss Michael as much as...as much as...uh, I do," Liz said in amazement.

"I mourn no one," Garrett replied stiffly, exhibiting the best poker face Liz had ever seen. But he didn't fool her. Now she remembered where she'd seen a likeness of the darkly handsome man who had cradled her in his close embrace. With whom she supposedly shared a house and a history. She'd bet her collection of compact discs that on the black Carrara marble mantel over the library hearth sat a silver-backed daguerreotype of a youthful Garrett Rowland standing in affectionate camaraderie beside his elder brother, Michael.

Garrett had opposed his family during the Civil War, joining the North and being branded a scoundrel by his Confederate father. From that moment until his parents' death, he had not been allowed to set foot on Rowland soil. Later, his brother had forgiven him his transgressions, yet they'd never completely reconciled their differences. Garrett had chosen to live a solitary existence far from the plantation life he abhorred.

Garrett Rowland, last descendant of the Rowland dynasty; black sheep, libertine, professional riverboat gambler...and accused murderer.

Liz almost laughed. She should have recognized Garrett instantly! She'd been fascinated by the house and despite the legend, half in love with him ever since she'd come to work at Rowland Plantation. From his picture, she'd decided he was one of the most attractive men she'd ever seen. Now here he was. Very much alive. And every bit the hunk she'd imagined he'd been.

"I see it, but I don't believe it. This can't be happening to me. Time-travel just isn't possible," Liz mumbled in acute amazement as what little nerve she'd managed to muster deserted her. She didn't know whether to laugh or to cry.

"What did you say?" Garrett breathed against her ear as he kicked open the master bedroom door, the brush of his lips so sensuously erotic that a tantalizing tremor rocked her body, even as she fought the dangerous attraction he held for her.

"N-nothing," Liz stammered, her thoughts a frantic jumble of times and dates, people, places and things. It seemed impossible, but if her suspicions proved correct, she'd somehow been zapped into the past, compliments of an evening thunderstorm!

Liz sprinted past shock, grappled with disbelief, and hurtled the impossible to finally face reality head-on.

"You're trembling. It's those wet undergarments. We've got to get you out of them before you catch your death," Garrett insisted, finally standing her on her feet.

"I'm fine. Really I am," Liz said, teeth chattering as she withdrew her arms from around Garrett's neck, once again folding them protectively across her breasts.

Garrett wouldn't be distracted. "You're cold and you know it. I'm cold myself, Elizabeth."

Because she was so afraid of him killing her, as history recounted that he had his wife, she said, "I'm not Elizabeth."

Garrett gazed at her wordlessly for a long moment, then scowled.

"You've tried those tricks before. They didn't work then, and they won't work now. You're not wiggling out of our bargain. I suggest you refrain from saying silly things in an attempt to do so, because I won't listen to them.

"I'm not—"

Scowl deepening, he interrupted her. "Don't push me, Elizabeth."

Liz tried again. "But I'm only trying to clear—"

Garrett yanked her back against him, trapping her arms between them as he shocked her into silence with a sizzling kiss. One that delved and bruised. And ravaged her mouth, along with her soul.

Too surprised to fight him, Liz melted into Garrett's rough embrace. Then, as abruptly as it had begun, the kiss ended.

"Things are all too clear as it is," he finished for her, thrusting her from him.

The lump forming in her throat threatened to close off her windpipe. It was obvious that telling Garrett the truth wasn't going to save her from him. In fact, it would make things ten times worse. Shaken to the core, Liz realized her only recourse was to backtrack.

Struggling for her own sense of identity, she forced her voice around the lump. "I only meant that I would prefer to be called Liz."

A mirthless smile twisted Garrett's lips. "You want *me* to call you by my brother's pet name for you? You said you couldn't bear to hear it upon another's lips."

"I've . . . changed my mind."

"I suppose it's a woman's prerogative, though I don't pretend to understand it," he said with an arrogant shrug she might have found offensive if she weren't frightened half out of her wits.

With a wicked-looking poker, Garrett stirred the banked coals in the marble-manteled fireplace until a flame flickered up through the smoldering embers. He selected a handful of wadded vellum sheets from the brass wastepaper can, along with several sticks of kindling from a stack on the hearth. Then, crisscrossing them in layers atop the flame, he fed the hungry fire.

"Why don't you light a candle, so we can see what we're doing?" he said over his shoulder. Even squatting to adjust a cedar log on the crackling kindling, he dominated the chamber with his presence.

Tearing her eyes from his broad back, Liz scanned the room, spying a dipped candle and pewter candlestick on the writing desk. With a grateful sigh, she put the desk between herself and Garrett, eyeing the candle.

"What's wrong? Go ahead, light it," Garrett prompted several moments later.

Liz didn't much care for the idea of open flames, but without electricity, it seemed she had no choice in that matter. Besides, her hesitation was beginning to make her look suspicious.

Propelled by the thought, Liz reached for the tinderbox and ignited the aromatic bayberry candle. An amber glow suffused the room, and shadows waltzed across the red-and-black flocked wallpaper.

"That's more like it," he said.

Rising from the fireplace, Garrett crossed the room. Flinging open the rosewood wardrobe, he retrieved a handful of nightgowns. Turning, he tossed the lacy confections on the half-canopied bed and eyed them critically.

"I think we could both use a good night's sleep. Choose one," he commanded.

A hasty glance told Liz she didn't care for any of them. They all seemed too sheer, too provocative and far too revealing for the pajama-type woman she was.

"I can't."

"Don't be coy. It doesn't become you."

Neither will that nightgown. "I'm not trying to be."

"Difficult, then?"

Liz shook her head.

Garrett frowned. "Fine. In that case, I'll choose for you."

He plucked a blue peignoir from the top of the pile and thrust it toward Liz, crushing the soft material into folds beneath his fingertips. His sharp movements told her more successfully than words could have that she was testing his patience again.

She gingerly accepted the peignoir, careful not to brush his hand.

Garrett stilled.

Liz followed suit.

"I'm not a leper, Elizabeth," he stated solemnly following a dramatic pause that assaulted her already badly battered composure.

"Liz," she said tentatively. "And I never said you were."

"You didn't have to."

His tone reeked of suppressed anger, though she suspected she'd hit another sort of emotional target. Surely she couldn't have hurt his feelings?

For a moment, her heart actually softened toward Garrett Rowland. "I didn't mean—" she began.

As if he'd peered into her brain, read her mind and seen the path her thoughts were strolling, he quickly cut her short. "I strongly suggest you put that on. Or else I'll be forced to do it for you."

"Is that an ultimatum?"

"You may consider it so—for your own good."

She blinked, hating that he'd witnessed her fleeting moment of compassion. It made her all the more vulnerable to him.

Liz protected herself against Garrett by hiding behind a wall built of pure bravado. "Wait outside, then."

"We're not exactly strangers," he commented dryly.

Liz didn't care for the suggestive glint in his eyes. Or the way he scanned her damp clothing.

"We're not exactly best friends, either," she said.

Garrett refrained from further comment, allowing his eyes to do the talking as he glanced pointedly toward the dressing screen Liz had somehow missed in her perusal of the room.

Garrett Rowland was becoming less and less a stranger and more and more an intimate, even as they spoke—whether she wanted it or not, Liz mused.

She tried again. "Don't you want to go to your room and clean up while I change?" She desperately needed time to sort this whole thing out—to study the fantastic implications of the chain of events that had led her from the present to the past, to the master bedroom of Rowland Plantation, and into the arms of a rogue like Garrett.

But Garrett seemed disinclined to take even the broadest of hints. Instead, he opened the top drawer of one of the chest of drawers and extracted a brocade smoking jacket and fresh trousers while Liz looked on helplessly.

"I have everything I'll need right here," he said, patting the stack of neatly folded clothes. The glint in his eyes died, replaced by an inscrutable expression that made him seem still more dangerous.

Liz glanced nervously toward the room's inanimate objects in hopes of the understanding Garrett denied her, deciding this must be the way the house had looked in its youth. Some of the things were familiar; many were not.

Prominently displayed on the dressing table were two brushes—a man's, and a woman's—a perfume vial, a straight razor and shaving mug.

Liz panned the room, squinting to take in even the dimmest of recesses this time around.

Situated beside the miniature dining table at the foot of the bed stood a pair of claw-footed side chairs, complete with heavily padded footstools. Twin china place settings graced the table. A decanter of bloodred wine and a crystal stemware duet rested cozily on a nearby side table.

How had she missed it? The bedroom shouted of a pairing. Of shared intimacies. She was amazed such intimacy could have soured, digressed into resentment and ended in *murder.*

The rich aroma of the bayberry candle suddenly made Liz nauseous. She fought the sick feeling in the pit of her stomach even as she grappled with the truth. And still she refused to believe fate could be so cruel and calculating and downright thoughtless. She had to hear it from Garrett's own lips to be thoroughly convinced.

"We sleep together?" she rasped weakly, as his face undulated before her eyes and the floor rushed up to greet her.

CHAPTER THREE

Liz's eyes fluttered open to discover the hand holding hers was attached to a body stretched out beside her. A man's body, freshly shaved and smelling tantalizingly of soap mixed with bay rum, fully clothed and taking up a considerable portion of the unfamiliar bed. With his piercing sky blue eyes closed, Garrett Rowland didn't appear as sinister as history had painted him. Then again, murderers never did, Liz ruminated.

Moistening her dry lips with the tip of her tongue, she decided to bluff her way through the inevitable confrontation with an attempt at humor. "You sure know how to keep a girl in line. That's a great left hook you've got there. I feel as if I've been worked over with a set of brass knuckles."

Garrett slowly opened his eyes to the sound of her voice. His blank expression was speedily replaced by a faint, sleepy smile that relieved the normal severity of his tanned countenance.

"What would a lady know of brass knuckles?"

"A lady would know they would hurt if she got hit with them. And I hurt," Liz said, eyes shining fervently, unable to believe she was still tangled in the past.

"I don't doubt that," Garrett drawled. As if he couldn't help himself, he reached over to lightly smooth an unruly curl away from her forehead. The action was unconsciously seductive.

He seemed entirely ignorant of the influence his nearness exerted on her—the rush of pleasure she experienced at his touch, the illicit thrill of dabbling with something potentially dangerous, like lighting fire-crackers on New Year's Eve, even though they were outlawed. Then again, perhaps he was as much a master at hiding his emotions as he was his questionable past.

His voice dropped low and husky as he commented, "Do my eyes deceive me, or has your hair dried fairer than I remember it?"

Body stiffening, Liz primed herself to pull away, though, oddly enough, it was the last thing she felt inclined to do. "It must have been the river water."

"Wouldn't that make it darker?"

Fear of him suddenly resurfaced, and she said hastily, "Don't change the subject. Did you, or did you not, hit me?"

Garrett withdrew abruptly. "No matter what sordid tales Michael might have related to you before he died, I did not hit you. There are more subtle ways to control a disobedient wife. You whacked your skull against the writing desk when you swooned. I had no idea that marrying you necessitated the added cost of installing a fainting couch in the house."

"I fainted? Impossible," Liz said, with all the vigor her languid mind could muster. "I've never fainted in my life."

"You did this time. The bruise proves it," he assured her.

Stretched flat on her back, Liz tipped her pounding head slightly to gaze squarely into Garrett's eyes. Her own eyes narrowed in concentration. "Do you have this effect on all the women?" she questioned, drawing his face into sharp focus, thinking what beautiful eyes he had—for a lunatic.

Garrett met her gaze eye to eye. "Only the ones I've made love with."

Mesmerized, Liz's breath caught in her throat. She hated being vulnerable, and at the moment she felt more so than at any other time in her life. She might just as well be honest with herself, she decided. To her dismay, an undeniable chemistry existed between them. Regardless of the fact that history had branded Garrett a murderer. Despite the fact that he repelled and fascinated her at the same time.

"I think this is where I came in. Or, should I say, went out." Liz bunched the ivory silk bed covers up to her chin as best she could with Garrett reclining on top of them.

"I admit the consummation of our marriage wasn't the most fulfilling encounter either of us has ever experienced, but we agreed it was necessary so that the marriage couldn't be annulled on a technicality."

"What do you mean?" Liz squeaked, desperately attempting to assimilate his words into her mind.

The present situation was inconceivable. Not only did he think she was married to him and carrying his brother's child. Garrett Rowland actually believed they'd been intimate. More astonishing and disconcerting still was the fact that fate expected a contemporary woman to step into Elizabeth Rowland's shoes without batting an eyelash.

The whole thing was just too bizarre . . . totally absurd . . . and well beyond her acting capabilities. And it wasn't as if she believed in the supernatural possibility of time travel, even though some people professed everyone had a double somewhere, and she might be Elizabeth's.

Garret brushed back the mosquito bar veiling the bed, breaking into her chaotic thoughts and tugging her back from her silent reverie. He stretched, rising with an easy athletic grace Liz found amazing, considering his reputation as a man who played cards all night and slept all day.

Day!

It suddenly dawned on Liz that milky morning sunlight was filtering in through the lace curtains. Just outside the lead-paned window, in the crown of an old poplar tree, a flock of ravens vocalized, while inside the bayberry candle guttered into a waxy puddle of its own design.

Where had the night gone?

"Oh, good grief! It's Monday morning! I'm late for work!" Liz exclaimed, jumping up, only to dive beneath the covers again when she recalled the sheerness of her blue gown.

Trapped in time and more than a hundred years away from her job, concentrating on the mundane made her feel less displaced and helped keep her mind off more important matters. Consciously combatting the creeps, she worried about how her co-workers would proceed at the library without her. It was far easier than thinking about the day in store for her here in the past.

A glint of something dubious lurking in the depths of his eyes, Garrett all too soon pulled her abruptly back to *his* reality.

"The house can wait. You've got all the time in the world to put it in order. You've had a rather difficult time of it up until now, and you need all the rest you can get."

"What I need are some clothes!" she countered. She felt at a definite disadvantage—a woman was always better able to cope when fully dressed!

Liz experienced a moment of panic, the same sort of helpless sensation she felt when the alarm clock failed to go off and she overslept, when she knew there was nothing she could do to prevent herself being late for work.

"I've got things to do that can't wait," she insisted. *Like jog on down to the tomb and hitch a ride back to my own time.*

"If it will pacify you, I suppose there's no harm in helping the housekeeper start the cleaning this morning. I'm sure Mrs. Crawford would appreciate the assistance, and it might help your state of mind to stay busy."

"Exactly. Now, how about my clothes?"

Garrett cocked an eyebrow at Liz. "Some of your dresses are in the wardrobe. The others are folded in the trunk at the foot of the bed. You haven't unpacked them yet."

Liz glanced at the iron-banded leather trunk. "How silly of me to forget. It's been the, um...move back from, uh...Baton Rouge, I guess." *And what a move! Whoosh! All the way from the twentieth century on the tail of a mystical lightning bolt!*

"I realize it's been difficult, leaving behind your personal maid." He squared his shoulders. "The fact is, I simply couldn't afford her."

Calvin had implied Elizabeth possessed a substantial dowry. Liz could only surmise Garrett was too proud to take more than he needed for the bare necessities.

"Believe it or not, I can dress myself."

A smoldering glow danced in Garrett's brooding eyes. "Do tell," he commented appreciatively.

Glancing down at her gown, then over at her undergarments, which were drying by the open window, Liz groaned silently.

She had a million important questions, but could think of only one at the moment. "Did you put the nightgown on me?" she asked, her voice soft and resonant.

"It seemed a good idea at the time. I didn't feel like battling a case of the ague, to top everything else you've put me through."

Noting the cleanliness of her bare arms, Liz slanted a glance at the commode and washbasin. "I suppose you engineered the sponge bath too," she commented, goose bumps rising on her flesh at the idea of his hands smoothing a washcloth over her body. Hands that could be gentle enough to bathe a woman without waking her and yet, according to historical records, murder without remorse.

"I closed my eyes," he responded in a deep voice.

Liz stated in a breathless voice, "Then you, Garrett Rowland, must be inhuman."

"I've been called that before, along with unmerciful brute, devil, beast, wretch . . . you name it."

"If it's all the same to you, I think I'll pass. I've heard it isn't nice to bite the hand that feeds you."

Garrett forgot himself so much as to laugh out loud, fine lines crinkling at the corner of his eyes. "Strangely enough, I find you more of a challenge this way. Besides which, it's a definite improvement over the weeping creature I wed," he said, moving toward the bedroom door.

Left tongue-tied by his abrupt admission, Liz could only stare after him.

"Speaking of nourishment, I'll have Mrs. Crawford bring up breakfast in a little while. Eggs? A beefsteak? Milk toast? A *beignet?* Coffee? Chocolate? Which do you prefer?" he asked over his shoulder.

Liz hesitated.

Turning to face her, he scowled. "Come now, I swear, no matter what your cousin has been telling you, I won't lace your meal with arsenic. As for the laudanum, the doctor prescribed it. If you feel well enough to leave it off, I won't force it on you this morning."

"Have you been forcing it on me?" Liz felt compelled to ask.

He glared at her. "I said I'd leave it off this morning."

"I'm not sure I should trust you."

"I'm not sure you should, either, but you have no recourse," he said tightly.

True. With Calvin gone, she had no one to turn to, Liz reasoned, feeling suddenly ravenous. She hadn't eaten since lunch the day before—tofu stir-fry and a garden salad washed down with a bottle of carrot juice purchased from a health-food store located off the interstate near the homesite exit. And in her present situation, it was mandatory she keep up her strength. One never knew what fate might throw at one next.

"I think I'll have a little of each, if you don't mind. I feel like a big breakfast," Liz said.

Garrett turned, a quizzical expression crossing his face as he backed the remainder of the distance to the door. "You haven't eaten that much food in weeks."

"I guess I'm finally on the road to recovery," Liz countered, feeling self-conscious, for herself and, oddly enough, for Elizabeth Trexler, who had married Garrett as a convenience and wound up with far more than she bargained for.

He paused, his fingers resting negligently on the silver doorknob. Almost as an afterthought, he said, "Perhaps later this afternoon you'd like to take a ride over the estates with me. The tenant farmers I've employed should be moving into the cabins near the south field. I'm sure their wives would appreciate a visit from you. You might even find a suitable girl to come around once a week and assist with the heavier household chores, since Mrs. Crawford is likely to be the only full-time retainer within the house for quite some time."

Liz had an overwhelming desire to explain that he was mistaken about her. That she shouldn't be hiring new employees in place of his wife, reasonably priced or otherwise. That she was a time traveler, drafted at random as a stand-in for the genuine article.

But she didn't have any proof. Her gown, with its precise sewing-machine stitches and its perfect buttonholes, her petticoats, with their modern zippers, even her tennis shoes and footie socks, had been lost to the river. Rather than look crazier than she already felt, she'd simply have to play along with fate's practical joke while accumulating as much knowledge as possible, in the hope that it would assist her in returning to her own time before she created irrevocable damage in this one. Or vice versa.

"An outing might be...nice." *Maybe some fresh country air will help to clear the cobwebs out of my head,* Liz thought.

He paused. "I never thought to ask you before now. You do know how to ride, don't you?"

Her grandmother had been a firm believer that lessons made the child—all kinds of lessons. So Liz had been given art lessons for a time. Horseback-riding lessons, until she'd fallen off a frisky gelding as they sailed over a jump, breaking her collarbone in the process. Viola and piano instructions throughout private school and well into college. She'd even dabbled in the world of dance, though fencing would have been her preference, given the choice, Liz thought. Her grandmother had preached the necessity of lessons until the day she passed away in her sleep; Liz had been a grown woman, well endowed with lessons by that time.

"I do. Hunt-seat," Liz said. Thank goodness for Grandmother Hayden.

Garrett seemed gratified by her affirmative response. "I have an appointment in the library with the estate ledgers this morning, but I should be finished going over them in time to meet you at the stables by nine. Can I assume that you will behave while I wind up my financial business? That you won't be tempted to try another stunt like that dip in the river?"

"That was an accident."

"Regardless, I'd like your word that you'll behave." His eyes questioned her integrity.

Liz frowned. Unaccustomed to being the object of someone's distrust, she said, "To the best of my ability."

"That sounds dubious," Garrett said.

Liz shrugged. What more could she say? That even though she resembled his Elizabeth, the clockworks inside were entirely different. That she was not now, and had never been, suicidal. Nor did she plan to allow outside circumstances to drive her to such an extreme.

"I can see by the petulant set of your chin, you don't intend to be pressed. I suppose that's a good sign." He hesitated. "I must warn you not to underestimate me, Elizabeth. I'll brook no more nonsense from you." His hand rested on the hilt of the knife at his waist.

Liz fidgeted under his easy surveillance. She'd come to terms with the fact that she'd somehow managed to travel backward in time. She had not come to terms with her association with Garrett Rowland, however, or to the unpredictability of his mood swings.

"I've been a burden to you since the wedding, haven't I?" Liz asked, wishing the moment the words were out she hadn't spoken so boldly.

"It's no secret I'd rather have been shot than marry."

"You blame..." Liz stopped, swallowed, then began again. "You blame me for this, don't you?"

Undoubtedly Garrett had decided he'd had enough, for he did not deign to answer her question. Instead, he said, "By the way, I've never seen a birthmark shaped like a pear before."

Liz turned twelve shades of pink, but not from embarrassment at Garrett's having viewed the strawberry birthmark on her hip. She blushed because in her heart of hearts, as depraved as it might seem, she wished she'd been awake to enjoy his ungentlemanly ministrations. Despite everything, she was physically drawn to him, and she was woman enough to admit it to herself.

"I thought you said you didn't look."

"I lied," he confessed. He twisted the doorknob, opening the door and crossing the threshold.

"Garrett?" Liz asked swiftly just before he closed the door behind him, scrambling from the bed to stand in the center of the room, wrapped in the silken bed cover as if it were the finest of imperial cloaks.

He stuck his head back inside. "Yes?"

"I know this is going to sound absurd. But you see, I've been in and out of it so much lately, what with the funeral . . . and the, ah, the wedding, and the drugs and all, that the days have sort of blurred together and become sketchy."

Garrett raked his fingers through his sable hair. "What are you asking of me?"

Chin up, careful to maintain an even voice, Liz finished the improvisation. "That you fill me in." Perhaps if he did, she could get an approximate fix on the date.

Garrett inclined his head, indicating that she should go on.

Compelled to find out a little bit about the woman she'd somehow replaced, Liz willed herself to continue. "Exactly how long have we been married?"

Solemn-faced, Garrett said, "Three weeks yesterday."

"What about the customary year of mourning?"

Garrett's mouth compressed into a thin line. "Let's just say I can be most persuasive when I want to be. Acquiring the special license was mere child's play."

"Do I have a ring?" she asked, attempting to keep the lines of tension from her face.

Liz could have sworn he flinched before saying, "You refused to wear any other than the gold band Michael gave you—an heirloom from our mother." His words held a faint note of mockery—whether for himself or for her, she wasn't sure.

Liz stared down at her left hand. Her fingers were bare.

"It seems I've . . . um . . . lost it," she said in a small voice.

Garrett glanced at her hand, the scar on his face coloring. "So you have. How extremely charming," he noted, mood swinging in an abrupt about-face, sarcasm dripping from his tongue.

"Perhaps it's down at the tomb, or even somewhere in this bedroom," she said quickly, fishing for an explanation for having lost a ring she'd never seen, much less possessed.

"Or in the river," he said dryly. Like a rapier, his eyes skewered her, accusing her of a range of things, from willful misconduct to carelessness.

"I'll look for it," she offered lamely.

"See that you do. It's been in our family for generations."

Without further ado, he closed the bedroom door between them. She stared at the smooth surface of the cypress door for several long moments, holding her breath, waiting for a key to scrape in the lock. She relaxed when, instead of a key, she heard Garrett's footsteps receding down the stairs.

He'd taken her at her word, after all. But she had no way of knowing how long it would last. If he ever found out she was an impostor...

Liz contemplated the leather trunk, temporarily rejecting the notion of dressing. Fighting a sudden weariness that was almost as draining as the river's current had been, she crossed the length of the bedroom. Crawling back into the rosewood bed, she curled into the fetal position in the center of the feather mattress, arranging the bed cover over her head. With a deep, heartfelt sigh, she wondered aloud beneath the muffling material, "Why me? How am I supposed to deal with this?" And then, more softly still, "If I'm here, where the *heck* is Elizabeth right now?"

Could her appearance have displaced Elizabeth Rowland? Liz wondered. Might they have switched places? While she was worrying about climbing aboard a horse and meeting Garrett's tenant farmers, might Elizabeth simultaneously be concerned over driving a car through morning traffic to a job at the public library?

And, though her mind shied away from it, Liz finally admitted there remained an even worse scenario to contemplate—that she'd somehow popped into the nineteenth century at the moment of Elizabeth's murder. Which left things wide open to all sorts of ghastly supposition.

It was not the smoke, but rather the scent of Cherokee roses, that awakened Liz from a deep sleep. Opening her eyes, she swam to the surface of consciousness, only to realize that a stifling haze hovered about her. For a split second, she sensed a malevolent presence in the bedroom. And then she heard a whisper of movement, the creaking of a floorboard, and the telltale click of hardware as the door opened and closed.

Her breathing labored, she sniffed the air. Something about it reminded her of the sickening smell of burning skin.

Something's on fire!

Liz automatically glanced toward the fireplace. Nothing more than dead gray ash remained of the merrily burning logs. Heart palpitating, Liz untangled her legs from the covers, springing from the bed. She scanned the room, searching for the source of the fire. Orange flames licked at the crushed sheets of vellum brimming the brass wastepaper can.

Spying the commode, Liz stumbled toward the washbasin, only to find it empty of water.

Throwing her hand over her mouth, she pivoted toward the can. If she could pick it up, she might be able to toss it into the fireplace before the circular rag rug, and possibly even the flooring beneath it, caught on fire.

Sprinting to the bed, she yanked the pillow case from the feather pillow, fashioning a sort of pot holder for her hand. Advancing on the wastepaper can, she bent from the waist, feeling the flames singeing her hand through the material. She quickly recoiled, backing up until the bed frame stopped her retreat.

She was panicking now, her thoughts veering toward escape. Tossing aside the pillowcase, she dashed to the door, frantically twisting the knob.

Locked from the outside.

Liz jiggled the silver knob, simultaneously using her weight in an attempt to somehow wrench the door from its frame. The hardware held firm.

"Someone! Anyone! Help! Let me out!" she screamed, hammering on the wooden panel.

She pressed her ear to the door. Silence reigned in the hallway.

Spinning, she darted to the window. She could see Garrett below in the yard, strolling toward a huge black horse. She beat at the sash in an attempt to raise the double-hung window. As if sealed from the outside, as well, it refused to budge.

He'd said he wouldn't lock the door. He'd told her she could ride with him. Had he lied on both counts, simply to gain her confidence, to lure her into a false sense of security? To what end? Or had he perhaps seen the real Elizabeth, thus discovering he'd been duped?

Liz's mind raced like a cornered doe, even as her eyes darted toward the wastepaper can.

What about a more simple explanation?

Garrett had probably realized from the way she'd been acting and the things she'd said that she feared fire. Could this be one of the macabre jokes Garrett was famous for? A means of control over her? Or perhaps he was angry with her. Might he have entertained second thoughts concerning their outing since he learned about the missing wedding ring?

Or maybe he was simply fed up with the notion of marriage in general, felt suffocated and confused and panicked—as she did now.

Liz clawed at the wooden muntins, rattling the panes, attempting to attract Garrett's attention. She could have sworn he glanced up, yet he mounted the horse and trotted out of the yard anyway. Too late, she thought of throwing the shaving mug through the glass.

Coughing and clutching her throat, Liz wheeled away from the window.

Trapped just as her poor, dear parents had been! she thought as tears rolled down her cheeks and the noxious smoke thickened, overpowering the scent of roses.

CHAPTER FOUR

"Have mercy on my soul!" an astonished voice exclaimed from the doorway. "Whatever are you about, ma'am?"

Life-giving oxygen assailed Liz's senses. She swayed forward, peering through the haze as it writhed, fighting against the hallway's ventilating effect. A wide-eyed, horse-faced middle-aged woman in black teetered as if frozen on the threshold of the bedroom. She wore a darned apron and carried a weighty breakfast tray.

Liz dashed toward her, nearly upsetting the tray as she snatched up the *veilleuse-théière*, removing the teapot from its night-light warming base and dumped its contents into the wastepaper can. The fire sizzled out, and the aroma of scorched chocolate replaced that of burning skin.

That accomplished, Liz turned on her rescuer. "I presume you're the housekeeper." Her voice sounded unnaturally high-pitched, and her throat was parched and scratchy from the smoke.

"Y-yes, ma'am," Mrs. Crawford stammered, an incredulous expression punctuating her reply.

"Do you have a key to the door?"

"No, ma'am," the housekeeper said. Thawing, she advanced cautiously into the room.

"But it was locked from the outside. How did you get in?"

"It wasn't locked."

"Yes, it was."

"I had no trouble opening it, ma'am."

"Are you sure?" Liz asked.

"No . . . I mean, yes, ma'am."

Liz fired another question. "Has the door ever stuck before? I mean, so that you couldn't open it from the inside?"

"Not that I recall."

"Did you see anyone in the hallway when you came up the stairs?" Liz asked. She moved to replace the porcelain teapot on its base upon the tray and to select a glass of milk instead. She downed the soothing liquid in one clean gulp.

"No, ma'am. No one."

"Positive?" Liz asked. Licking the milk from her upper lip, she set the empty glass aside, moving to examine the door.

"Positive, ma'am," the housekeeper responded.

Determined to discover what was going on, Liz jiggled the doorknob, opened and closed the door several times, and tested the mortise and retractable metal tenon that had earlier held the door in a fixed position. The door worked perfectly.

A deep frown furrowed Liz's normally smooth brow. Liz shivered involuntarily.

"What about Mr. Rowland?" she asked as her heart finally decelerated to its normal rhythm. Garrett was moody. She'd learned that from her tour-guide training. She'd also learned from the history books of his known deviousness.

Mrs. Crawford balanced the tray on one hand while she suppressed a cough with the other. "I believe he's left for the day."

"But we planned to ride together this morning," Liz said, telling herself she couldn't trust him. That she dare not let her guard drop where he was concerned.

"I wouldn't know about that, ma'am," the housekeeper said, placing the tray on the dining table.

Mrs. Crawford was watching her closely—too closely. Had she been hired solely to keep house? Or was she Garrett's spy . . . a keeper for Elizabeth? She had to be, Liz decided. Otherwise, Garrett would never have felt comfortable leaving the plantation for the day.

Liz contemplated Mrs. Crawford as she crossed the room, pulled a nail from the sash, twisted the latch and easily lifted the window. She used her apron to fan fresh air into the room.

Like a disembodied spirit weary of resisting an overzealous exorcist, the smoke glided outside to disperse in the atmosphere of the open yard.

Bidding it a silent and heartfelt farewell, Liz fought to regain her equilibrium. That accomplished, she redirected her attention to Mrs. Crawford.

Hoping she didn't appear to be in need of chronic supervision, Liz finally asked, "Did Mr. Rowland tell you where he was going?"

Mrs. Crawford appeared momentarily confused. "Mister Rowland isn't in the habit of confiding in me, ma'am, though I have a message for you," she replied.

Another faux pas—probably only the first of many.

In nineteenth-century America, a servant wouldn't be taken into the master's confidence, especially a female servant, Liz told herself. Where was her brain? She'd best find it, and start using it, if she planned to survive out of her own element.

Liz drew herself up to her full height. "Well, stop dilly-dallying and let's have the message," she said. She incorporated her most imperious tone as she attempted to cover her mistake by acting and speaking as she thought Elizabeth might.

The housekeeper stopped fanning to reach into her ample apron pocket, extract a sealed envelope and extend it to Liz.

Liz gingerly accepted the envelope, which was marked Elizabeth. She peeled the seal open with her fingers and slipped out a sheet of black-bordered stationery. It was the first time in her life she'd opened someone else's mail.

Liz felt almost criminal as she took a deep breath, unfolded the note, and silently read, "Meet me in the gazebo an hour before sunset." The words were penned in slanting letters that slashed the page like knife strokes. It made Liz think of the ivory-handled blade sheathed and resting upon Garrett's muscular thigh. Did she dare meet him in the rose garden? Did she dare not?

If only Garrett had not been a prime suspect in Elizabeth's murder. If only she could be sure of his intentions. If only they'd met under more promising circumstances, in another time and another place.

Her time. Her place.

If only there weren't all these unanswered questions hanging over her head like so many guillotines.

Liz glanced again at the bold handwriting, so like the man himself. How arrogant of him, not to even bother to sign the note.

"Did Mr. Rowland tell you how long he'd be away?" she asked, wishing to reaffirm the strange summons she'd read.

Rubbing her nose with her index finger, Mrs. Crawford said, "As I recall, he mentioned something about nightfall, ma'am."

Liz refolded the note, replaced it in the envelope and tossed it on the writing desk. She'd have ample time to stroll down to inspect the tomb and see what she could dig up in the way of a ticket home—before the extraordinarily charismatic and potentially dangerous Garrett Rowland returned to dissuade her.

"Have you known Mr. Rowland long?" Liz asked speculatively, intent on gleaning as much information as she could while she had the chance, just in case she needed it at some later date. Not the biographical stuff, but the deep-down nitty-gritty that only those closest to him could accurately recount.

Liz felt she knew the basics—at least, what the historians believed to be the truth—but something told her she didn't know the whole truth. Not yet, anyway.

There was a lot of information on Elizabeth's cousin Calvin. He'd become prosperous after the Civil War. A pillar of society. A man to look up to. He'd cared deeply for his cousin, keeping her welfare at heart to the bitter end. He'd been the one to accuse Garrett of duplicity in Elizabeth's disappearance, and he'd been responsible for bringing him before the court of inquiry, only to be stunned by his acquittal. Later, he'd sponsored a school for well-bred ladies in memory of Elizabeth,

There were documented details available on Michael and Elizabeth, as well. A portfolio of love letters. A personal Bible.

But there was next to nothing on the mysterious Garrett Rowland beyond the legendary hearsay. He was a gambler who survived by his wits. A maverick. A loner. A man who lived by his own rules and sense of morality. Proud. Resentful. Perhaps murderous.

"I haven't known Mr. Garrett long, ma'am."

Liz glanced up, looking directly into the woman's dark eyes. "But you are familiar with the family?"

The housekeeper shot her an oblique smile. "I should think so."

Liz watched as she strolled to the rosewood wardrobe and selected an ankle-length brocade dressing gown, much like Garrett's shorter smoking jacket.

"Perhaps you'd like to put this on, ma'am, so you can enjoy your breakfast while it's still hot."

Liz shrugged into the dressing gown without comment. The material felt heavy and unfamiliar, yet oddly comforting. Almost as comforting as Garrett's large hand encompassing her frailer one. Or the warmth of his body when he'd held her in his powerful arms, forcefully ministering to her river-chilled body....

Liz shook herself. It would be sheer insanity to trust Garrett Rowland. She must remember that, if nothing else.

"Tell me, do you live here on the premises or in a...a village, or something like that?" Liz asked as she tied the drawstring tightly about her waist, giving the knot a final pat, as if it were somehow a talisman against her wayward thoughts.

Mrs. Crawford looked puzzled. "I have a cottage a mile or so down the road. Don't you remember?"

"I'd...forgotten. I'm afraid I seem to have trouble remembering things lately," Liz said, falling back on the same line she'd sold Garrett.

"Not so peculiar. I should think extended illness would have a tendency to cause such things," the housekeeper said.

Her tone was far too patronizing for Liz. She didn't need mothering; she needed information concerning Garrett. She also needed to gauge where Mrs. Crawford's loyalties rested.

Liz said, "I'm better now."

"Of course you are. I can see that with my own two eyes. You have a decided blush to your cheeks that was missing yesterday."

Liz couldn't decide whether the woman was being kind or condescending, so she let it slide.

"So...exactly how long have you been with the Rowland family?"

"Well now, let me see." Mrs. Crawford puckered her lips as she slowly recounted the years on her fingers. "Going on thirteen summers I suppose. Old Mr. Rowland hired my late husband as an overseer. When he passed away, I stayed on as housekeeper. Times were hard, what with the end of the War and all."

Liz's heart sank as she recalled that at age sixteen Garrett had run away from home to join the Union army—before Mrs. Crawford's time, it seemed.

Warming to her subject, Mrs. Crawford continued. "When Old Mr. Rowland and his wife died in a carriage accident, it was...uh...the eldest in the household, home from the War, that kept me on as housekeeper."

Noting the housekeeper's reluctance to mention the name of Elizabeth's dead husband, Liz prompted her. "And later?"

Mrs. Crawford's expression clearly indicated she'd rather not continue the discussion, though she finally responded cordially enough. "Why, I've the same arrangement with Mr. Garrett as I did before—cottage and board."

So, in a backhanded sort of way, Garrett had inherited the housekeeper, along with Elizabeth, Michael's unborn child, and a failing plantation he would probably just as soon have seen go down the tubes. For a man who'd spent his adult life footloose, fancy free, and avidly skirting responsibility, he was now in it up to his disarming blue eyes in responsibility, Liz surmised.

Liz had not failed to notice that while they'd been talking, the housekeeper had worked her way back across the bedroom toward the wastepaper can. Now she peered inside. Shaking her head and clucking her tongue, she retrieved a piece of tightly balled vellum from beneath the writing desk.

"What's this, ma'am?" she asked as she unwadded the sheet. "Why, it's a page from your lovely leatherbound journal. So that's what you've been burning. Now, why ever would you want to do that? I thought you treasured that book. Such an expensive wedding gift, too, with paper so dear."

Sensing a juicy tidbit of information, Liz perked up perceptively. "From Garrett?" she asked, more sharply than she'd intended.

The housekeeper swallowed, the color in her own cheeks high.

"From Mr. Garrett?" Liz reiterated, forcing her to answer though she realized the older woman would rather avoid the question altogether.

"Why, no, ma'am. The journal was a specially commissioned gift to you from, uh...from Mr. Michael," she explained finally. She pronounced the name softly, almost carefully, as if she expected Liz to dissolve into a fit of uncontrollable weeping.

Liz resisted the impulse to assure her that mention of the name did nothing more than arouse her curiosity. And to explain that someone else had burned the journal. Perhaps to frighten her, perhaps to destroy documented information—she wasn't sure which one. But now that she was calm, she realized the fire had been superficial. The burning book cover had created the smoke, and as soon as it disintegrated into ashes along, with the journal's vellum pages, the danger would have died away to less than nothing.

Which meant the fire had been intended as a psychological rather than a physical threat.

"I... There were personal things in it I didn't want anyone to see," Liz said hurriedly. She snatched the vellum from Mrs. Crawford's fingers, in hopes of discovering a clue to the diabolical reasoning behind the incident. But the page was blank.

The housekeeper looked so astonished, Liz felt compelled to apologize for her rash behavior. "I'm sorry. That was rude of me. I'm afraid I haven't been myself lately." It was the understatement of the century, present *or* future, Liz thought.

The expression on Mrs. Crawford's face cleared somewhat.

"I quite understand. No need to apologize, ma'am. I've been widowed myself—twice, in fact. Then again, you've got something I never had to wear upon your mind and make the situation all the more difficult."

"What's that?"

"Why, a babe on the way, of course."

"Oh, that." So, her suppositions had been correct. Garrett had wasted no time in apprising the housekeeper of the precarious state of Elizabeth's health, as well as the pregnancy.

"Which reminds me. Mr. Garrett asked Dr. Breninger to stop by later this afternoon."

Dr. Breninger! The same Dr. Breninger Garrett had threatened to contact before she fell in the river? And she'd imagined things couldn't get any worse! The last thing she needed right now was an obstetrical examination. If word got back to Garrett that she wasn't pregnant...

She'd just have to think of an excuse to avoid Dr. Breninger. But how? It would look suspicious if she locked *herself* in her bedroom. Garrett would ask questions. She'd have to explain her actions, and she couldn't. Not now, possibly never!

Liz closed her eyes in an attempt to collect her thoughts, to plan her next several steps. When she reopened them, the housekeeper was lifting the lid of the trunk at the foot of the bed.

"Which gown would you like for me to put out for you?"

A vision of Garrett, crushing the blue pegnoir in his strong hand, popped into her head. Liz had had enough of people choosing her clothes for her.

"You needn't bother. I'll pick out the one I want to wear."

Mrs. Crawford's eyes clouded, and for a moment Liz thought she was actually going to protest. Then she relented.

"Yes, ma'am. I suppose... if you insist."

"I do."

Still, she hesitated. Liz belatedly realized that Garrett had probably leaned on the housekeeper to help with Elizabeth, and that the housekeeper might be genuinely concerned for her.

"Really, it's all right." *I'm all right!*

"Very well."

Mrs. Crawford crossed the room, hesitating once again at the door. "Please, if you don't mind, no more fires today, ma'am."

Liz almost smiled. "No more fires." *If I have anything to say about it, that is.*

"I'll show the doctor up when he arrives."

"No," Liz said quickly. She had no intention of allowing the doctor's visit to become even remotely intimate. "I'll come downstairs."

Mrs. Crawford raised a brow at her. "The house wants cleaning, ma'am. It's been shut up for a while now. I've only just finished this bedroom and the library. As for the parlor—"

Liz cut her short. "The library will do nicely, Mrs. Crawford." Once inside the library, perhaps she'd feel as if she were on an even footing again. After all, she was a librarian.

"But, ma'am, I . . ." Mrs. Crawford paused.

"Speak up. Tell me what's bothering you."

"Uh, yes, ma'am. It's just that you've never greeted visitors in the library."

Before Liz could bite her tongue, she asked, "Why not?"

As if she couldn't believe her ears, as if Elizabeth had never asked her anything of particular importance before now, Mrs. Crawford croaked, "You're asking me for my opinion, ma'am?"

Liz nodded.

The housekeeper looked thoughtful for a moment. "Well, I suppose it's because you always considered the library a man's domain, too masculine for the likes of a fashionable young lady...reeking of cigar smoke and brandy and fish stories, as you called them. Why, Mr. Garrett spends hours in there, poring over the ledgers. He meets his business associates there. He sometimes even takes his meals there. But you never—"

"The library will do nicely," Liz said, interrupting her.

The Rowland family library was the perfect spot to learn more about the darkly handsome man she'd supposedly married. And she could hardly wait to get a good look at the daguerreotype on the mantel. It had always fascinated her, and she'd never really had a chance to study it in depth, because the room was always roped off at the door with red-and-gold cording.

That should adequately occupy my thoughts until I can slip down the oak alley to the tomb and...

"I'm afraid Mr. Rowland might disapprove if we use the library," the housekeeper said, breaking into Liz's partially formulated thoughts.

It suddenly occurred to Liz that Mrs. Crawford's loyalties resided in her own sense of security, that she was a woman accustomed to straddling both sides of the fence on an issue, and that she'd do what she must to maintain her position at Rowland Plantation. In this particular situation, however, Liz had the upper hand, and she knew it. And she wasn't above using it as a means to reach her own ends, either.

Liz decided to bluff her way through Mrs. Crawford's obvious misgivings. Calling on her natural sense of authority, she firmly reminded, "But Mr. Rowland isn't home, and I am."

It's the moment of truth. Show your true colors by making a choice. Stand firm or back off.

"Yes, ma'am," Mrs. Crawford responded tightly.

Liz relaxed, allowing a sigh of relief to escape her lips. It felt absolutely *wonderful* to win this clash of wills and regain some semblance of control over her life; she'd just have to worry about Garrett's displeasure later.

"See you shortly, then," Liz said in parting, hoping to hurry Mrs. Crawford along. She had much to do, and little enough time before sunset to accomplish it.

The housekeeper exited the bedroom, muttering to herself about the taxing whims of high-strung, pregnant, newly remarried widows, and the questionable absences of their husbands.

Driven by the prospect of shortly returning to her own time, Liz enthusiastically turned toward Elizabeth's trunk, gazing down at the neatly arranged, tenderly preserved tissue-papered contents.

It was like peering into the heart of an open wound.

Revolted, yet intrigued, Liz stepped forward and knelt somewhat reluctantly before what amounted to part and parcel of another woman's personal life.

Elizabeth's trunk contained treasures the new curator of the homesite's historical museum might willingly give his right arm to obtain intact, Liz decided. Things lost to age and time and the general insensitivity of modern man.

She took her time sorting through the trunk. After all, if she was to impersonate Elizabeth for even an afternoon, it couldn't hurt to know something about her, Liz rationalized, subduing a nagging sense of guilt.

The crisp rose-colored tissue paper protested with a whisper of a sigh as Liz lifted out a trio of gowns and placed them on the foot of the bed. The first was an expensive number fashioned from ebony silk, the second an umber gabardine traveling dress studded with frilly bows and boasting a matching spencer, and the third an indigo cotton day dress cut in crisp lines and edged with smart black braid.

Funny, Liz thought. She'd expected a woman of Elizabeth's status to own more than three gowns. Perhaps there were others in the wardrobe, as Garrett had suggested. But she didn't have time to look now. The number of gowns Elizabeth owned was really irrelevant.

Liz dug deeper in the trunk.

Arranged beneath a layer of undergarments and pliant leather-soled slippers, she discovered a book by the Reverend W. K. Tweedie entitled *Home, A Book for the Family Circle,* complete with its own tasseled bookmark. Beside that rested a stereoscope and a stack of three-dimensional photo cards.

A reticule of crushed red velvet held an amazing array of memorabilia—from a broken string of amber beads and a shell cameo to an empty ebonized pillbox and a miniature china mule purchased at the world's fair. Liz also uncovered an inlaid leather workbag complete with a wooden darning egg, rapier-pointed scissors, needles and thread and a mother-of-pearl thimble secreted inside an acorn case.

And then there were the really personal items. Soulful things that silently recounted the installments of Elizabeth's life. The kind of stuff that made Liz's heart twist slightly and her breath catch in her throat.

Like a wax doll with a stuffed calico body and shiny glass eyes.

A creased advertisement from a Saratoga resort, and a jar of sand from some unknown shore.

A headache bag filled with dried mint, vanilla and spices.

A Confederate medal for bravery, pinned to a woman's lace handkerchief.

A heavy album bound with metal clasps containing pressed rose petals faded with age to the rusty red of dried blood, a collection of dance cards, two of which had been ripped in half, several valentines, and a handwritten marriage proposal tattooed with tears.

And, doubly poignant, an incomplete layette for a child who had never been given the opportunity to draw its first breath. A baby entirely overlooked by history, for Liz had read nothing in the tour guide's manual about Elizabeth's pregnancy.

All represented pitiful reminders of Elizabeth's life with Michael, yet nothing tender was included to acknowledge her marriage to Garrett. What had she thought when she discovered she was pregnant with Michael's child... perhaps on the eve of his funeral? Had she panicked at the thought of raising the child alone? Had she been forced into marriage with Garrett during a period when she was vulnerable and overly susceptible to the powers of persuasion?

Liz could almost feel Elizabeth's suffering. Her despair and confusion.

It drew her.

Gnawed at her.

Beseeched her.

And it also scared the hell out of her, because the more deeply she became enmeshed in the past, the more convinced she became that some tragic fate had befallen Elizabeth!

Suddenly uneasy, Liz hastily repacked the trunk with everything except the indigo day dress, a clean shift and slippers, gently easing the lid shut, as if in doing so she might somehow close off her own thoughts.

Poor Elizabeth, Liz mused, despite herself. How ghastly it must have been for her. Her life had been nipped in the bud, along with that of her unborn child. She'd been cheated, and she deserved to have her mysterious disappearance and death resolved. She deserved...

Liz tried to blank out the thought that seemed to bombard her from every angle, tried to defy the sympathetic stirrings of her heart.

Someone needs to investigate. But that someone isn't me!

Liz dropped her robe and peignoir to the floor and shrugged into the cool shift and the businesslike indigo gown. She had to be objective. Methodical. Practical-minded. Pragmatic!

"*I* deserve to go home, before I get hurt for being in the wrong place at the wrong time," Liz muttered aloud. If she stayed too long, she'd have to start wearing some sort of padding beneath her clothes to simulate an advancing pregnancy. And at the end of nine months... well, Garrett would be genuinely surprised when she delivered a bouncing baby *pillow.*

She imagined his knife would come in pretty darn handy then. She could almost feel the cold blade against her throat right now.

Of course, at the appropriate time of the month, she could fake a miscarriage. Then again, Garrett would probably accuse her of neglecting herself at the expense of the baby. Besides, she despised lying. It made her feel cheap.

"It's really not ethical to get involved here, anyway. When I get home, I'll do some in-depth research at the library, comb the homesite for clues. Uncover the ways the legends were right, and the ways in which they're wrong," she told herself as a form of self-pacification.

The bottom line was that she feared knowingly tampering with the past. She might be able to uncover the hidden truths, to bring someone to justice, if she played the sleuth long enough, but at what cost? If she changed the past, might it not also reflect on the future, and where would that leave her? Would it close her avenue of escape? Could she become entrapped in Garrett's world forever?

Get your priorities straight! she cautioned herself.

But even as she fought it, Liz felt her resistance weakening, sensed herself being sucked, atom by atom, into a past thick with shadows.

CHAPTER FIVE

Conscious of her gown's trailing skirts and of the soft leather slippers she wore, Liz carefully negotiated the staircase down to the central hall with her breakfast tray in her hand, wishing she still possessed the skid-proof tennis shoes she'd lost to the gluttonous Mississippi River. She'd almost made it to the last step when she slipped and would have fallen, if not for the balustrade.

The dishes on the tray toppled, and Liz tried unsuccessfully to catch them before they rolled off the fluted edge. Wobbling off its tall base, the porcelain teapot hit the floor with a shattering crack. It died a quick and brutal death.

"Oh, no," Liz groaned, gently gathering the sharp pieces, only to glance up and find the keen-eyed housekeeper watching her.

"I broke the teapot," Liz explained unnecessarily, extending the spout toward Mrs. Crawford.

"Yes, ma'am. I can see that. You didn't cut yourself, did you?" she asked, rescuing an unbroken cobalt-blue china cup.

"No. I'm so sorry."

"No harm done. It was an old thing, anyway," the housekeeper assured her as she took the spout from Liz's fingers.

"Yes, I know," Liz said sadly. That was what hurt so much. She loved old things. Next to her absorption with Garrett, prompted because she was at heart a sleuth, that was one of the primary reasons she'd volunteered at the homesite—so that she could enjoy the priceless collection of antiques on a continuing basis. And here she'd broken one of her favorites. Ordinarily it was encased in glass, untouched, protected. She wondered if the *veilleuse-théières* now no longer existed in the future. Or if it did in jagged bits and pieces of porcelain.

I'm damaging the past and therefore the future, Liz thought. *I have to get home. And soon!*

Mrs. Crawford took the tray from Liz, saying, "I'll just get rid of this, and then we'll begin—"

"No, don't trash it!" Liz cried.

The housekeeper looked stunned. "What?"

"I mean, don't throw it away. Please, put all the pieces in something and put them . . . somewhere."

Mrs. Crawford hesitated. "Where would you have me put them, ma'am?"

Somewhere safe, so I can ask the new curator about piecing them back together when I get home. If I get home.

"How about in a box . . . up in my room."

"A hatbox, ma'am? One from your wardrobe?"

"That'll work." Liz had recognized the rosewood wardrobe as part of the collection at the homesite.

"I'll see to it right away."

Poor Mrs. Crawford. She must think Elizabeth's illness has turned her into an eccentric, Liz thought as she watched her reorganize the items on the tray.

The housekeeper paused. "I've straightened up in the library...drawn back the drapes to let the sun in, opened the jalousies to let out some of the cigar smoke. I did not touch the clutter on Mr. Rowland's desk, however."

"Fine," Liz agreed, trying not to sound too anxious, though she could hardly wait to view the daguerreotype of Michael and Garrett. She had no qualms about riffling through his books and papers, either.

Liz turned to the left at the bottom of the staircase.

Mrs. Crawford scooted around her, preceding her down the hall to a familiar set of paneled pocket doors. She ushered Liz through them, quietly sliding the doors closed behind her.

The essence of the high-ceilinged room was the same as Liz remembered—troweled plaster walls, rosettes in the ceiling, a brown cypress floor that would eventually turn black from years of polishing—but there the familiarities ended.

As her eyes adjusted to the light, Liz realized she'd been introduced into a library utilizing none of the furnishings from the homesite collection.

Instead of open-shelved bookcases lining the walls, a single rosewood breakfront bookcase supplied the room with hardcover reading materials. Beside that stood a baize-covered mahogany card table complete with matching chairs. A masculine-looking kneehole desk, littered with paperwork, and his well-used leather armchair dominated one wall. A cloak-draped coatrack postured in one corner. And, rather than a settee, a pair of tapestry and velvet wing chairs hugged the hearth.

As she'd suspected, however, a daguerreotype of Michael and Garrett as young men graced the Carrara mantel.

But something else caught her attention—something both fascinating and frightening. An elegantly appointed full-length portrait framed in carved gilt was displayed above the oak mantel clock.

Never before had her displacement been so graphically enforced, Liz thought, her gaze riveted on the startling oil on canvas. She felt as if she been dashed in the face with cold water.

The model for the portrait was none other than Elizabeth Rowland. She was dressed in Lincoln-green silk, holding a bouquet of Cherokee roses, and wearing a sparkling ruby necklace at her throat and an etched wedding ring upon her slender finger. Though her own features were more refined than Elizabeth's—her hair honey-blond rather than dishwater, her eyes a deeper brown, her lower lip fuller—Liz now knew for certain why she'd won the homesite's look-alike contest.

There existed between them an uncanny resemblance. She and Elizabeth could have been sisters. No, it was more than that. Liz didn't like to think it, much less say it aloud, but they could almost have been . . .

"Mirror reflections," she marveled. She stepped more deeply into the room, to better study the woman fate had ordained she impersonate.

Elizabeth's lips had a slightly petulant tilt that Liz knew hers lacked. Her eyes were more rounded and her teeth less straight—at least they appeared, to be judging by the portrait. Yet she had the same decisive chin, the same oval face, and a similarly fair complexion.

Still, it was their figures that astonished Liz the most. *No wonder Elizabeth's clothes fit me,* Liz mused. She'd heard of body doubles, but this was ridiculous! It gave her the creeps. It was now crystal-clear to hear how Garrett had mistaken her for Elizabeth.

Liz reached for the daguerreotype. A young Garrett, face unscarred and smiling, stared back at her. He seemed happy, and yet a haunted expression marred his beautiful eyes.

She tentatively traced the lines of his face and body, wondering why his arm was in a sling. Had he been a rambunctious teenager? Had he fallen from a tree, or perhaps a horse, Liz wondered, recalling the huge black stallion he'd seemed to control as easily as a rocking horse. Or had he and Michael gotten into a tussle, as siblings were prone to do? And if so, who had been the victor?

There was so much room for speculation....

Liz almost jumped out of her skin when Mrs. Crawford eased the library doors apart and stuck her head inside.

"I've put the broken teapot in a hatbox in the wardrobe, as you requested."

"Good," Liz managed, in a strained voice.

"Pardon me, but is everything all right, ma'am?" the housekeeper asked from the doorway.

Liz cleared her throat, replacing the daguerreotype on the mantel. "Yes. Why wouldn't it be?" she asked distantly.

"No reason, ma'am, it's only that...uh...I thought I'd best let you know the doctor has arrived. He's outside on the veranda, asking to be received."

Great! Liz thought. The moment she'd been dreading had finally arrived.

Liz took a deep breath and exhaled slowly, rubbing her arms, which had been wrapped in an unconscious hug about her upper body.

"Give me a minute and then show him in."

Liz hurried to the wing chair facing the door and eased into it. Sitting ramrod-stiff, she smoothed her skirts across her lap, pasted a smile on her lips, and waited.

Within minutes, a gallant old gentleman who reminded her of Colonel Sanders stepped into the room. He stopped short when he saw her, bowed with a practiced flourish, then advanced toward her chair, hand extended.

Mrs. Crawford stood like a sentinel by the door.

"My dear," he chortled, taking Liz's hand in his own gnarled one and patting her knuckles. "Mrs. Crawford told me you were up and about. I can't tell you how charmed I am to see it for myself. I've been concerned about you."

"The feeling is mutual," Liz said with a gracious smile. She tactfully extracted her hand from his.

"I take it the morning sickness has ceased?"

He reached for her wrist this time, looking toward the rosette on the ceiling as he calculated her pulse.

"I guarantee it," Liz said.

"And what of the melancholy?" He released her hand to pull up an eyelid and gaze into her eye.

"Nothing out of the ordinary, considering."

"Have you been sleeping?"

"Like a rock." *Normally.*

"I suspected as much.... Eyes as clear as a bell. Taking walks to help with the circulation?"

"As often as possible."

"Stick out your tongue, my dear."

Liz did so, somewhat apprehensively.

"Good color there, too."

"Is she eating her calf's liver Mrs. Crawford?" he asked over his shoulder.

"No, sir," the housekeeper said from the doorway.

The doctor frowned at Liz. "You should be, you know. It's good for the baby."

"I don't like liver," Liz remarked.

The doctor chuckled. "Elizabeth, you sound as if you've finally got some life back into you. I hereby pronounce you fit as a fiddle."

"That's all?" Liz asked. This was the strangest doctor's visit she'd ever participated in.

"All what, my dear?"

"All there is to the examination?"

"Well, what did you expect?"

Liz almost laughed. Her fears had been entirely unfounded. She should have realized that in a day and age when women weren't allowed to show their ankles, an doctor's examination would be only cursory. How women had survived childbirth with such haphazard prenatal care was a mystery to her.

"I'm so happy you could stop by, Doctor," Liz said, ignoring his question. It was true. Perhaps now Garrett and Mrs. Crawford would get off her back.

"Glad to do it. Send Garrett around, if you need me. Otherwise I'll plan to see you again this same time next month, as he's instructed."

I certainly hope not! I have no intentions of hanging around here that long. "Yes, you do that."

"By the way, I passed Garrett on the River Road. Seemed in a mighty big hurry." Dr. Breninger said. "He was preoccupied—did no more than nod in my direction."

Liz wondered fleetingly if Garrett had timed the incident with the wastepaper can in the hope that the doctor would catch her overwrought and prescribe further sedation for her. If he had, he'd be bitterly disappointed when he learned the doctor's verdict.

"You'll have to excuse Garrett," Liz said, because the doctor seemed to expect a response from her. "He's had a lot on his mind lately." *Mainly how to get rid of an unwanted wife.*

Liz rose to escort the doctor out, but Mrs. Crawford beat her to it.

"I'll see the doctor to the door," the housekeeper offered.

"Thank you," Liz replied. She heard the front door open and close. Presently, Mrs. Crawford reappeared.

"I'll be out back in the kitchen if you need me, ma'am," she said.

"I won't be needing you."

With the raising of a brow, Mrs. Crawford asked, "No tea today, ma'am?"

"Not today." Not any day. She hated hot tea. "You go ahead, though."

"And what might your calendar be, if you don't mind me asking?"

Liz smiled. Mrs. Crawford didn't fool her one bit. Obviously Garrett had asked the housekeeper to keep an eye on her for him. The woman wouldn't have been so bold otherwise.

"I think I'll rest here for a while, perhaps catch up on my reading, and then I plan to take a stroll down by the river."

"I'm not so sure Mr. Rowland would—" the housekeeper began.

Liz interrupted her. "You heard Dr. Breninger. To quote, I'm 'fit as a fiddle.' And he as much as prescribed long walks for my circulation. Now, if you'll excuse me...and close the door behind you," she said firmly.

Mrs. Crawford gave a curt nod and backed out of the library.

Liz sat for some time in the wing chair, gazing up at the portrait of Elizabeth, finally turning to Garrett's desk when she felt sure that the housekeeper was otherwise occupied in the kitchen.

The clutter Mrs. Crawford had referred to turned out to be a mass of sympathy letters, along with an equally large stack of bills held together with a brass paper clip. It seemed Michael's creditors had fallen on Garrett like a flock of vultures, Liz thought, flipping through the paperwork. Many of the bills were duns from millineries, seamstresses, and jewelry shops—duns with staggering totals.

Now wait just one minute! Something wasn't adding up here, she thought, reviewing the lists of feminine purchases.

Nothing she'd found in Elizabeth's trunk had suggested she was such a spendthrift. Perhaps that was what Garrett had been referring to earlier, when he mentioned Elizabeth's shopping sprees to Natchez. He must have been attempting to sort through the bills and ledgers and settle some of the accounts this morning, though by the look of things it would take a pretty penny to get the estate out of debt.

Liz jiggled a few drawers, hoping to find the ledger book Garrett had mentioned. She quickly discovered that he kept all the drawers except one locked, and the unlocked one contained nothing except an inkwell, blotting paper and a stamp box. She'd learn nothing of personal value from the desk, she decided. She had, however, discovered the kind of financial pressure Garrett must be living under.

Why didn't he sell the plantation? Pay off the creditors with the profits? Get out from under the gun?

Liz realized the answer to that question, at least, was relatively simple. Though he would not admit it, he had loved his elder brother. And his brother had loved Rowland Plantation.

And Elizabeth.

Tossing the bills atop the sympathy letters, Liz left the desk altogether, wandering over to stand before Elizabeth's portrait again. Oddly disheartened, she stared into the eyes of the true mistress of Rowland Plantation.

"What sort of woman were you, Elizabeth Rowland?" Liz asked aloud. "What did you do with all the clothes and jewelry those bills imply you owned? The facts seem so elusive, so contradictory.

"Did you really love Michael to distraction, as the historians believe?" Liz asked the life-size portrait. "Were you happy together? Were you thrilled to be carrying his baby—the Rowland heir?" She sighed. "Or is my sympathy misplaced? Were you simply a heartless troublemaker who disappeared and left me holding the bag?"

The clock on the mantel chimed loudly, breaking into Liz's thoughts, demanding her immediate attention. Her gaze drifted from the portrait down toward the clock's glass face.

Four o'clock in the afternoon already? Where had the day gone? She'd have to get on the ball if she planned to visit the tomb before Garrett returned.

Liz made it out the back door, across the veranda and down the path beyond the free standing kitchen, only to be drawn back to the small brick house by the aroma of jambalaya simmering on a wood stove. Enthralled with the contents of Elizabeth's trunk and anxious to begin her search for the path home, she'd hardly touched her breakfast. Now her stomach grumbled in acute protest.

Telling herself she could use an energy pick-me-up, she dallied in the kitchen long enough to sample a dish of the highly seasoned mixture of chicken, sausage, shrimp, oysters, tomatoes, and okra poured over a bed of fluffy white rice.

Her visit, and the praise she bestowed on the food seemed to mollify Mrs. Crawford. Once she finished eating, Liz had surprisingly little trouble slipping down the quarter-mile oak alley toward the last place in the world she really wanted to visit—the Rowland family vault.

Buck up, kiddo, Liz told herself as the tomb came into view. *It's your ticket home.* "I hope," she added aloud as her steps slowed to mincing proportions.

Today, in the late-afternoon light, the tomb seemed almost benevolent with its solid plaster veneer and its fresh coat of white-wash. Not half as imposing or brooding. And definitely less sinister.

But looks could be deceiving.

A brilliant flash of crimson shot through the trees, startling Liz—a redheaded woodpecker fed by hunger and bent on destruction. Claws extended, it landed under the eaves of the vault. She listened to its rapid peck-peck-pecking, wondering if its sharp little bill had contributed to the wood damage the restoration society in her century was pledged to restore. Thoughts of the bird took her mind off other matters. Off her fear of approaching the tomb. Of what it might hold for her today.

Or what it might *not* hold.

Liz took a tentative step toward the vault. Then another. And another. Until she stood a yard from the marble door.

Nothing happened.

Of course nothing's happening, Liz admonished herself. *You sheltered inside the doorway during the storm. Not out here, three feet from the doorjamb.*

She shuffled closer. Still nothing happened. No keening. No blackness. No nothing.

"This isn't doing me a bit of good," she said out loud.

Liz exhaled, clenching her fists at her sides. She had to open the door and step within. That was all there was to it. If she wanted to get home badly enough, she'd open the door and ease inside. She *had* to make herself do it. She couldn't stay here. Not in the past. Not with Garrett Rowland, pretending to be someone she wasn't, forfeiting her own destiny for that of a woman who had lived a century before her.

She wouldn't do it; she couldn't do it.

She had to move while she had the chance.

Go for it! she told herself, forcing her hands to unfurl. She released the outside catch and flattened her palms against the cool marble panel, making her muscles strive, her feet move forward.

Liz suddenly sensed a presence behind her. Before she could wheel around, she felt a large hand splay across her back. Cruel fingers dug into the soft flesh between her shoulder blades. Fingernails pinched her skin, compelling her to move forward in order to keep her balance. The pressure against her spine intensified as she was propelled against her will through the partially opened door and into the dank mustiness of the Rowland family vault.

Before she quite knew how it happened, the door slammed with a horrifying thud behind her, sealing her within the profound and stifling darkness.

Blinded by the truancy of the light, Liz fumbled at the door. She frantically traced the width and height of the wooden doorjamb with the tips of her trembling fingers. Over and over and over again.

Finally, with a severe sense of terror that stilled her hands and stabbed at her heart, she acknowledged that the door possessed no latch on the inside.

CHAPTER SIX

Horrified, Liz turned away from the door and stretched out her arms, intent on discovering another means of escape from the black netherworld. Her fingers met with something hard and unyielding. Something with cold metal handles and squared sides. Something shrouded in a blanket of dried blossoms that rustled like crushed tissue paper when her hands brushed against them.

Liz felt the blood drain from her cheeks.

A flower-draped coffin! Michael Rowland's coffin.

"No," Liz croaked. She shook her head as she backed away from the coffin, coming abruptly up against the slick, moisture-laden inner wall of the vault. Silently she cautioned herself not to hyperventilate. Not to give in to hysteria.

"This place feels...like a...sauna," she whispered. Her mouth felt as dry as chalk dust as she nervously thumbed open the buttons at her throat, trying her utmost not to panic. Her statement was echoed eerily back at her, strained and unfamiliar, as if rasped by the voice of a stranger.

Slumped against the wall, Liz strained to see through the pitch-blackness, while the ensuing minutes whittled away at her peace of mind and her badly shaken composure. It was too dark for her eyes to adjust. She fought the panic welling within her, suffocating her in her own fear.

Don't be ridiculous! Think positive! There's nothing in here that can hurt you. And the vault isn't hermetically sealed. You can breathe! Now breathe! Deeply. Hold it. Now exhale, slowly, Liz coached herself as she tensed and relaxed her fists.

It was a foregone conclusion that sooner or later Mrs. Crawford would come searching for her, Liz told herself. Probably sooner rather than later, knowing Garrett's housekeeper. Then all this would seem like a bad dream.

As the fire in the bedroom did now.

A coincidence. An accident. Just one of those things.

Liz swallowed, listening to her heart as it pounded madly in her ears.

Only this wasn't an accident. She'd felt the fingernails digging into her back, forcing her forward. And she'd never forget the sensation of the door being slammed against her. Never!

Lord, how she wished she had her cordless phone, so that she could dial 911 for assistance! She wished plenty of things right now. Most of all she wished she didn't once again suspect Garrett of arranging this incident to frighten her into behaving. If he'd come home early to discover her visiting the tomb, he'd have been incensed, she reasoned. Perhaps enough to play a callous trick on her as a warning.

At least she prayed it was a warning, rather than an out-and-out attempt at relieving himself of the burden of an unwanted wife.

In all probability, Garrett was waiting just outside the marble door, listening for her to start screaming her lungs out. She wouldn't give him the satisfaction, Liz thought.

By the time she had slowly counted to 5,250 Liz had changed her mind. Screaming didn't seem like such a bad idea after all. If nothing else, it might relieve some of the anxiety she felt inside.

She opened her mouth, but nothing came out.

She cleared her throat and tried again. Finally her vocal cords decided to cooperate.

The words came out softly at first, growing stronger with each passing second, until her cries sounded like those of a banshee on the prowl. "Help! Somebody out there, help me! I need help! I'm locked in and I can't get out!" Liz punctuated her cries by pounding on the door with the flats of her hands.

To her relief, within minutes the door swung inward. Liz started, blinking at the infusion of dusky light, like a bat disturbed in its cave by the direct beam of a flashlight. She inhaled deeply of the summer fragrances borne into the vault on the wings of a cooling breeze— fresh water and clean air and the ethereal fragrance of roses swelling around her.

"Elizabeth? Is that you? Good God, it is you! How long have you been trapped in there?" a welcome voice asked.

"Not too long . . . an hour, maybe. I'm . . . not sure," Liz said as she tumbled gratefully into Calvin Trexler's comforting arms.

"Thank heavens I heard you call out. It was a good thing I decided to come to the gazebo this way," he murmured, gently smoothing a tendril of hair from her eyes.

"Someone pushed me inside and shut the door," Liz explained in a tremulous voice, nearly in tears now that she was free.

"I'm here now," he reassured her with a warm smile. "You are safe."

It was obvious Elizabeth's cousin was concerned for her, that he wanted to help. She wanted to trust him. Not only that, she feared she might really go nuts if she didn't voice her suspicions about Garrett. If she didn't confide in *someone*. And Calvin was the logical choice.

"I'm afraid Garrett is trying to kill me," Liz confessed in a rush.

Calvin's eyes narrowed. "I have advised you repeatedly that you cannot trust the man, but you refuse to listen."

"I had ample time to think about things in the vault," Liz faltered. "Garrett carries this knife in a sheath at his waist, and when I contradict him he rests his fingertips on the hilt as if he'd love to use the blade on my throat."

"Despite what you believed when you married him, he harbors no love for you or the child you carry. You finally understand that now, don't you?"

"I think so," Liz said, hoping to learn more about Garrett from him by allowing Calvin to fill in the blanks.

"If only you had listened when it happened the first time." He gave her a tight bear hug of assurance. "I could have saved you from this episode."

Liz realized she had to be careful. By all accounts, Calvin had been extremely close to Elizabeth. Closer than Mrs. Crawford. Or Garrett. Perhaps almost as close as her husband, Michael. It would be so easy to make a misstep with him and incriminate herself.

"I'm afraid I don't remember being shut inside the vault before today," she said.

Calvin looked incredulous. "You do not recall the incident at Michael's funeral? Barring the fact that the minister rescued you rather than me, it was a mirror reflection of Garrett's recent attempt to frighten you."

There are lots of things that seem fuzzy since my fall in the river," Liz hurriedly informed him.

"Well, fancy that—gaps in your memory," Calvin said.

Liz nodded.

"I have heard of that before. During the War. Sometimes men with head wounds would suffer from it."

"It—" Liz began.

Calvin interrupted her. "You poor, brave, dear. When I think of the hell that blackguard has put you through in the name of brotherly love, it turns my stomach."

As he spoke, Calvin slipped an arm around her waist. With a short sigh, he drew her down the twisted garden path, toward the gazebo and the benches lining the interior.

"Tell me, sweetheart—do you recall how you fell in the river the other day?"

History said she could trust Calvin with the truth, Liz reminded herself.

"Garrett was angry because Eliz—I'd visited the tomb. I was running from him. I accidentally tripped off the dock."

For a moment Liz thought she saw a rush of relief on Calvin's face, but she quickly realized she must have misread his expression. Garrett had her so shaken, she could hardly think straight.

"I am glad I sent the note to you this morning," he said, settling down beside her on one of the seats, his arm securely around her shoulder.

Taken aback, Liz stared at her hands, more confused now than ever.

"You sent the note? But how? I thought—"

"I know what you thought," he assured her gently. "You thought I would not dare cross Garrett, even though I vowed to you that I would return to the plantation."

"You shouldn't be here, not after the way he—"

"I am not afraid of Garrett," Calvin said quickly. "Not when it comes to you. I hold you in high esteem, Elizabeth. You have always been special to me. Even as children, playing in the stockroom of our fathers' mercantile in the French Market on Decatur Street."

He paused, as if recalling something especially pleasing to him.

"And in the Vieux Carré, how you would dance and sing to entertain the elite as they promenaded through the square toward Saint Louis Cathedral and their stuffy religious services. You were such a pretty little thing. Always laughing. Always gay. Always so amusing."

She'd never done any of those things, Liz thought. But she couldn't tell Calvin that. He would think she'd gone off the deep end.

"But how—" she began.

Seeming to interpret the question before she had completely formed the thought, Calvin interrupted her. "My horse is tied over yonder, in the forest. I decided to remain overnight with friends, farther down, along the River Road...to be near you, Elizabeth. Just in case you needed me."

"Why take such a chance? Garrett might have seen you. What would you have done then?" The imaginary confrontation played over and over in Liz's mind, like a film clip. It wasn't a pretty scene. She couldn't help cringing.

"I would have crossed that bridge when I came to it...*if* I came to it," Calvin commented.

There was a hint of something elusive in his voice. Something she couldn't quite clamp on to. Before she could consider it further, Calvin dug deep into his coat pocket and extracted a velvet-wrapped parcel.

His hazel eyes alive with excitement, he said, "I brought you something." He unwrapped the parcel and pressed a small jeweled casket into Liz's hand.

"I stopped by the jeweler's in New Orleans a few days ago, but I never got around to presenting this to you. It is one of the reasons I felt I had to see you today. Please, go ahead, open it," he said encouragingly.

Liz lifted the lid and peeked inside. A mourning brooch fashioned from a lock of sable hair shot through with gold thread and framed in black enamel and seed pearls, rested on a cushion of plush red satin. Encircling the brooch was a matching bracelet of braided hair.

There was no doubt in her mind that the hair, so like Garrett's in color and texture, had to be that of Michael Rowland.

Liz almost grimaced at the macabre pieces of memorabilia. Glancing at Calvin, who was rigid with expectation, she consciously turned her frown right side up.

He visibly relaxed. "You are pleased. I knew you would be the moment I saw them," he said.

"They're...something else."

"I realize you had these commissioned several weeks ago. I also know Garrett is keeping a tight rein on the purse strings, so I took it upon myself to collect them for you."

Calvin proceeded to lift the pieces from the box.

"Consider them a gift—from me to you."

Liz knew Calvin was attempting to be thoughtful, and she appreciated his generosity and kindness in purchasing the items for his cousin. But the jewelry made her skin crawl. How could anyone ever get over the tragedy of a life cut short when wearing such intimate reminders? It was morbid. And potentially unhealthy. At least as far as she was concerned.

"Here. Allow me. I want to see how they look on you."

Hesitant to disappoint him when he was so obviously pleased with the gift, Liz reluctantly presented her arm for him to loop the bracelet around her wrist, staring at the gold clasp created from a miniature of Michael framed in pearls.

"Quite a nice likeness," he commented.

"I suppose so," Liz responded. Brooch in hand, Calvin glanced at the bodice of her gown. She saw the direction his gaze had taken, realizing belatedly that a nineteenth-century woman would never show her bosom before late evening. It just wasn't done.

"It was hot...inside the vault," she said quickly, reaching up to fumble with the buttons of the bodice.

"I am sure it was," he said, not unkindly. "Do not look so stricken, Elizabeth," he added, impatiently sweeping her hands away. "Social dogma is of no consequence between us. We have known each other far too long for such as that."

He pinned the brooch to Elizabeth's indigo gown, near Liz's collarbone, tentatively slipping his fingers beneath the material to ensure that he did not stick her. Their gazes met, and Liz saw a warm flicker of something register in his eyes—a glimmer of the long-standing friendship he'd mentioned, she guessed.

"You shouldn't have gone to so much trouble," she said politely.

"It was no trouble," he replied with an indulgent smile.

"Well . . . thank you."

"You are most welcome."

"I appreciate the thought."

"I am glad to hear it."

His expression suddenly grew quite serious. "You are so formal today, so cautious with me," he said in a pained voice. "Is this what marriage to Garrett has done, driven a wedge between us?"

"I . . . don't know what to say," Liz said. It was true. She didn't know how to respond to him.

"I want you to remember that I am one of the lucky ones, Elizabeth. I have come up in the world since the war. My investments have paid off admirably. I am—how shall I put this without being indelicate?—financially secure. Suffice it to say, I now move in the finest circles in New Orleans. No door is closed to me, Elizabeth."

Liz didn't have the faintest idea what Calvin was getting at. Before she could question him, he blithely supplied the answer.

"I could take you away from all this . . . now, if you want." A frown of concern marred his fair complexion. "All you have to do is say the word. Garrett has a volatile temper. It cannot be easy living under the same roof with him.'' He cast her a hard look.

Calvin had hit a vital spot. No, Garrett wouldn't be easy to live with...not on an extended basis. Not because of his legendary temper, but because he aroused in her something she would rather not face just now. A darker, more remote side of herself that she had never known existed.

Avoiding his eyes, Liz glanced toward the Rowland family vault. She had been incarcerated inside the tomb for nearly an hour, and yet she had remained firmly entrenched in the past. Still, she felt convinced the tomb was her only key to returning to the future.

If she left the plantation with Calvin, she had no doubt but that there would be extreme repercussions— she might jeopardize her chance to return to her own time. Therefore, she had to remain with Garrett, even though history had taught her that Calvin was an honorable man and that she could feel secure in his company.

''My needs are adequately provided for,'' she said finally, although she knew there was nothing she needed more than a good friend right now.

''*Your* needs? What of my— Oh, never mind!''

Calvin's angry vehemence, like a gray cloud passing over the face of a golden sun, surprised Liz. She glanced up into his guarded eyes.

He shuffled his feet beneath the bench, studying her with a quiet regard that might have left a weaker-willed woman shattered and clinging. Finally, he said in a softly coaxing voice, ''Do you not think you are carrying this obsession a bit too far? I can do more for you and the child than Garrett can. Besides, the man can be explosive. You have seen that for yourself.''

"I'm safe as long as I carry Michael's child," Liz said, though the words sounded ludicrous to her. She was safe only as long as she could keep up the pretense, and she knew it.

The upward slant of his fair brows gave Calvin a sensitive appearance. That, in conjunction with the defeated look in his eyes, told her she'd wounded him with her rejection.

"Come with me, Elizabeth," he pleaded, arms stretched forward, palms up.

Liz was touched by Calvin's gift and by the fact that he cared enough about her—about Elizabeth—to try to take her away from Garrett and the danger he represented. But as tempting as his offer sounded, she couldn't leave the tomb and the doorway back to the future.

Liz bowed her head. "I can't."

"Cannot—or will not?" he asked grimly.

Liz bowed her head, wondering why Calvin was pressing the issue. In his time, divorce was a horrible burden for a woman to bear. Why wouldn't he be concerned with his cousin being branded with the shame?

Because he intends to shelter Elizabeth, she told herself.

The problem was, she wasn't his cousin. She could put her trust in him, but she couldn't do as he suggested, because it wasn't in *her* best interests.

"Both," she answered honestly.

He dropped his hands to his sides.

"I came here in the hope of talking some sense into you. I can see now the futility of my visit. You are not ready to relinquish your hold on the Rowland family," he said with elaborate casualness.

"I guess not."

He folded his hands across his chest. "You are determined to see this thing through?"

"To the best of my ability," Liz said softly, though she realized they weren't talking about the same thing. Calvin was talking about marriage and babies; she was talking about finding a way back to her own century.

Calvin gazed out over the garden, saying in a distant voice, "Strange how quickly the weeds take over an untended garden, strangling the more tender plants."

Liz followed his lead, glancing out across the chaotic garden.

"It doesn't take long without a gardener's care," she said.

"Exactly," he said.

Calvin turned toward Liz again and caught her hand. Flashing her a shy smile that said he forgave her for turning down his offer, he raised her fingers to his mouth and gallantly brushed his lips lightly across the back of her hand.

"So be it, then. I shall give you some time to think over my proposition."

"I won't change my mind," Liz warned him.

"Perhaps not. We will meet again soon, regardless," he promised, reluctantly releasing her hand. "And, by the by, wish that husband of yours all the best for me."

Liz arched a brow at Calvin.

"I mean it," he said.

"I doubt that. You don't give a fat ra—uh, a fat fig— about Garrett Rowland."

He actually chuckled. "You know me too well," he said, adding more gravely, "Take care, sweetheart."

And with that, Calvin tipped his hat and carefully descended the steps of the gazebo, favoring his right leg.

Left alone, Liz pondered her conversation with Calvin. At best, the encounter had been unsettling, leaving her drained and uncertain. At worst, she'd practically alienated the only friend Elizabeth seemed to have in this world.

Liz remained in the gazebo, watching Calvin limp toward the forest without benefit of his cane. She watched as he melted into Louisiana's dense summer foliage, until the sun was a mere memory of itself and the mists rising from the Mississippi River curled inland toward the garden. Until she could no longer put off the inevitable.

CHAPTER SEVEN

Liz hurried through the swirling mists toward the plantation house. Sprinting up the wooden steps and across the veranda, she let herself in the back door and slipped down the central hall toward the stairs, intent on ridding herself of the mourning brooch and bracelet. They were Elizabeth's mementos, and Liz believed they belonged in her trunk, along with the other memories of Michael she'd so carefully preserved.

But before she could reach the stairs, a masculine voice halted her. "A moment of your time, if you please."

Liz pirouetted toward the open doorway of the candlelit library. Realizing she'd really botched it this time, she had an insane desire to run the other way.

But she could tell by his voice that Garrett would only follow her, growing angrier by the minute as she sought to escape his summons.

Liz suppressed her trepidation, squared her shoulders and stepped gracefully across the library threshold. And paused.

How could she have forgotten in a single afternoon what a hunk Garrett Rowland was? Everything about him was perfect. At least on the outside. The inside was harder to fathom, she decided as she slowly advanced into the room.

"You saw him today, didn't you?" Garrett asked.

Rather than confirm his suspicions concerning Calvin, Liz said, "I didn't know you were home."

"Obviously," he said, his voice thick with menace. Sprawled in a wingback chair, he rolled an empty glass between his palms. Liz shot a sidelong glance at the Waterford brandy decanter on his desk. It was unstoppered and empty, while a plate piled with a serving of jambalaya sat untouched beside it. Catercorner on the desk rested the cloth-bound ledger she had searched for earlier in the day.

Smoothing her palms along the side panels of her skirt, Liz said, "I'll have Mrs. Crawford warm your supper for you." Sensing that the jewelry might upset him, she edged toward the desk in hopes of escaping Garrett long enough to stow it away.

She knew he watched her like a hawk as she sidled across the room toward the plate, though the oil lamp's wavering light phantomed his features. Feeling at a distinct disadvantage, she longed to flip a switch and flood the room with the gaudy glow of a hundred-watt bulb. Was it only yesterday she'd taken shadow-chasing light at the touch of a button for granted? And air-conditioning? Short skirts? Microwave ovens? Headache tablets?

How long was she expected to remain a misfit in an alien environment, in a tug-of-war between two men she hardly knew?

"Mrs. Crawford has already left for the evening," Garrett said, jarring Liz from her mental reverie.

So, she was alone in the house, with no one to act as buffer between her and Garrett. She stopped in the center of the room, halfway between the door and the plate.

"Then I suppose I could—" she began.

He scowled, the crow's-feet around his eyes deepening. "I'm not hungry."

"But—"

"The food is of no consequence. Leave it!" he exclaimed impatiently, raking his fingers through his already tousled hair.

Thoughts, like wary adversaries, circled in Liz's head as she watched him rise from his chair. His disdainful gaze immediately fell upon the brooch—the very thing she'd wanted to hide from him. A sardonic smile flitted across his lips as he strode toward her. He stopped when he was practically toe-to-toe with her.

The scowl that had begun at his mouth spread to his eyes as he glared down at her.

She swallowed, wanting to tell him that he was invading her space, and that she'd appreciate it if he'd just back off!

Under the circumstances, she didn't quite dare. He appeared weary, harassed—and far too volatile to cross just now.

"What a lovely piece," he said, though from the sound of his tone and the lowering of his brows it seemed he thought the brooch anything but lovely.

Liz's hand strayed to the brooch Calvin had pinned to her gown. She realized it wouldn't matter at this point if she explained she'd been under the impression the unsigned, black-bordered note was from him. He wouldn't believe she hadn't recognized her own cousin's handwriting—she could only carry the amnesia bit so far before someone caught on to her.

Liz stepped back, first one pace, then another.

"The brooch . . . arrived today."

"By special messenger?" His gaze challenged hers. She wanted to tell him Dr. Breninger had dropped it off.

But under such a direct and biting onslaught, she knew, she couldn't, because he would see through the lie.

"No. Calvin brought it," she admitted, lowering her hand to her side.

His mouth twisted in disapproval as he advanced toward her once again, cutting her off from the doorway.

"It seems you insist on repeatedly defying me where your cousin is concerned."

She'd never stopped to consider why Garrett would ask to meet her at the gazebo when he could just as easily have seen her at the house when he returned. Now she could have kicked herself for not realizing something didn't quite make sense.

"You've got it backward, Garrett. Calvin came to me. I didn't go running to him."

"And because he defied me, it is permissible for my wife to do so, as well. Is that what you're saying?"

She shook her head. It seemed she had a knack for putting her foot in her mouth. "Not exactly."

"I'll be damned if I'll be betrayed by my own wife! I've compromised my integrity and my livelihood on your behalf. My God, a man can be pushed only so far before he does something—"

Garrett stopped suddenly, reaching up to pinch the bridge of his nose. Recalling Calvin's warning concerning Garrett's explosive nature, Liz instinctively retreated until her back was literally against the wall. In his present temper, he might go berserk if he discovered she'd not only seen Calvin, but visited the tomb, as well. And then what would she do? She was in the house with him. Alone.

Garrett matched Liz's steps until he was so close to her his breath blew across her perspiration-dampened skin, cooling the sensitive area above her breasts. Now she wished she hadn't unbuttoned the bodice of her gown and folded it back to expose the top of her shift. It put her at a distinct disadvantage, for the summer warmth was nothing compared with the heat radiating from Garrett's eyes. Heat that branded the swell of her breasts, making it difficult for her to breathe normally.

Glancing furtively toward the door, Liz shifted in an attempt to draw away from him. He would have none of it, stepping closer still as he flipped the cloth of her bodice upright to better inspect the partially covered brooch.

Liz wondered frantically whether, if worse came to worst, she could race ahead of Garrett up the stairs and lock him out of the bedroom. And then what? Did she sit and wait and sweat until he found a key? Or kicked the door in? Or could she climb out the second-story window and shimmy down the tree without breaking her neck?

She doubted it. And even if she could, what then?

Liz glanced up, surprised to see a hint of amusement playing in Garrett's eyes. Was it possible he knew her thoughts? That he was actually enjoying watching her squirm? What kind of man *was* he?

Liz told herself that she must not allow Garrett to further unnerve her. Lifting her chin a notch, she said, "Calvin wished you well."

Garrett's sharply sardonic expression scared her. "Hah! I just bet he did. I suspect the man would give his good leg to see me dead. Do you have any idea what your precious cousin has been up to?" he hissed.

Liz shook her head at the man towering above her.

"Then allow me to apprise you of the latest developments. I received a telegram by courier from New Orleans this morning."

"I didn't see a courier." She wished he would move back a step, but he remained too close. And he was too unpredictable for her to take the initiative and move away from him.

"He came and left while you were sleeping."

"Oh."

"The bank president in Baton Rouge refused to transfer my funds to an account I opened in the city. I rode into New Orleans, only to find I must travel to Baton Rouge and sign for the transfer in person."

So that's why he was gone all day, Liz thought, wondering if the fire in her wastepaper can might have been an accident. Wondering if she'd overreacted because smoke to her was worse than any bogeyman.

"I would bet my last dollar Calvin Trexler is somehow responsible for this day," he concluded.

"I don't think Calvin would intentionally gum up the works," Liz said slowly, wondering if she could relax and let her guard down now that his anger seemed somewhat defused.

Garrett frowned. "Gum up the works?"

Liz realized she'd been thinking aloud. She'd have to watch her slang, she admonished herself. Garrett already thought of her as unbalanced. If she started talking in strange tongues to boot, he might check her into the nearest loony bin.

"I mean, I don't think Calvin would do that," Liz amended quickly.

"I don't care what he's convinced you of, he would and he did." Garrett's words were fierce, contemptuous and venom-filled, fed by acute frustration.

"But how?" she asked, feeling as if she were walking on eggshells as she watched his anger rise again.

"My lawyer in Baton Rouge warned me Calvin and the banking authorities in New Orleans were as thick as thieves. By God, I should have listened to him when I had the opportunity!"

"Are you saying Calvin is corrupt?" Impossible! As a tour guide, she knew his credentials were impeccable.

"I understand your divided loyalties. I do not condone them, however. The man is devious. He intends to thwart me at every turn. He thinks that by withholding my funds he can force me to sell off..."

As if he'd said more than he wanted to, he allowed his words to trail off.

"Perhaps it's just a mix-up. Things happen," Liz said.

"Where Calvin is involved, they most certainly do," Garrett agreed scathingly.

"What makes you think he had anything to do with this?" she asked in a hushed tone. Even in her day of modern, computer-aided banking, financial institutions made mistakes.

His jaw tightened. "Because, my dear, I have something he wants. Badly."

"I beg your pardon?" Liz said, surprised in spite of herself. "I'm not sure I understand what you're implying."

"Only that you look quite fetching today," he said with a longer-than-acceptable glance that made her distinctly uncomfortable and curiously elated at the same time. "There is a carelessness, a sweet disarray, about you that I've not seen before."

She was disheveled because she'd been scared stiff. But he didn't need to know that. Let him think it was natural, she decided as he continued.

"Any man would be, shall we say, tempted to compromise you. Even Calvin."

Liz didn't want to be so easily flattered by the backhanded compliment, and yet she couldn't help herself. His choice of words sounded so literary... so cultured... so very romantic. Even when he was angry, he somehow managed to navigate the complex labyrinth of her heart and hit home each and every time.

It was disconcerting.

Exhilarating.

And dangerous, she reminded herself. Garrett Rowland might sound like Romeo. He might even look like Romeo. But according to Calvin, he had the heart of Dr. Jekyll and Mr. Hyde. In addition to that, she was alone with him in a day and age when men considered it acceptable to force their wives to perform their "duty."

Garrett captured her hand, physically bridging the tiny gap between them as he examined the braided-hair bracelet. When she would have pulled away, he resisted, weaving his fingers through hers.

"Calvin doesn't think of me as a woman to be... compromised."

"I beg to differ. Attraction between cousins is not uncommon."

Maybe in your world. But not in my genetically enlightened one, Liz thought, saying instead, "If I didn't know better, I'd think you were jealous."

"Perhaps I am. You can only push a man so far," he rasped softly. Twisting a loose curl from her chignon around the finger of his free hand, he asked, "Why did you do it?"

Before she could gather her scattered thoughts and respond coherently, he continued. "Why marry me? Is it because I resemble Michael that you consented to make my life a living hell?"

Why hadn't she noticed before the way his voice level dropped low, and soft, when he was uncertain? Liz wondered. Was it because until now she'd never seen him uncertain about anything?

Liz glanced into his eyes, seeing a haunted expression that disturbed her. As if she were the one who had him cornered, rather than the other way around.

Her gaze darted to the portrait over the mantel.

"I'm not sure," she answered honestly, with an attempt at a lightness she was far from feeling. She had no idea why Elizabeth had married Garrett. Judging that the best defense was a good offense, she asked, "Why did you marry me?"

He laughed. The sound was far from pleasant.

His mouth mere inches from hers, he said, "Damnable pride. Pride is a curse. Did you know that?" he asked, squeezing her fingers.

Liz wasn't sure she knew what he meant. She did know that pride made people do and say things they might later regret. And that, much to her chagrin, she was suffering from a total lack of it, for, even in her fear, she was thinking what a handsome man Garrett was. And how she wished they'd met under better circumstances.

Liz said with bravado, "I know that pride has been the downfall of many prominent men throughout history."

"And you hope it proves to be mine, as well," he bantered, tightening the curl of her chignon almost to her earlobe. He used it to tug her face even closer to his.

For a split second, Liz could have sworn Garrett intended to kiss her. She saw it in his eyes, sensed it in his touch, as a heady rush of anticipation coursed through her body.

He wasn't fooling her with his somber expression. He'd felt it too. In that instant, Liz experienced another startling revelation—Garrett Rowland was a man who hadn't been happy, *really* happy, in a very long time.

Sympathy and raw desire warred with her better judgment.

Liz almost leaned into Garrett's embrace.

Almost opened her mouth to his.

Almost.

She caught herself just in time, reaching up to disengage the curl from his fingers.

She belatedly realized nothing she said tonight would make any difference. He was too angry for her to reason with him, too intent on intimidating her, on making her pay for Calvin's assumed treachery and Elizabeth's supposed betrayal.

Even if she threw caution to the four winds and explained that she was a time traveler and reluctant impostor, she doubted he was of a mind to listen to something so outrageous.

Fearful that she must somehow discover the answers to the questions and veiled innuendos that surrounded Garrett before she would be allowed to return home, Liz realized she needed to buy herself some time. Time in which she need not be constantly on guard, furtively looking over her shoulder while expecting the worst from Garrett.

Deciding to try one last time to relieve the tension between them, Liz drew an imaginary *X* across her chest with her index finger. "I swear, I'm not a threat to you, Garrett. Cross my heart and hope to—"

She broke off abruptly, stricken by the realization of what she'd been about to say.

Liz knew her eyes must have reflected her consternation, for Garrett's answered hers with a dark flame that seared straight through her skin to blister her very soul.

"Die," he finished for her.

Liz felt suddenly so weary she wasn't sure she could beat her way out of a wet paper bag, much less resolve their obvious differences tonight. Finally, before her composure slipped completely and she dissolved into tears, she said, "I'm tired. It's... uh...been a long day. If you'll excuse me...."

For a fleeting second, she thought she saw concern replace the hostility in Garrett's eyes. "Go to bed. Things will look better in the morning," he suggested, in a voice that held an almost tender quality. Then, as if he'd suddenly realized he'd made some kind of unpardonable slip, his voice hardened again as he added, "They always do."

He abruptly released her hand, stepping back and away from her.

Concealing the movement in the folds of her skirt, Liz flexed her bloodless fingers, staring out into the darkened hallway.

"Will you be coming up soon?" She hated to ask, and yet she felt she must know.

She forced herself to look Garrett directly in the eye. An impassive expression shadowed the straight lines of his autocratic countenance, but his eyes suddenly turned as cool and hard as topaz.

"Is that an invitation?"

"You know it isn't."

"I didn't think so."

He studied her intently for a moment before advising her, "I'll be up later. Leave the bedchamber door open."

Shaken, Liz realized that if Garrett took it into his head to exercise his husbandly "rights" tonight, if he decided not to take no for an answer, there was no one to protect her from him. Worse still, she wasn't entirely sure she'd want to be protected, if it came right down to it. She didn't like the idea of being alone in an enormous bed, in a strange room and a dimly lit house.

She wanted to go home. As soon as possible, before things grew any more complicated. Before she became so deeply involved, or so resigned, that she became stuck in the past.

Liz grappled with her feelings, glancing up to find Garrett smiling ruefully down at her. As if prompting her to action, he handed her the spatter-glass lamp from his desk.

She hesitated. "If I take the lamp, you'll be left in the dark," she said, wondering why in the world she cared one way or the other.

He laughed shortly. "The darkness agrees with my twilight disposition. You should know that by now. Besides there is a full moon. The natural light is enough . . . more than enough.

He was being poetic again, Liz thought. It was one of the things about him that touched her, swayed her toward him against her will. That made her long to feel a wall pressed against her back with no avenue of escape from him readily available.

Garrett must have sensed her inner turmoil, for he repeated slowly, "Go to bed, Elizabeth."

He took her shoulders, turned her around and gave her a little push in the right direction. "Go—now."

Fearing her voice might crack if she attempted to once again remind him to call her Liz, she simply nodded.

Plagued by doubts, she mounted the stairs to Elizabeth's bedroom, wondering how Rowland Plantation had managed to fall under the spell of such a dark enchantment.

Once inside, the bedroom felt too close and the night too oppressive, even with the door wide open. To combat the mugginess, Liz crossed the room and raised the double-hung widow as high as it would go. Light from a white moon spilled through the protective curtains, mimicking the lace with patterns that laved her skin as she stripped down to her cotton shift. She opened the trunk and dropped the brooch and bracelet inside, then hung the indigo gown in the wardrobe, pointedly ignoring the sheer peignoirs.

Still thinking of Garrett and his accusations against Calvin—and, more importantly, of their near kiss—Liz brushed back the mosquito netting and climbed into the huge feather bed, wondering if perhaps she might be suffering from PMS. It always made her do and say things contrary to her nature and seemed to temporarily increase her sexual desire. . . .

But no, it wasn't the rise and fall of hormonal levels that made her do and say the things she did. Garrett was the cause of her emotional and physical frustration. She might as well admit it and stop making up invalid excuses. The man titillated her. Aroused her. Attracted her—like a moth to a flame, as her grandmother Hayden had been fond of saying. And if she wasn't careful, she was going to get her wings singed but good.

Tense and apprehensive, Liz lay awake, peering beyond the netting, through the semidarkness, and out into the hallway. It seemed extremely quiet without the benefit of a radio or television. Breathing in short, shallow breaths, she listened to every squeak, every groan, every creak, as the house settled in for the duration of the night.

She dozed fitfully while straining her ears for the added sound of Garrett's footsteps on the stairs. Wondering if he might yet demand from her his conjugal rights. Wondering whether or not, if push came to shove, she had the stamina to deny him something she herself wanted.

Garrett paced the library, berating himself for leaving Elizabeth alone with only a weak-willed housekeeper to supervise her movements. What was it about Elizabeth lately that taxed his composure and sent him reeling toward the limits of masculine endurance? It hadn't always been that way. Of that he was positive.

Garrett twirled on his heel, staring at the elegantly appointed portrait over the mantel. Elbow propped on his fist, chin resting across his knuckles, he studied the painting critically by the full light of the moon streaming in the window.

It was a superb piece of work. Michael had procured the best immortalizer available in New Orleans to capture the image of his beautiful bride on canvas. Still, the painting didn't quite do her justice. Her eyes seemed a sultrier brown in real life. Her lips more sweetly curved and alluring. Her hair fairer, more lustrous. The col-

umn of her throat more finely turned. The upper curve
of her breasts...

No, in that respect, at least, the artist had captured
her to perfection. The softly rounded mounds rose high.
Proudly. And torturously.

Garrett whirled away from the painting and glared at
the empty brandy decanter on the desk, acutely aware
of her, even with his back turned toward her image. In
his mind's eye, he envisioned her lithe body. Her
moistly parted lips. Her devastatingly expressive eyes,
which appeared guileless one moment, shrewd the next.

His growing need for her was a contradiction within
itself. Desire tore at him, causing his temper and temperature to soar. He prided himself on his self-control.
Lived by it. Demanded it of himself. She'd destroyed
that, encouraging him to act like the animal his family
had branded him during the War.

Damn Calvin Trexler! And damn Elizabeth for making him want her so desperately...excruciat-
ingly...without half trying.

What would she do if he ascended the stairs, un-
dressed down to bare skin and slipped into bed beside
her? If he pulled her into his arms? If he kissed her inviting lips? Laved her throat? Teased her breasts?

He could do all those things. And he might. But only
on his own terms.

Perhaps there would come a time when she put her
grief for Michael aside and he could tell her she set him
on fire. That he'd wanted her since the moment he
dragged her from the river, wet and pliant and fighting
for her life. That the spark he'd seen in her whiskey-
brown eyes had ignited something within him that had
been buried away for years. Something that had grown

by leaps and bounds with each and every confrontation between them since that moment.

But the time wasn't now because it would give her too much power over him.

There was something about Elizabeth that he couldn't quite put his finger on. And he'd be damned if he was going to be led into a trap before he figured out what it was about her that touched him against his will!

Garrett slammed his fist on the desk. The ledger book he'd shoved to the corner of the desk when he could no longer stand to contemplate it toppled off. It smacked to the floor, opening to a seemingly endless line of figures. He stared at the total for a moment, acutely aware of the jeopardy Rowland Plantation faced if the crops failed this year.

He slowly bent and retrieved the book. Closing it with a snap, he tossed it atop the stack of bills awaiting his attention.

The plantation was dangerously low on capital, and it was imperative that he make the trip to Baton Rouge in the morning and sign for a transfer of personal funds from bank to bank. Funds necessary to their survival over the next few months.

If only the trip were not so supremely ill-timed.

Elizabeth had clearly proven today that he could not risk leaving her behind and open to the influence of a cur like Calvin Trexler. She suddenly seemed so much improved—both physically and emotionally. He couldn't take a chance on her swaying back the other way. Back toward a world of grief and pain and laudanum-induced sleep. Things that couldn't possibly be good for the baby she carried.

He was stuck with a woman he couldn't trust farther than he could throw her, and a cousin-by-marriage bent on ruining him, one way or the other.

Only one solution remained. Though it meant they would be thrown into an atmosphere of even more intimate contact, he would make Elizabeth accompany him to Baton Rouge—for the sake of Michael's unborn child.

He would deal with Elizabeth after the baby arrived.

CHAPTER EIGHT

Liz awoke, immediately realizing she was still in the
past. Garrett, freshly shaved and fully dressed, relaxed
in one of the bedroom's claw-footed chairs, long legs
stretched before him and crossed at the ankles. He
sipped from a steaming china cup.

Yawning, Liz asked, "What time is it?"

Garrett nodded toward the red-gold light filtering
through the curtains. "Dawn," he said, an edge to his
voice.

Liz turned her heavy-lidded gaze toward his side of
the bed. The silk quilt was smooth, the feather pillow
undented.

"You didn't come upstairs last night," she commented.

"I had work to do in the library."

Liz had the distinct impression that Garrett was me-
thodically working his way around to telling her something she didn't want to hear. Feeling slightly self-
conscious, she sat upright in the bed, punching her pillow up behind her back and tucking the covers about
her waist.

"No sleep?" she asked.

"As I said, I had business to attend to. Ledgers don't
add themselves."

"You must feel like death warmed over," Liz said,
although in actuality he looked quite handsome, with

his damp hair slicked back away from his face, his sleeves rolled to the elbows and his shirt unbuttoned to the middle of his chest. Handsome, and quite pleased with himself, as he stared at her for a moment over the rim of his cup.

"Is that concern for me I see in your eyes?" he asked. He casually reached for the silver pot on the table and tipped it to fill a second cup.

Her hand fluttered to her chest, and she felt her skin grow warm, as it invariably did under his acute surveillance.

"No, it's concern for me. I know what I'm like when I don't get my eight hours. I can imagine what *you're* like."

"You needn't worry that I've been lying in wait to nip your head off again this morning. As a matter of fact, I had a swim before daylight to ensure my good humor. They say exercise is good for the soul—soothes the savage breast, so to speak."

"I thought it was beast," Liz said.

"Beast? I don't think so—not according to William Congreve," Garrett said thoughtfully.

Liz didn't have the faintest idea who William Congreve was, but she didn't need a crystal ball to tell her Garrett was up to something. He was far too cordial. Too solicitous. Too... agreeable this morning.

She felt herself tensing.

"Beast, breast, whichever... same difference," Liz said, recalling her inadvertent dip in the mighty Mississippi and the hands of the beast on her breast as he forced water from her lungs.

"You sound a bit tense," he said. "Here, have a few sips of this. Perhaps it will help." He surprised Liz by offering her the cup he'd poured.

"I can tell this is going to be a bang-up day," Liz said sarcastically, her apprehension concerning Garrett growing by leaps and bounds.

He arched a brow questioningly. When she failed to respond he asked, "Bang-up?"

"First-rate," she explained.

"Ah, you mean excellent. Indeed it will be," he agreed.

Liz accepted the cup gingerly, sniffing at its contents and wondering what Garrett meant. But the aroma wafting from the cup in her hand soon sidetracked her thoughts.

Coffee. Wonderfully rich, fresh-brewed, mouth-watering coffee. Not hot tea.

Garrett had remembered. Not only remembered, but acknowledged her preference.

Liz paused for a moment, savoring the heady steam and thinking of the stainless-steel brewing machines in the cafés throughout the French Quarter that spat out eight different flavors of perfectly brewed coffee at a dollar fifty a cup. Café au lait was her first choice. But this didn't smell bad. Not bad at all.

When she hesitated before tasting it, Garrett drained his cup and reached over to refill his from the same silver pot.

"Don't worry," he said, settling back in his chair. "There's no laudanum in it, if that's what's bothering you." As if to prove his statement, he took a healthy swig from his cup.

"That wasn't what I was thinking."

"What then?"

It was strange how cozy they seemed this morning, Liz mused. Like an old married couple. Only they weren't old and they weren't married. And they didn't know each other well enough to be so darned companionable.

What *was* he up to? No good, most probably. Therefore, she'd best not let down her defenses entirely, Liz told herself.

"I don't normally drink coffee black and without a sugar substi—uh, sweetener." Liz followed Garrett's lead, sipping from her cup. "But this is good."

He actually smiled, and for the first time Liz realized he had dimples. They softened the harsh lines of his face, overshadowing the scar marring his smooth cheek.

"I'm glad you approve. I made it myself before the housekeeper arrived. And, speaking of Mrs. Crawford, as soon as you've finished your personal toilette I'll send her up to help you pack your portmanteau."

Wondering if there was a medical term for a psychopath with redeeming qualities, Liz slowly lowered the cup away from her lips. *Here it comes,* she thought.

"My portmanteau?"

"I've run up the signal flag this morning," he stated matter-of-factly.

As if that was supposed to mean anything to her, Liz thought.

"Signal flag?" she asked, lifting the cup once more to her lips.

"Out on the boat dock—to alert the captain of our intention to board. I plan to take the steamer into Baton Rouge. And I've decided that you shall accompany me."

Surely Garrett wasn't talking about packing an overnight bag and taking a steamboat ride down the Mississippi River! Liz thought.

"Impossible," she sputtered into her coffee.

He frowned. She saw the question in his eyes before he voiced it.

"Impossible? Are you saying you don't own a portmanteau? I could have sworn you did."

Liz didn't know if Elizabeth had owned one or not. And even if she had, Liz had no intention of packing it. She'd turned down Calvin's invitation to escape the plantation so that she could remain near the tomb. She certainly didn't intend to turn right around and depart the estate hugging Garrett's arm.

But she couldn't very well tell him that.

"I'm trying to explain that I can't leave the plantation right now." She chased through her mind for a feasible explanation for her defiance, in her agitation nearly sloshing her coffee onto her shift. "I've got some things that have to be done today. You see, the garden is in such, uh...lousy shape. I thought I'd do some pruning."

"Lousy shape?" he asked, as if she'd spoken to him in Swahili.

"Weedy. Overgrown. In desperate need of attention," she elaborated.

"The garden has waited these past few months. It can wait a few days more."

"No, it can't! For real." The words tumbled off her tongue and over her lips before she could properly weigh and measure them. "I mean, I hate to put the skids on your travel arrangements, but the weeds are strangling the rosebushes. The Spanish daggers are drooping. The, uh...holly is wilder than a—"

"What do you know of gardening?" he asked interrupting her.

"I have a shotgun duplex full of potted—" She stopped herself in the nick of time. Garrett didn't want to hear about her pink splash hypoestes. Her aloe. Her cactus. Her airplane plant. Her whiskey begonias and crimson geraniums. "I mean, people tell me I have a green thumb."

"Elizabeth, you never cease to amaze me."

I never cease to amaze myself, either. "Liz. I asked you to call me Liz," she said, struggling to maintain a modicum of her own identity.

"Where in the world did you ever learn such strange phrases? Death warmed over. Shotgun duplex. Green thumb."

Not in your world, that's for sure. "I'm half-awake. I . . . don't know what I'm saying."

"Half the time, neither do I," Garrett said dryly. "But that is neither here nor there. Drink up. We leave for Baton Rouge within the hour."

"Seriously, I can't be ready in an hour," she said. Perhaps if she stalled, the steamer would leave them behind.

"We will breakfast on the steamer," he said.

"I'm not worried about break—"

"I want you with me," he said, with a cold authority that brooked no opposition.

"But I don't want to go. Not just now."

"Mrs. Crawford told me the doctor pronounced you—"

"Fit as a fiddle," Liz finished for him. She'd never dreamed the cliché would come back to haunt her so vividly.

"Therefore you have no alternative, Elizabeth." His words were measured, chiseled in concrete and reinforced with steel as he pointedly ignored her request to be called by the name she preferred.

Startled by the rush of irritation that momentarily clouded her brain, Liz said, "You only want me with you so that you can keep an eye on me—and I've asked you more than once to call me Liz." Her voice sounded far more curt than she'd intended.

Garrett placed his empty china cup in its matching blue saucer and spun them across the table like a Frisbee. To Liz's relief, they stopped just short of the other side.

"You're quite full of yourself this morning, aren't you?" he ground out.

"Am I?" she asked, thinking, *I'm certainly trying to be full of myself, not Elizabeth.*

Garrett nodded. "Most definitely."

He vaulted from the chair and moved to stare moodily out the window toward the river. Hands pushed deeply into his pockets, he continued, "I thought the idea of a trip into the city would please you. I'd imagined it to be one of your favorite pastimes. The ledgers do not lie."

Liz wanted to tell him to chill a minute and give her time to think and to curb the unreasonable annoyance she felt. *She wasn't a spendthrift, and she hadn't run up an exorbitant amount of bills for personal gratification, because she* wasn't Elizabeth Rowland!

But then, Garrett didn't know that. And right now she dared not attempt to appraise him of the situation.

Calming somewhat, Liz finally managed to say, "I've . . . changed recently."

He rotated on his heel to gaze at her. "You're saying that I've misjudged you?"

"You don't know me well enough to misjudge me," Liz said quietly.

Expression dark, he declared, "I've made my decision concerning Baton Rouge. Don't force me to do or say something you'll regret."

"I'll regret?" Liz glanced at the ivory-handled knife riding on his hip.

After only two days in his company, she could tell by his erect posture, his set jaw and his compressed lips that Garrett was bracing himself for battle—if it came down to that. But she wouldn't oblige him. She wasn't up to one. Not this morning. Not when she had awakened in the past for the second morning in a row. Not with so many questions running like water through her mind. Questions she wished she could turn off with the twist of a handle like the chlorinated tapwater back home.

How many more dawns would the light of a nineteenth-century sun rouse her from sleep? Liz wondered. How many more lazy summer afternoons would she play mistress to an antebellum estate that didn't really belong to her? How many more trips would she make to an unobliging family vault where stale roses draped a wooden coffin? A place she must now overcome her fear of after being trapped inside it.

And how many more nights would she be consumed by fearful anticipation as, alone and unprotected, she awaited Garrett's footsteps on the staircase?

The answers were suddenly more daunting than the notion of a steamboat trip down the Mississippi with Garrett Rowland.

She would just have to go along with him and bide her time. Though she'd never been any good at waiting.

Liz sighed. "How long will we be gone?" she asked at last.

"Several days."

Days spent away from the plantation. Away from the tomb. Away from a chance at escape.

"How many? Two? Three? More?"

"A day and a half. Perhaps two," he said, visibly relaxing.

"Two?" She could zoom down to Baton Rouge from the Crescent City in an hour on I-10. Of course, that was in her time, not Garrett's, Liz reminded herself.

"New Orleans to St. Louis one way takes four days, and that's at full steam and racing the wind . . . so pack accordingly."

Pack accordingly. If only Garrett knew packing accordingly to her meant a black silk dress and heels, a couple of T-shirts, shorts, jeans, tennis shoes, a bra and several pairs of high-thigh panties.

What would "pack accordingly" mean to Elizabeth?

As much as she hated to admit it, Liz supposed just this once she'd have to lean on Mrs. Crawford for guidance.

An hour later, Liz stood on the dock, gowned in the umber gabardine traveling dress, minus the bows, and a sun-shielding straw bonnet that made her feel like Rebecca of Sunnybrook Farm, Elizabeth's portmanteau at her feet and Garrett at her side. He wore a tailored broadcloth suit, and a panamalike hat tipped at a jaunty, devil-may-care angle, which she found acutely attractive.

Keep your mind on the boat, she told herself each time she caught herself sneaking a peek at the handsome man beside her. A man any woman would be proud to walk beside.

If she dared.

"Here she comes, right on time," Garrett said. He pointed toward the bend in the river.

Liz squinted. "There's a man standing on the deck with a telescope."

"He's looking for the flag."

"Look, the boat's turning this way."

"They've seen us. Good."

Together they watched as the flat-bottomed paddle wheeler maneuvered toward them, tied up to the riverbank and lowered its wooden gangplank for them to board. Wasting no time, Garrett took her elbow and assisted her across the wooden plank, probably because he was afraid she'd break and run, Liz suspected.

The deck shuddered and shimmied beneath her feet when she stepped aboard, almost unbalancing her. Garrett's grip tightened as he steadied her.

Eyes wide and confidence shaken, Liz asked, "What was that?"

Garrett cast her a perplexed look.

"What was what?" he asked.

"That rumbling sound. For a minute, the deck felt like it was breathing," she exclaimed, thinking how notorious steamboats were for catching fire.

"The engines are beneath our feet," he explained.

"Yes, of course. I knew that," Liz amended quickly, wishing she hadn't asked the obvious. Naturally the engines would make the deck shudder.

She'd been boating on Lake Pontchartrain. She'd crossed the Mississippi on a great purring ferry. She'd even taken a cruise ship from New Orleans to Jamaica. But she'd never ridden a steamer. It was fascinating the way the twin stacks belched smoke and fiery sparks as the boat eased away from the dock and headed northwest, using its paddle wheels to churn the water into spume as it navigated the treacherous sandbars that dotted the channel. She marveled at the red-and-white superstructure, the gay flags fluttering in the breeze, the triple decks.

But most of all she marveled at Garrett's face as, with a teakettlelike shriek from the whistle and a cough of the engines, the helmsman guided the ship out into the flood-deepened waters of the river and away from Rowland Plantation. His expression eased perceptibly with what she could only term as genuine relief.

He must have felt her eyeing him, for he said, as he relinquished her to a man attired in a spotless white uniform, "The porter will see you to the stateroom."

"Where will you be?" Liz asked uncertainly.

Their gazes briefly met. "I'm going to the purser's office to pay for our passage. I'll be along shortly."

"Shortly," she repeated softly. She glanced away first, almost guiltily, unable to suppress the feeling that she'd glimpsed something she shouldn't have. Something buried deep within Garrett. Something painful and personal and not easily shared. Maybe one of the demons responsible for his dark moodiness.

The sensation was most unsettling.

Liz watched Garrett tip the porter. The man in turn shouldered their luggage and headed along the main deck toward a set of stairs leading up to the promenade deck. Liz had no choice but to follow him as Garrett disappeared through one of the many doors that graced the oblong superstructure.

A few moments later, the porter escorted Liz into a long, narrow cabin sumptuously furnished with Brussels carpet, gold-framed paintings, a tufted settee and linen shades. And brass-framed twin beds.

"Have a nice trip, ma'am," he said as he backed from the room.

A polite smile curved her lips. "Thanks," Liz said.

After he had gone, she untied the satin ribbons bisecting her jawline and tossed the bonnet Mrs. Crawford had insisted she wear onto one of the beds. Decorum via the perfect chapeau had gone out with the Jackie Kennedy era, Liz thought as she pulled the pins from her hair and ran her fingers through the dampened tresses.

Of course, with the summer sun beating down on her head, a broad-brimmed straw hat did have its advantages. The spencer, however, had absolutely nothing going for it, she decided as she shrugged from the tight-fitting jacket and added it to the growing heap on the bed.

Liz stretched and strolled to the window to peer outside her plush, hotellike room. She watched a flock of mockingbirds flit among the branches of the oaks along the banks. A pair of snowy egrets waded through the shallower waters in search of minnows. A beaver with a water-slick coat scampered near a dam of fallen saplings. She even saw a fawn standing at its mother's side in the shadow of a spreading magnolia on the lawn of a Greek Revival plantation house. With wide, innocent eyes, the doe gazed out across the water toward the lethargic steamer.

Along with the wildlife, Liz spied men fishing along the river. With the water high, the paddle wheeler passed so close to the bank that at times she felt she could almost reach out and touch the tips of their poles. No fiberglass rods and metal reels. No nylon line and artificial bait. Only cane, and string, and wiggling bloodworms.

The abundance of wildlife along the Mississippi, the harmony of nature and the languid life-style of these people only served to forcefully remind Liz of who she was. And where she came from. Of her own society, where time was money. Where hurry up and wait seemed the main buzzwords. And the story of one's life could be read through the typed lines of a credit report.

Liz abruptly pivoted away from the window. She didn't want the nineteenth century to become an attractive alternative to her own fast-paced society.

She couldn't stay.

She didn't *want* to stay. She wanted to go home, to the twentieth century, where she belonged . . . and leave Garrett Rowland in the past, where he belonged.

With a start, Liz realized she was lying to herself. Alarmed by the possible repercussions of such thoughts, she vehemently denied her growing emotional involvement. Strong coffee on an empty stomach had her wired, and Liz restlessly paced the stateroom, thrusting the bewildering thoughts from her mind as she awaited Garrett's return. She didn't have to wait long.

Garrett entered the cabin, glancing at the beds, as if to make certain the sleeping arrangements suited him, and then over at her.

"Did you get everything settled?" she asked.

"Yes," he said. "Do the accommodations suit you?"

"They're fine."

Garrett scanned the room. His gaze rested momentarily on the bonnet and spencer. As if staking a claim, he aimed his panama at the remaining twin bed.

"I thought they would be," he drawled as they both watched the panama settle in the center of the bed, as neatly as a nesting bird.

Liz filled in the motives behind his actions out loud.

"Together, yet separate," she commented, surveying the two very different hats resting on identical beds.

"That was the bargain between us," he said, seeming reticent and somewhat withdrawn now that the steamer was under way.

"Was it?" Liz asked, before she could stop herself.

"More or less," he responded.

Their eyes locked.

"I see. I'd...forgotten," Liz said, strangely troubled by his affirmation. Garrett's and Elizabeth's relationship seemed such a cold and calculated proposition. In marriage, at least, Liz believed love to be a mandatory commodity.

Garrett's eyes narrowed as the silence between them lengthened. "Once upon a time, outward demeanor meant everything to you. How is it that you've forgotten so much in a matter of days?"

Because the woman you married wasn't me, Liz was tempted to confess. Instead, she asked, "Could we please change the subject?"

"Why? What are you afraid of?"

That you'll find out too much about me. That I'll never find out enough about you to be comfortable in your company.

Liz dropped her gaze so that he couldn't read the truth in her eyes.

"The only thing I'm afraid of is dragging this little chat out so long that they stop serving breakfast before I get there," Liz said, bluffing her way past his query. "And having to make it to lunch on a cup of black coffee. And then getting sick to my stomach afterward because of it."

"Of course. Your delicate condition. How remiss of me," Garrett said after a short and far too thoughtful pause.

Liz nodded, encouraging him to think of the baby. She hated playing on a nonexistent pregnancy, but she was desperate to end this conversation, and it seemed to be Elizabeth's only ace in the hole as far as Garrett was concerned. Nothing else swayed him. Nothing else touched him. Nothing else mattered.

"There are several guests on board today," he added. "I suggest we remove to the dining salon before it becomes overly crowded." He proffered her his arm. "May I?" he asked.

"I suppose, if you insist . . . for appearance's sake," she said, trying to act for once as she thought Elizabeth might.

"But of course," he said smoothly.

Hesitantly Liz slipped her arm through his. Her fingers tingled where they rested on the solidity of his muscular arm.

Garrett silently escorted her along the promenade deck and down to the dining salon. As he opened the door for her to pass through, the clink of crystal and the clatter of silver upon china greeted her, along with the aroma of freshly baked muffins. She allowed the beauty of the salon's old-world decor to take her mind off Garrett's nearness. Off the way her heart palpitated and her knees weakened each time he touched her. Off the question of why he affected her in such a way.

They were seated at the linen-draped table by the maître d', and had barely ordered their broiled mutton chops and scrambled eggs and been served by the waiter when Liz caught sight of a fair head bowed over the remaining morsels of a huge breakfast spread on a table situated on the far side of the salon.

Calvin Trexler glanced up from his meal, and for an infinitesimal moment Liz could have sworn she smelled an evanescent hint of roses. When Calvin winked at her, she almost dropped the fork from her suddenly nerveless fingers, thanking her lucky stars that Garrett's back was turned to Elizabeth's debonair cousin.

With a frown, Garrett asked between bites of a buttered muffin, "Are you all right? You look as if you've discovered an eggshell in your breakfast."

"No eggshells... Perfectly fine," she said quickly, praying Calvin would remain seated. Or leave. Or something. *Anything* other than what she sensed he was about to do.

Holding her emotions at bay, she watched in horror as he tossed his crumpled napkin onto the table, pushed back his chair and rose to his feet. Leaning heavily on his gold-knobbed cane, Calvin weaved his way through the occupied tables, pausing every now and again to deliver a politely murmured "Good morning" to an acquaintance.

Unerringly he made his way toward her table.

CHAPTER NINE

Liz grimaced in anticipation of the forthcoming fireworks. Her practical side told her to brazen her way through the confrontation. Her spontaneous side advised her to run as if the devil chased her.

Garrett must have seen the anxiety on her face, for he turned in his chair and cast a swift glance over his shoulder. She watched his fingers constrict around the stem of his water glass, though his expression remained bland.

Clad in summer colors that complemented his golden good looks, Calvin reminded her of Robert Redford in *The Great Gatsby*. He smiled at her in greeting as he reached the table, reinforcing the impression.

Garrett's fingers whitened.

Liz expected the stem of the glass to snap like a fractured bone. Or for Garrett to stand, throw the water in Calvin's face and challenge him to a duel—just like in the movies.

The ninety-degree summer temperature seemed to escalate. She plucked at the constricting collar of the umber traveling gown, pulling the fabric away from her throat, only to feel beads of perspiration pop out on her forehead.

"Fancy coming upon you two here," Calvin drawled.

Garrett tilted back his head. Looking up at Calvin through half-closed lids, he surprised Liz by responding in a moderate voice, "Fancy."

It was far from the volatile reaction Liz had anticipated. She suspected Calvin experienced a similar sense of astonishment, for his smile slowly faded, and he continued with a cutting jab. "How touching—a second honeymoon, Garrett?"

Garrett lifted the water glass to his lips and slowly drained it before repositioning it on the table.

"I don't believe that's any of your business, Trexler," he said.

"I make it my business to know what you are up to."

In the same composed voice, Garrett said, "I assure you, I hold no illusions on that point."

Calvin shifted his weight to his left leg, leaning heavily on his cane.

"Elizabeth, you look well this morning...and drinking coffee, too, I see. I thought you were more inclined toward hot tea."

Liz's heart fluttered slightly. Of course Calvin would know Elizabeth's preferences. He would be more prone than Garrett to notice and question discrepancies. After all he'd grown up with Elizabeth.

She had always perceived knowledge as an asset. Now she realized it could also be a threat. Perhaps it was a good thing Garrett frowned on their association, she reasoned. It would save her lots of explaining.

"I've had a certain...craving for coffee recently," Liz said, alluding to her supposed pregnancy in the hopes that it would get Calvin off her case.

It worked like a charm.

"Entirely understandable," he said agreeably. He directed his attention toward Garrett. "By the by, who is looking after the estate in your absence? Surely a ten-thousand-acre plantation cannot run itself."

"Why should that concern you?" Garrett asked. He folded his napkin in a neat rectangle and placed it atop his plate.

"Because Michael—"

Calvin paused while a zealous waiter buzzed up, refilled Garrett's water glass and whisked away his plate.

After the waiter had moved on, Calvin tried again. "Because Michael would have wanted me to—"

This time, Garrett interrupted Calvin. "We both know Michael's interests have nothing whatsoever to do with this little tête-à-tête."

Calvin straightened. "Elizabeth is my cousin."

"I need not be reminded of that."

"I have her welfare at heart."

"How admirable," Garrett said, with a hint of sarcasm Liz found oddly reassuring. Garrett under tight control made her more nervous than Garrett flinging angry words around like a rotating lawn sprinkler. With the one, she knew where she stood. With the other, she could never be sure.

"How can you doubt it?" Calvin asked, as if highly insulted by the veiled insinuation.

Elbows on the table, fingers steepled before him, Garrett asked, "Has anyone ever told you that you're quite a tedious fellow, Calvin?"

Liz decided Garrett deserved a medal for his cool reserve—especially with Calvin pushing all the right buttons.

"Tedious or not, this is a public steamer, and I have a right to speak with my cousin."

"I don't recall expressing anything to the contrary."

"Back at the plantation house, you threatened to—" Calvin began.

Garrett once again intruded, and Liz suddenly realized it was his way of dominating the conversation.

"As you've so aptly pointed out, this is indeed a public steamer. If Elizabeth wishes to converse with you, by all means, be my guest. You won't mind, however, if I insist on being privy—husband's prerogative, you know."

Liz glanced around. The dining room had grown quiet. Every eye seemed trained on their table, every ear tuned to their next exchange. She decided Garrett had realized it, too, and was acting appropriately—polite, indifferent, and unperturbed by Calvin's determination to cause a scene.

Liz felt a grudging respect for the way Garrett was handling himself.

Calvin said, "I see that you are not wearing the brooch, Elizabeth." His tone sounded wounded, accusatory, as if she'd somehow let him down.

"We packed so hurriedly this morning, I forgot to include it," Liz said, wondering why she felt she must explain.

"I see." He glanced at Garrett.

"You need not look at me that way, Calvin." His voice dropped several decibels, so that only the most immediate tables could follow their conversation. "The brooch is nothing new to me, though I would have preferred to collect it myself, following our journey to Baton Rouge."

"I doubted that you would. That is why I delivered it myself."

Garrett's pupils dilated with rage, and yet his demeanor remained as cool as a cucumber. He didn't accuse Calvin of freezing his funds in Baton Rouge, as Liz half expected. Instead, he said simply, "Believe what you will." With a fluid gathering of muscle, he stood, which only served to emphasize Calvin's physical disadvantage. "And now, if you'll excuse us, my wife and I have some unpacking to do."

Liz could only assume Garrett was the kind of man who refrained from airing another man's dirty laundry socially. It occurred to her that the same couldn't be said for Calvin. She'd come from the future, where historically he was known for his savvy; yet today he was coming off as a twit. Then again, Calvin had been pushed to the limits by recent events—his best friend's death, his favorite cousin's remarriage to a person he disliked. To add to that, Garrett was a man who by his very nature made others feel inferior.

Liz believed Calvin had Elizabeth's best interests at heart, but because she wasn't his cousin, his kindness suggested a threat to her. It wasn't the same type of threat Garrett posed by his dangerous control over her, but it was just as real.

Calvin looked pitiful, and Liz felt sorry for him. But she couldn't let sympathy get in the way of good judgment. Not in this instance.

Her meal half eaten, Liz rose on trembling legs. Calvin stood his ground, his fine hazel eyes capturing and holding hers.

"My offer of yesterday still stands," he said quietly. "You need not remain here. I leave the steamer this evening . . . near Vacherie, when we anchor to take on coal. Come with me, Elizabeth. I'll protect you."

"You must be joking," Garrett said in a barely audible whisper.

Liz immediately recognized Calvin's angle. He had been baiting Garrett because he thought that, now that the secluded plantation was behind them and they were the center of attention, she might feel comfortable enough to accept his offer. He had intended to show Garrett up from the very beginning. Goad him into a display of temper, complete with witnesses, thus making it easier for her to gracefully leave Garrett.

Only, Calvin's ploy had backfired.

Poor, brave, misguided Calvin, Liz thought. He was trying so valiantly to be gallant in the face of overwhelming odds. He couldn't possibly understand that being away from the tomb with Garrett constituted only a temporary hitch in her plans. If she ran off with him, her displacement in the past would become a permanent situation, because Garrett wouldn't allow her near the Rowland family vault again in a millon years.

Her chance to return home would vanish in a puff of bluer-than-blue smoke. She dared not let it happen.

What a dilemma! She suspected that Garrett's marriage to Elizabeth was based on stubborn pride, and that Calvin's interest in Elizabeth was wrapped up in love of family. She admitted that two handsome men arguing over her proved flattering. But when it came right down to it, she had only one real choice. And she must make it now.

Liz slipped her hand over Garrett's arm. She felt his muscles tense as he pressed her arm to his torso. She was totally unprepared for the deliciously dangerous surge of electricity that zipped through her body when he reached over to cover her hand with his free one.

Nonplussed, Calvin stared at her for several long seconds before recovering himself. "Is that the way it is to be?'' he asked. His voice was strained, and his determination seemed shaken.

Though her heart went out to him, Liz nodded. "For the time being."

She knew he thought she meant until after the birth of the baby. She felt guilty, but couldn't afford to save his feelings by correcting him.

Calvin extracted his distinctive pocket watch and clicked it open to examine the time before he extended it toward Garrett.

"An incredible likeness of Elizabeth, don't you think?" he asked, as if determined to regain the advantage in this power play.

"The artist outdid himself," Garrett drawled. His fingers tightened across the back of her hand in much the same manner as they had on the stem of the water glass.

As if he had suddenly noticed the movement of Garrett's fingers upon her arm, Calvin said, "The miniature was painted from the one on display in the library. Michael was particularly fond of it."

"I wouldn't know," Garrett commented.

"Of course you wouldn't," Calvin said slowly, as if savoring every thrust. "You two weren't particularly close, were you?"

The scar on Garrett's cheek blanched a bloodless white. "Not in recent years."

"Not since you were a boy."

Garrett's jaw tightened, "I was a man when Michael and I parted ways."

"Barely sixteen, as I recall."

"Sixteen was considered a man during the War."

"So it was," Calvin said thoughtfully, and Liz had the feeling he was extremely satisfied with himself for some reason.

Calvin smiled toward her again, saying, "Well, I suppose it is time I was on my way."

"High time," Garrett agreed.

Calvin ignored the remark. "Good day to you, Elizabeth." He flipped the watch shut and pocketed it.

"Good day," Garrett answered for her.

With a slight bow, Calvin pivoted and limped from the dining salon. The clatter of cutlery against china resumed.

With a forced smile, Garrett steered Liz from the salon.

Once outside, Liz said, "Something bothered you in there."

"How astute of you to notice," Garrett said dryly.

Liz ignored the sarcasm in his voice. "It was something more than Calvin. What was it?"

He frowned. "I don't know what you're talking about."

Liz sensed that the pieces of the mystery were slowly falling into place. Now was not the time to wimp out, she told herself. Even if Garrett did look like he wanted to bite her head off.

"I think you do," she said, determined to drag the information from him.

"Calvin only does that to infuriate me, you know," he muttered through clenched teeth.

"You mean confront you in public?" Liz asked innocently.

"No," Garrett said finally. "Fiddle with that damned pocket watch—the one my brother bequeathed to him on his deathbed."

* * *

Back in the stateroom, Garrett turned on Liz.

"You were rather hard on Calvin back there," he said. "That's not like you."

Liz could only stare at Garrett, wondering at his unpredictable, lightning-like moodiness. It frightened her. Made her defensive.

"Isn't it?" she asked.

"No. Why didn't you go with him?" Garrett pressed, watching her a little too carefully. "It would have been so easy just to walk off the steamer on *his* arm. I couldn't have stopped you. Not without living up to the reputation Calvin has actively peddled since our marriage."

Garrett was fishing for something. It worried Liz that he might suspect something about her. It was also clear he was losing patience—with Calvin, with the upheavals in his life-style and with her. Would he revert to threats of locking her in her room because of it? She didn't think so. But the alternative of becoming a wife in more than name only concerned her more than ever.

Because she wasn't his wife.

And because the idea of being Mrs. Garrett Rowland didn't frighten her one-tenth as much as it had at the start.

"If I'd sided with Calvin, would you have let me leave with him when we reached Vacherie?" she asked.

Garrett grimaced. "Over my dead body, and you know it. Which leads me to believe you knew this episode was going to take place."

He had opened up to her when he told her about the pocket watch. Now he seemed intent on shutting down the lines of communication by accusing her of duplicity.

"You must have known Calvin was going to be on board the steamer," he continued. "Did you plot that rebellious outburst against him in detail when you met with him in the gazebo?"

Rebellious outburst?

Astounded by the question, Liz stammered, "How—how could I have known it was going to happen beforehand? I didn't even know *we* were going to be on board. Not until I woke up this morning and you announced—quite forcefully, I might add—that we were heading to Baton Rouge. I tried to tell you I'd rather not come along. But you insisted."

The man standing before her, so obsessed with the notion of his own freedom, was slowly chipping away at her right to be considered innocent until proven guilty.

"I could have just as easily stayed behind at the plantation," she said. "I'm accustomed to being in control, enjoying a certain freedom . . . like yourself."

"You had Michael wrapped around your little finger, didn't you?" Garrett asked bitterly.

Liz didn't know anything about Elizabeth's and Michael's relationship, so she hedged. "What has that got to do with anything?"

"You did, didn't you?" he insisted.

"We had an . . . understanding," she improvised.

"So do we," he said harshly.

"Do we? Funny. Right now, I couldn't quote it if my life depended on it," she said, rather more flippantly than she'd intended.

Garrett scowled. "Three lives hinge on *my* remembering it. Yours. Mine. And Michael's child's."

"What about Calvin? He has a stake in this, too." As far as Elizabeth was concerned, Liz thought.

Garrett ignored the question as if it were insignificant. "I take it you're denying prior knowledge of his presence on board."

"You're badgering the witness, Counselor," Liz said, using her best quote from Perry Mason.

Of course, it made no impression whatsoever on Garrett.

"Are you denying it?"

Liz sobered. "You betcha."

Almost before she finished voicing the denial, Garrett crossed the stateroom in three angry strides, and Liz began to fear she had chosen the wrong man.

Might she have been better off to leave the steamer with Calvin, and spend the rest of her life attempting to trespass on Rowland property and visit the tomb? Rather than remain on board to deal with Garrett?

Facing him now, it certainly appeared that way.

Garrett stepped even closer, and the scene from the plantation library flashed through Liz's mind. Feeling like a moth flirting with its own destiny on the altar of an open flame, Liz realized that this was a moment she had feared, and yet hoped, might repeat itself.

"Perhaps I should have taken Calvin up on his offer after all," she said under her breath.

"Perhaps," he said. His mouth was mere inches from hers.

"You agree?" she asked, determined to face him without flinching. She'd had enough of feeling her back pressed against a wall. Or a tomb door. She wanted to get inside Garrett's head and try to determine what made him tick. She must find out where the historical facts concerning this dark and secretive man had been right. And where they had been wrong.

Garrett nodded in answer to her question.

"I'm not sure I understand," she said, her voice faltering despite her resolution.

"Neither do I. You see, as improbable as it might seem, as inappropriate, as unjustifiable, I suspect I'm developing a fatal captivation for you—like a grandaddy longlegs for his mate."

As a research librarian, she was familiar with a hodgepodge of assorted information. And one of the things she'd learned from a children's workshop on spiders and snakes was that granddaddy longlegs mated with, and later might be feasted upon by, the more aggressive female spiders.

Only in this particular case, she suspected Garrett had the consequences backward.

"There's something else," he said.

Their eyes locked.

Boy, ask for crumbs and you get loaves of bread thrown at you, Liz thought, her sense of expectation unwinding like thread from a bobbin.

"I lied," he confessed.

"To me?"

"No, to Calvin. The miniature inside the pocket watch doesn't do you justice."

He reached out and tipped her chin up with his index finger to gaze deeply into her eyes.

She inhaled sharply.

"You feel it, too, by God!" he said, and Liz knew Garrett's patience had finally come to an end.

Her hands flew up to ward him off as he slipped his hand beneath her hair. But instead of hurting her, he kneaded her neck beneath the stiff collar of her traveling gown, relaxing the tension and heightening the desire that spiraled through her like fudge swirls in vanilla ice cream.

Sensing the emergence of yet another facet of Garrett's character, a side zealously guarded and rarely exposed, Liz feared she might be swept away on a current of liquid emotion and further trapped in his time. Her heart beat faster as she acknowledged that this was a side of him she could not easily combat. "Please. Don't," she protested.

He seemed to consider her plea. Consider and reject it, just as she had feared he would.

Instead, Garrett combed his fingers through her hair above her ears, holding her face steady. Tilting her mouth toward his, he tugged her against his hard body.

Liz felt her control slip. "This really isn't such a hot i—"

Garrett's lips slashed off her words, curtailed all coherent thought, immersed Liz in a liquid pool of sensation that sent common sense fleeing to the deepest, darkest recesses of her startled mind.

Caught off guard by the rush of passion his mouth evoked, Liz unconsciously leaned into the sweet punishment of his embrace. The pressure of his lips increased as his hands moved lower to rest on her hips. With teasing nibbles, he urged her lips open, intimately testing the soft inner lining of her mouth with his tongue, taking her to the edge of madness with his skillfully explicit kiss.

This man is... dangerous... dangerous... dangerous.... echoed her brain. The warning in her mind flashed like the emergency lights on a fire engine.

She willfully disregarded the signals and allowed her powerful craving to chart her reactions and assuage the burgeoning ache within her. Garrett's arms felt so good around her. So strong. So... right.

She was a lonely outcast in an alien world. She yearned to indulge herself in another human being's touch.

Garrett's touch.

In a moment of solace.

The kind of solace she knew he could provide. If only she wasn't riddled by misgivings.

As Garrett's hands slipped still lower, as he splayed his fingers in a possessive caress across her buttocks, Liz decided he had lost his mind. And she hers. She knew from history that he was a driven man. Everything he did, he did with a passion. Nothing halfhearted. Nothing without premeditation. She could be so easily crushed beneath his heels, and yet she blithely tripped along in his footsteps.

Fate had never before seemed quite so cruel and calculating. Nor had complete euphoria ever seemed so easily attainable.

Liz struggled with her feelings, wondering what it might be like to flout fate and defy the burdens it had placed on her reluctant shoulders. What would happen if she gave in to her susceptible heart, savored the moment, and simply surrendered to Garrett Rowland?

The idea was oh, so tempting.

Garrett tasted like expensive Colombian coffee. The rich flavor tantalized her.

He smelled of spiced brandy and ginger tobacco. The masculine fragrances intrigued her now as much as they had on the day she'd met Garrett.

Liz relinquished herself to his druglike kiss.

She gave as good as she got; he willingly accepted as much as she gave.

She was vulnerable; he was sweetly debilitating.

Together, they frightened each other.

And yet...

"Damn," Garrett exclaimed huskily against her lips, though the word smacked of a caress more than a profanity.

Liz felt him withdraw from her. Not just physically, but emotionally, as well.

Garrett backed away, putting one step between them.

Then another.

And another.

He drew a shaky breath once he was safely on the other side of the room. An inhalation that Liz unconsciously mimicked.

He raked his hands through his dark hair. "What are you trying to do to me?"

"I was wondering the same thing about you." Liz wasn't surprised that her voice was trembling. Her whole body quaked inside.

Garrett bunched his hands in his pants pockets as if it were the only way he knew to contain them.

"I'll be damned if I'll step into Michael's shoes! If I had any sense, I'd walk away from this whole damn affair—let Calvin have you and be done with it."

Liz advanced toward Garrett, forgetting herself so far as to reach out, intending to touch his arm. He flinched away.

"There are several books in your portmanteau I asked Mrs. Crawford to pack for you—*The Art of Needlework,* by the Countess of Wilton, and *Little Women.* You may want to read to pass the time of day."

Garrett's arrogance had returned, along with his resentment, and the wariness that often hooded his bluer-than-blue eyes. Fingers resting on her now tender lips, Liz plummeted back to reality. To her precarious situation and defenseless position.

"What? No *Tom Sawyer?* I would think that would be more appropriate, considering the adventure we've embarked upon together," Liz quipped. She blinked back the tears, and damned the pain that threatened to engulf her.

Garrett cleared his throat.

"I fear I've been unable to obtain a copy of that book for our library. It is too newly published," he said, as if they were carrying on a normal conversation. As if he hadn't just yanked the carpet from beneath her feet and watched her tumble flat on her face without lifting a finger to break her fall.

"I see. That's too bad. It's one of my favorites," she said, her voice growing stronger by the moment.

"You've read it?"

"I have," she boasted.

"How interesting."

"It was," she said, bluffing her way through the heart-wrenching aftermath of an otherwise delicious kiss.

"Tea is served at four o'clock in the dining salon. Most of the ladies on board will attend. You are welcome to join them."

Liz nodded.

"Otherwise, you may order cabin service so that you won't have to dine alone. Just pull the bell cord over by the bed. It rings in the steward's cabin. Someone will be along directly to attend to your needs."

"Oh," Liz said, realizing he intended to leave her to her own resources longer than she'd expected. She felt suddenly deflated, and acutely bereft outside the circle of Garrett's arms. Before she could stop herself, she asked, "Why did you draw away from me? Are you afraid I'm more woman than you can handle?"

Dropping the pretext of small talk entirely, Garrett breathed, "Brazen baggage."

"If that's what you call a woman who speaks her mind, then I suppose I am."

Garrett inhaled deeply. "When I take you, Elizabeth, it will be on *my* terms. Not Calvin's. Not yours. Mine, and mine alone."

"That sounds a little one-sided to me," Liz said, letting indignation carry her through the disappointment she was feeling.

"I'm going to go down to the gaming salon and attempt to recover some of the money I spent on our passage," he said abruptly.

Liz was reminded that Garrett was a black sheep. A riverboat gambler. A card shark, a notorious womanizer, and an accused murderer. History had blackened his name with conjecture and slandered his soul with speculation. He couldn't be trusted.

But all that seemed strangely irrelevant at the moment, as she struggled to regain her shattered equilibrium.

"Don't expect me to return to the stateroom before dawn," he continued.

Garrett's legendary reputation suddenly seemed insignificant, compared to the fact that here and now, though he'd certainly been fishing for something earlier, he was letting her escape the hook. Again.

Only this time, Liz hadn't wanted to be set free to swim her own way. For a single, self-motivated, independently minded woman of the nineties, it was a sobering realization.

She couldn't allow herself to become involved with a man like Garrett Rowland. Could she?

"We should dock in Baton Rouge by late afternoon tomorrow."

Still shaken from his devastating kiss, Liz said, "Fine."

"And, Elizabeth?"

Trying to come to grips with her attraction for Garrett, Liz lowered her hand from her lips and looked him squarely in the eye. It was her way of coping with things—facing them head-on.

Call me Lizzz.... "What?"

"Don't try anything with Calvin. You should realize by now I've got a sixth sense where he's concerned."

And a void in your heart the size of the Grand Canyon, Liz thought, wondering what it would take to fill it. She understood that Garrett's threat to her had expanded to both a physical and an emotional level. And that she was ill equipped to deal with either one.

The past sucked at her, drawing her more deeply into its whirling vortex. Step by step. Cell by cell. Emotion by complicated emotion.

Swallowing the lump in her throat, she attempted to harden her heart against Garrett.

"I've made a public announcement where Calvin is concerned. After this morning, I doubt he'd take me away from here when he disembarks if I presented myself to him na—" she paused, for once stopping her tongue from running ahead of her brain "—on a silver platter."

"I doubt he would, either. But then again, stranger things have happened."

And I'm living, breathing, proof! Liz thought.

CHAPTER TEN

Wearing the indigo gown and the loathsome bonnet, which she had to admit shaded her eyes from the ninety-degree sun almost as well as a pair of sunglasses, Liz leaned over the railing and stared into the murky waters that lapped at the steamer's wooden hull. What would the afternoon bring?

Following Calvin's disembarkation, Garrett had settled into much the same routine they shared at the plantation. He rested while she was up and about. Worked while she slept to avoid intimate contact with her. Was attentive in company, and kept a wary distance in private.

Would things be different once they docked in Baton Rouge? She didn't think so. The tension between them was like a ticking time bomb. They had shared a kiss. An extremely satisfying kiss. A kiss that might have led to all sorts of compromise.

If *he* hadn't broken it off so suddenly.

Liz sighed. She no longer knew what to expect from one moment to the next. Not from Garrett, and certainly not from herself. He made her do and say things...think things...she had no business doing or saying or thinking.

Garrett Rowland was definitely beginning to get to her. Whether he'd planned it that way or not.

Tiring of the water, she let her attention wander to the thinning timber along the riverbank. A riverbank that should have been dotted with oil tanks instead of forests. Even the mighty Mississippi seemed changed from the way she remembered it.

Liz knew that twentieth-century engineers had modified the river's twists and turns with dredged channels and sluice gates like the Bon Carré to control the water's normal flow, though it had once been called the "most crooked river in the world." After observing its meandering passage for the past two days, she now understood the reason behind the nickname.

Liz wished she could fathom Garrett as easily.

"We're here," he said from behind her. His breath tickled her ear and sent shivers up her spine. He was closer to her now than he had been since their confrontation with Calvin.

Liz gathered her emotions, steeled herself to act casually, and half turned toward him.

"I didn't hear you come up," she said. She was rather proud that her voice sounded so composed and so indifferent.

"You were lost in thought."

And in time. "I was just wondering if I would be going to the bank with you, or if you planned for me to stay on the steamer and wait."

Garrett scanned the swarm of activity at the inland port.

"There should be a carriage waiting for us. Somewhere," he said evasively as the steamer bumped into its moorings.

Liz glanced toward the dock. Fish crows soared aloft, cawing in raucous glee as a fisherman deposited his catch near a mountainous stack of baled cotton. She could almost hear the heated bargaining between a vegetable vendor and a Creole woman with a basket tucked beneath her arm, while a tipsy sailor had his pocket picked clean by a streetwise kid who immediately lost himself in the milling crowd.

A world different from her own, and yet strangely similar.

Shielding her eyes, Liz looked beyond the dock toward a shiny black cabriolet parked on the street. Hood folded back, drawn by a single horse and attended by a black driver, it reminded her of the French Quarter carriage tours in contemporary New Orleans.

"Is that the one?" she asked. She pointed toward the cabriolet.

Garrett nodded. "It belongs to a friend of mine."

Liz raised a brow at him.

"Don't look so surprised, Elizabeth. I've been known to have a friend or two—despite my reputation."

That a man like Garrett might have friends didn't puzzle her half as much as the amused manner in which he looked at her bonnet. Or the fact that he had left his panama behind in the stateroom. Could there be a hidden meaning here somewhere? Had she missed something important?

When Garrett put his arm in a proprietary fashion around her waist and led her down the gangplank and unerringly through the throng to the street, she decided there was definitely something going on.

"Hello, Mr. Garrett, sir. Nice to see you again," said the carriage driver.

"Thanks, Sam. It's good to be back." Garrett replied.

"Been a while," he said, politely tipping his beaver hat toward Liz.

"A month of Sundays." Garrett smiled a genuine smile that danced in his eyes and drew the crow's-feet spidering at either corner into merry puckers.

"I was sayin' that to Mr. Charles only yesterday. And then, lo and behold, he got your telegram explainin' you were headed this way."

"I feared it wouldn't reach you in time."

"Well, it did, sure and certain. Next thing I knew, Miz Jackson had the maid dustin' the parlor."

Again the engaging smile lit up Garrett's face, chasing away the shadows and sending an arrow soaring straight toward Liz's heart.

"Miz Jackson had me polishin' silver. And ordered the cook to bake up a batch of those wheat crackers you like with the crabmeat spread. Imagine she intends to tempt you to stay over a few days," Sam said.

Garrett shot a glance at Liz. "I fear we must decline this time. Do you think she'll toss me out on my ear for causing her so much to-do over nothing?"

"Now, sir, you know Miz Jackson better than that."

Garrett nodded. "You haven't spoken of the boys—how are they?" he asked.

The driver's dark face shone. "Wild as Indians, and growin' like weeds. They were so excited when they heard the news about your visit, Miz Jackson could hardly get them to bed last night. Up and down like jack-in-the-boxes."

"Caused a stir, did I?" Garrett said.

Liz wasn't sure what he preferred the most—being made a fuss over or causing a stir. At least not until Sam unwittingly clarified it for her.

"Yessiree . . . and you know it." The driver grinned widely, displaying a mouthful of gleaming teeth. "Stir bein' caused, look for Mr. Garrett to be smack-dab in the middle of it, I tell 'em.''

While they conversed, Garrett helped Liz into the carriage. Sam climbed onto the driver's box and clucked to the horse. The animal leaned into its harness. With a lurch that almost unseated Liz, Sam steered the cabriolet into the street.

Lulled by the steady *clip-clop* of the horses hooves striking the cobbled pavement, Liz relaxed into the sunwarmed leather seat, determined to enjoy the ride.

Garrett stared at the back of the driver's head, showing none of the enthusiasm for the city Liz felt as they crossed intersection after intersection, slowly making their way toward the business district. Liz thought they were headed toward the bank, until they turned onto a particularly lovely street dotted with elegant homes and the horse picked up its pace without being directed. They braked outside a gingerbread house painted in multicolored earth tones, and the driver jumped down from the carriage to assist her to the ground.

She refused to budge, and Sam automatically looked to Garrett.

Garrett levered himself from the carriage and raised his arms to her.

"I'm not going to the bank with you, am I?" she asked woodenly.

Arms extended, he said, "Come." He encircled her waist with his hands. "There is someone I'd like you to meet."

Liz hesitated. For all she knew, this house might be the loony bin she'd worried about. A depository for wayward wives. A way to rid himself of her. Such calculated disappearances weren't uncommon in the nineteenth century. And even if his intentions were harmless, it was clear now that he planned to leave her in the company of strangers for the afternoon and had purposely kept her in the dark about it.

Liz's distrust of Garrett rushed to the fore. Determined to change his mind, she clung to his supporting arms, much as she supposed Elizabeth might do.

"I—" Her voice faltered.

His hands tightened around her waist. "You'll like them," he said smoothly. Liz noted that he incorporated the same coaxing voice he had used on the dock at the plantation, when he'd offered her rose-hip tea.

She took a steadying breath. "You planned to leave me here all along. Why didn't you tell me while we were on the steamer?"

He regarded her in silence for a moment. "I didn't want to upset you."

Was he being considerate or was he simply a good liar? she wondered.

With quivering bravado, Liz said, "I'm a big girl, Garrett. I'm not easily upset. Not any longer."

"I'm just now beginning to realize that," he mused out loud.

"When will you be back for me?" Liz asked, suddenly realizing how much she'd come to depend on Garrett. She might consider him dangerous, but she no longer considered him a stranger. And he was her only link to the tomb.

"Before dusk."

Wanting to trust Garrett, knowing it might be the worst mistake she had ever made, Liz stood, because she had no choice. Garrett swung her down from the carriage as if she weighed no more than a child.

Almost before her feet touched solid earth, the door of the house opened, and two children tumbled down the sidewalk toward them. One could have been no more than five. The other was eight or nine, Liz guessed.

"Uncle Garrett!" the boys shrieked in unison. The youngest made a mad dash for Garrett's knees, nearly knocking him off balance.

"It's been forever! Mother's made up your room for you. I helped her." His glance flicked beyond Garrett, and he scanned the empty carriage. "You've left your bags on the steamer?" he asked.

Garrett nodded.

Instantly crestfallen, the boy said in a dejected tone, "That means you'll be leaving before nightfall."

"I'm afraid so, Ben. This is a business trip. But perhaps there will be other visits when we can stay longer," Garrett said kindly, ruffling the youngster's unruly locks.

Here was a side of Garrett she definitely hadn't known existed, Liz thought. He liked children.

Grandmother Hayden had always said, "A man who likes children can't be all bad." Of course, her grandmother had been known to be wrong.

"Well, then, did you bring us something?" Ben asked Garrett, as if he expected compensation for being deprived of Garrett's company.

"Benjamin! Your godfather brought you a hug, and Thomas a handshake. That is enough," a statuesque woman standing on the porch called out. Her voice dripped with the syrupy sweetness of the born-and-bred Southern lady. Her gown was white, her hair dark as soot, and around her throat she had tied a cameo pinned to a black silk ribbon. She moved to stand on the top step with the grace of a swan gliding across a pond.

The man with her was flawlessly attired in a gray pin-striped suit. Wings of silver arched at his temples, enhancing his pale, aquiline countenance and hazel eyes.

The children looked remarkably like him. Liz found herself wondering if Elizabeth's unborn child would have resembled Michael, and therefore Garrett.

"You heard your mother..." the man began.

"A hug and a handshake," Garrett finished for him, and Liz could almost imagine the salutelike click of his heels as he hunkered down and gave Ben a hard squeeze. Then he turned to the older boy and, at eye level with him, exchanged a measured handshake. From her vantage point, Liz witnessed the marked softening of Garrett's face. She also saw his sleight of hand, and knew as he rose and stepped back that the child clutched two shiny coins in his palm.

Liz wondered if Garrett would truly be disappointed if he found out she wasn't pregnant. And if that disappointment would turn to vengeance against her.

She must find a way back to the future before he discovered her deception! With his precarious temperament, there was no way of telling whether he would swing with her... or at her.

"I saw that," the woman said crisply, breaking into Liz's thoughts.

"Saw what?" Garrett asked, with an air of innocence Liz found incredible for a man who'd been caught red-handed. Was he such a good liar all the time? And if so, what did that mean? She recalled now that he'd lied to her before. When he'd denied undressing her. She'd caught him at it only because he mentioned the pear-shaped birthmark on her hip.

"Do not play games with me, Garrett," she admonished him. "I know you passed something to Thomas. You will spoil the boys."

"A few coins, nothing more. You know it gives me pleasure to indulge them, and I didn't have time to stop off for proper gifts."

"We do not expect gifts—your presence is enough," the man interjected.

"Can we keep the money, Mother?" Ben asked, clasping the coin Thomas had furnished him.

A tolerant smile crossed her lips. "I suppose so, Benjamin...just this once. Now, run along to the nursery and ask Nanny to help you stow away your booty," she said. "Tell her I've said you two may come down to the parlor after tea and spend some time with your godfather."

As the boys scrambled back into the house, her gaze rested speculatively on Liz.

"Where are your manners, Garrett? Pray introduce us to your wife," she said, without taking her eyes off Liz.

The woman sounded as if she had a chicken bone stuck in her throat, and Liz had the distinct impression that she would just as soon they remained strangers. Liz tensed.

The shape of his knife sheath pressed through her gown and into her skin as Garrett drew her tightly to his side.

"Be gracious, Elizabeth. These are special people, and they know you only through hearsay," he cautioned under his breath as he propelled her toward the couple. Liz tripped along beside him, wondering what the woman might have heard that would cause her to react so negatively toward Elizabeth. She told herself not to take this personally.

As if for support, the woman slid her hand into her husband's. It was then that Liz noticed that one of his sleeves dangled empty at his side.

"Martha...Charles...I'd like you to meet Elizabeth Rowland, my wife." Garrett paused.

Why the pause? Liz wondered. Did he suspect something? Or was introducing her as his wife as awkward for him as it was for her?

"Elizabeth, meet Martha and Charles Jackson," he continued finally. "I served under Charles during the War."

That explained the arm. Charles Jackson must have lost it in battle.

Searching for an appropriate response, Liz promptly put her foot in her mouth by saying, "I haven't known Garrett long, but I imagine he must have been a handful to command."

As soon as she realized what she'd said, a dark stain spread across her cheeks. "I mean...he just doesn't seem like the sort...to take orders from anyone," she stuttered, trying hard not to let her eyes wander to the sleeve.

Garrett's expression darkened. It was a look that said, You can dress 'em up, but you sure can't take 'em out. Not with any measure of confidence.

Charles surveyed Garrett's face a moment, and then, as if making a spur of the moment decision, smiled benevolently at Liz. It was a sign of support, of empathy. Liz clung to it.

"I daresay it didn't take you long to discover that much about Garrett. He came near to a court-martial on more than one occasion," Charles said. "Makes up too many of his own rules, I fear."

Martha gazed up adoringly into her husband's eyes. As if taking her cue from him, she said, "I suspect he's still doing that."

"You were handy at bailing me out. Still are," Garrett said humbly.

"I was only able to do so then because I claimed a surname that carried some weight."

Liz looked blank. They were talking about the Civil War as if it had been only yesterday. Of course, for them, it had been, she reminded herself. They were much like the Vietnam vets of her own time.

Thawing somewhat, Martha asked, "Has Garrett told you anything about Cain Creek?"

Liz shook her head.

"How remiss," Martha said, going on to explain, "Our distant connection with Stonewall Jackson kept these two scamps out of worlds of trouble... until the day Charles was wounded and the Yankees thought they'd stumbled across the genuine article. There's a family resemblance between Charles and Stonewall, you see. Anyway, if not for Garrett, the Yankees would have cut Charles to ribbons and taken his head as a trophy. Garrett single-handedly fended them off until reinforcements arrived. Of course, in the process they left their mark on him...."

So that was how Garrett received the scar on his cheek. Defending Charles Jackson against a band of bloodthirsty soldiers. She wondered if there were other scars. Internal scars. Scars that had contributed to the dark and deadly reputation that had pursued him for more than a century.

"She exaggerates," Garrett told Liz with a roguish grin.

"Martha never exaggerates," Charles said levelly. "I owe your husband my life."

The Jacksons considered Garrett a hero. How interesting, Liz thought. Nothing she'd read or heard had ever recounted this story of heroism. It seemed it had been obliterated by the passage of time from Garrett's biographical profile.

"A debt paid many times over," Garrett said.

"A debt that can never be repaid," Martha said with a faint, sad smile. "Our two oldest children succumbed to diphtheria around that same time. If I had lost Charles, as well, I don't know what I would have done."

There were definite advantages to progress, Liz thought, tugging at the collar of her indigo gown. Like air-conditioning, and high-speed travel... and inoculations against childhood diseases.

Charles glanced her way and abruptly changed the subject. "Speaking of debts, the president of the Baton Rouge Bank and Trust awaits us in his offices," he said.

It dawned on Liz that Charles had misread the motivations behind the tugging of her collar. He imagined that Martha's reference to his near death had reminded her of Michael Rowland. Which would have been a rather astute observation—if she'd been Elizabeth.

A knowing look passed between the men, and Garrett actually grinned at Charles, as if thanking him for his demonstration of compassion. Actively pursuing the new topic, he asked, "How did you arrange a meeting?"

Charles returned the grin. "Believe it or not, the name Jackson still holds some weight in the South."

"You're a shrewd man, Charles."

"I'm a lawyer. It pays to be shrewd."

As she listened to their repartee, Liz decided the Jacksons could be invaluable in helping her delve into the heart of Garrett Rowland. More helpful than anything she might uncover riffling through his papers in the plantation's library. And definitely more insightful than Mrs. Crawford. Probably even better than plundering Elizabeth's trunk.

Perhaps whiling away the afternoon in Martha Jackson's company wouldn't be so terrible after all. Even though she would be stepping into the new and uncharted territory of a nineteenth-century woman's parlor.

Liz desperately cast about for something to say to redeem herself. An acceptable icebreaker. Something that couldn't be misconstrued or further alienate her. Her gaze flitted to the pot of a wilted viola tricolor hortensias on a stand in the corner of the porch. It needed help.

Feeling a little shy and a lot uncertain, she said, "My grandmother used to insist the trick to potting pansies is mixing peanut shells with the soil so their roots can breathe. Of course, they really thrive much better when they're planted in a garden." Quoting her grandmother helped her to keep in touch with her own reality. Because *this* reality, this dimension, whatever it was, wasn't wearing off, and it wasn't getting any easier to deal with.

Three pairs of brows winged skyward in skeptical disbelief.

"You know something about plants?" Martha asked, without even trying to hide her surprise.

"A little," Liz said. She'd planned to be a horticulturist before she realized her love of knowledge and books outweighed her fascination with plants. Now she wondered if she hadn't made a mistake in changing her major because libraries had become so computerized by the time she graduated that a librarian rarely experienced much real contact with the books.

Martha took a step toward Liz. "How delightful. Garrett, you never told me she was interested in gardening. Every well-bred young lady is expected to have her own garden when she weds, but I thought—"

"It seems I underestimated her," Garrett interjected thoughtfully, and Liz fought not to blush under his perusal.

Liz couldn't stop herself from asking, "What did you tell them about me, darling? You haven't been blackening my character, have you? That wouldn't be very nice." Bound and determined to push back just a little, she said it coyly. Almost flirtatiously. Underneath it all, she was dead serious.

"Oh, dear... I didn't mean... I assure you, getting information from Garrett is like squeezing blood from a turnip. I have friends in New Orleans who travel in your circles, Elizabeth—Cassandra Raintree and Rachael Davis and Katherine Barnes. You remember them, of course."

Liz nodded, thinking she would never be able to pass a polygraph test as long as she lived.

"We go out and have tea together when they're in town, and—"

"Gossip," Charles said with a wink.

It was Martha's turn to blush crimson. "Charles! We do not gossip. Yesterday when we had tea, we merely dis—"

"It's all right, my darling. I quite understand. Women will be women."

Liz understood he wasn't being condescending, only playful, and his thoughts were a reflection of the times. Her tour at the homesite had included a short talk on a woman's role in the Victorian age. The affluent men of the nineteenth century considered their wives decorative ornaments whose duties included the supervision of the household, child care, hostessing and homemaking. Their carefully chosen mates provided a luxurious haven from the business world. Occasionally, they were even well loved. As Liz could see in this instance.

"And men will be men," Liz muttered beneath her breath, feeling a sense of sympathy for Elizabeth and Martha, brought up in a world where women had so few human rights beyond the custom of afternoon tea.

Liz heard Garrett suppress a chuckle. She scowled at him.

"You're thoroughly enjoying this, aren't you?" she asked.

He sobered. "I always enjoy being with Charles and Martha."

Martha glanced from Liz to Garrett and back again. The indomitable hostess, plainly determined to avert a scene in her own front yard, said hurriedly, "I have an herb garden started beneath the crepe myrtle trees round the side of the house. The parterre is beautifully laid out, but the plants aren't doing too well. Could you... Would you like to see it?"

Liz's apprehension concerning a day in the company of Martha Jackson vanished. Garrett was right—the Jacksons were special people.

"Sure," she said.

Martha's face brightened as she hooked her arm through Liz's. "Well, no matter what Cassandra Raintree said, it seems we have something in common after all."

Martha stopped beside her husband and raised her face toward him.

Charles bent and planted a dutiful kiss on her cheek, saying, "Well, that's that. We'll be off now, my dear." He motioned to Sam, who resumed his seat in the carriage.

As Liz passed Garrett, he leaned toward her. Surely he wasn't going to kiss her cheek, too!

It was a matter of pride, Liz told herself. His damnable Rowland pride! He was playacting and pretending they were happily married in front of his friends. Or if not happily, at least satisfactorily.

She only wished it was true.

The thought startled Liz. *Get a grip on yourself! One passionate kiss and you've gone all mushy in the head.*

As his lips brushed her cheek, Garrett said in a low voice, "Take care, Elizabeth."

Liz read his farewell as a warning, an admonition to behave herself.

"I always do," she replied.

Instead of Garrett leaving her, as she'd feared, she left him—at Martha's urging.

Out of hearing range of the men, Martha said in a low voice, "I can tell by the way Garrett looks at you, you're quite special to him."

Liz tried to keep her astonishment from reflecting in her voice. "That's the same word Garrett used to describe his feelings for your family."

Martha smiled. "I'm not speaking of friendship, Elizabeth. I'm suggesting something much more...intense. Garrett has had other women here before."

"Other women?" Liz asked, startled by the jealousy that streaked through her. Martha made it sound as if her house possessed a revolving door that Garrett had used frequently. "Is this a benign way of warning me I should brace myself for a barrage of knowing looks and sly innuendos when we appear in public together?"

"Oh, dear! I didn't mean for it to come out that way. I don't think he's had that many—" Eyes wide, Martha's hand flew to her lips. "Good gracious, that sounds even worse, doesn't it?"

Liz nodded, staring up into the boughs of the crepe myrtle tree, wondering what kind of a lover Garrett was. Judging by his kiss, he would be fantastic. She wanted to kick herself for allowing such an extreme thought to tiptoe across her mind.

She shouldn't be thinking of Garrett in that light. She shouldn't care one way or the other whether he had made love to one woman, or one hundred and one.

But she did.

"What I'm attempting to say is that his were never serious. Garrett didn't look at the others the way he looks at you. I mean—" She broke off, glancing over her shoulder as if to assure herself that the carriage was pulling away from the curb. Confident that the men had left for the bank, she said in a conspiratorial voice, "Shall I just come right out with it and be blunt?"

Recovering from the initial shock, Liz was able to say in an almost normal tone of voice, "Please, be as blunt as possible." *For a nineteenth-century woman who probably considers sex a dirty word.*

"Well, Garrett looks at you as if he could positively eat you alive."

Liz laughed out loud. *As if he could strangle her* would be a more accurate observation, she thought, but she didn't try to explain to Martha.

"I'm sure he doesn't realize it shows," Liz said.

"Well, it probably doesn't—to others," Martha said. "But Charles and I are about as close to Garrett as he allows anyone to become. Except you, naturally."

"Naturally."

"You're a fortunate woman, Elizabeth, married to the master of a grand estate like Rowland Plantation. I don't need to tell you there are gentlewomen in this town who would faint and fall over dead to be in your shoes."

"You don't say."

"Indeed."

"Tell me more." *Share everything you know about Garrett Rowland with me.*

Liz spent an indolent afternoon seated in a padded rocker in a parlor decorated with gold-flecked wallpaper. The room was overrun with chairs covered in gold-and-violet silk and glass-domed butterfly collections, and sported a bay window that overlooked Martha's garden.

Liz had learned few cold, hard facts about Garrett's personal life beyond the names of his ex-girlfriends. On the other hand, she had witnessed firsthand many of the things she had explained on her group tours of the

Rowland Plantation homesite concerning the sheltered lives of the nineteenth-century woman.

Following Martha through the narrow hallways of the quaint gingerbread, Liz had seen the arrogance of the pre-Civil War door leading to Charles's smoking room and had experienced the frustration of a door built narrow on purpose, so that a woman's hoop skirts couldn't fit through it.

Martha had confirmed without realizing it that the abundance of chairs in the parlor was due to the fact that men stood when women entered a room. And since it was considered inappropriate for a woman to sit in a chair warmed by a man's body, a cool one must be present.

They had even touched on the subject of careers, though Martha had been adamant that work outside the home was beneath a wife and humiliating to her husband. She had gone on to say that, though she felt a certain leniency toward an acquaintance who had taken up journalism and sold her work to the newspapers under a male pseudonym, a woman's business was her home, husband and children. It seemed that a Victorian woman's success in life was gauged not by her own accomplishments, but by her family's.

Promptly at five o'clock, Martha fulfilled one of her many domestic duties by serving tea. Liz knew that tea with honey and lemon was good for stress, and she didn't want to appear rude by refusing, so she sipped at the bone-china cup. She also ate crawfish salad, and heart-shaped scones, roast chicken and pound cake topped with fresh fruit served from a low table set with silver and linen. They discussed Martha's charity work and the local Bible society while Liz strenuously resisted the impulse to inject into the conversation her modern ideas concerning the treatment of women. During the discussion, Liz watched her hostess do needlepoint.

Liz anxiously awaited Garrett's return, reaching up to occasionally massage the curve of her cheekbone, which still burned from the quick caress of his lips.

"The men should be returning shortly," Martha said finally, setting aside her canvas. From a salver on the table she retrieved a glass vial. She uncorked the top and poured a dainty portion of the liquid into the bottom of her teacup.

"Would you like some?" She offered Liz the bottle.

"What is it?"

"Violet water, to sweeten your breath," she said. "Charles is quite partial to it."

Liz thought she heard the anticipation of a welcome-home kiss in her voice. Intrigued, she accepted the vial, wondering if Garrett would think to kiss her hello. Reflecting on whether or not he might also like the flavor of violets, she tipped the bottle against her finger and dabbed the tip of her tongue with the floral essence.

It instantly set her mouth aflame. Reminded of the punch-colored Bourbon Street hurricane drinks so fashionable in her time, Liz dissolved into a pool of laughter.

"What is it? What's wrong?" Martha exclaimed.

"Now I know how you make it through these long afternoons," she said.

In the midst of pouring herself a shot of the tincture, Liz glanced up to see Charles and Garrett strolling through the garden toward the house. The men paused outside the bay window. Charles's back was to the window, while Garrett, the taller of the two men, stared over his shoulder and through the glass with alarming intensity. He listened attentively to Charles, nodding occasionally, but his chilling cerulean eyes never wavered from her face.

Liz's laughter faded.

Had she done something wrong? Said something improper? Could Garrett hear her teasing Martha about the hundred-proof violet water from his vantage point in the herb garden? And if so, why should she care? She was protected here by the Jacksons' hospitality.

Charles finally ushered Garrett into the house, and Martha rose to greet her husband. As she had anticipated, she received a kiss on the lips.

"Elizabeth isn't anything like we imagined," Liz heard her murmur to Charles. "She's been an absolute delight, and she's so knowledgeable about plants. I vow, my garden cannot help but prosper from her visit."

Beaming, Martha turned her attention to Garrett.

"We've had such an interesting conversation this afternoon. You'll have to bring Elizabeth to visit me again soon, Garrett. When you can both stay longer."

"Perhaps later in the fall, when we are more fully settled in at the plantation." Garrett glanced pointedly at Liz's teacup. She hastily set it down.

He moved to stand behind her. His hands on her shoulders, he kissed her on the nape of the neck. And then again, behind the ear. Gentle nibbling, more suction than bite, meant to be disarming—and to show her who was boss.

She wanted to be angry with him for his audacity. But she couldn't concentrate on anger with her knees turning to water and her heart pounding like a jackhammer.

"Did *you* enjoy your afternoon?" he whispered in her ear. His voice trembled slightly, and Liz had the distinct impression that the kiss had been more than show, and that he had enjoyed it as much as she—heaven help her.

"Y-e-e-s..." Liz replied breathlessly. For a woman accustomed to working forty-plus hours a week, it had been a lovely afternoon. "Did you...uh...get the stuff at the bank straightened out?" she asked, snatching at her chaotic thoughts.

"Stuff?" Charles asked.

"The transfer," Garrett supplied with a wry half smile, his arm draped solicitously around her shoulder. "And, yes, the 'stuff' is all settled."

Once again he was playacting, Liz decided. Putting on a display of affection for the benefit of his friends. In a way, though, he had also been shielding her from the jaws of social speculation. From gossipmongers like the Raintree woman, and any unconscious tidbits of information concerning their relationship that Martha might let drop during one of her teas.

Liz wondered why he had done it as he moved to accept a seat beside Martha on the cushioned settee. She doubted Garrett ordinarily took an interest in idle gossip. She supposed it was for the sake of the baby, and to ensure the dignity of the Rowland family name.

A few minutes later, Martha handed Garrett a cup of tea. He drank it, yet ate sparingly, sampling only a bite or two of the crabmeat spread Sam had mentioned earlier in the day.

During the ensuing hour, the men talked of President Rutherford B. Hayes, the withdrawal of federal troops from Louisiana, and the end of carpetbag control through the statewide election of Governor Francis Nicholls. It all seemed like some sort of bizarre history lesson to Liz.

Presently the children tumbled into the parlor like two unruly puppies. They dragged Garrett off to inspect their butterfly collection.

Afterward, Garrett politely declined Martha's invitation to dinner, and by dusk they were saying their goodbyes. The Jacksons accompanied them back through the streets of Baton Rouge to the boat. By full dark, they were steaming their way along the Mississippi.

The pleasant interlude in Baton Rouge behind them, the day-and-a-half return trip to New Orleans proved strained. And, like a cloud obliterating the sun, Liz felt a shadow of apprehension skitter across her heart as they rounded a bend in the river and isolated Rowland Plantation loomed into view.

CHAPTER ELEVEN

Alternating between exasperation, wariness and fascination, Garrett gazed down from the bedchamber window and out across the garden. With narrowed eyes, he watched the woman he had married kneeling on her hands and knees, weeding the rampant jasmine from around the legs of the garden bench.

In a matter of a mere week, she had managed to breathe life back into the desolate garden.

He wondered fleetingly if her hands smelled of crushed jasmine. Or the slender column of her throat, where she absently brushed it with her fingertips? Or the errant tendril of honey-blond hair she kept pushing back up into her chignon?

Garrett wondered why he did not follow his most basic instincts. Why not drag her upstairs, have his way with her and be done with it? She tempted him to do just that. Why hold back?

Because over the past few weeks his feelings had softened toward her, Garrett told himself.

He looked past her to the roof of the family vault, peeking through the trees. He knew she had visited the tomb several times since their return from Baton Rouge. But she no longer cried and carried on like a woman possessed. And he had noticed of late that her cheeks bloomed vivaciously, like the roses gracing the garden she toiled in so diligently day after day.

Garrett's attention returned to the woman in the garden. She seemed happiest with her gloveless hands plunged wrist-deep in dirt while coaxing the flowers to unfurl in honor of his brother's memory. He admired her newly surfaced spunk.

She wore her nails short now, and he racked his brain to recall when she'd cut them. She also refused to wear her bonnet. And she hummed romantic melodies in a sweet sing song voice as she worked.

It was as if he were looking upon a new woman.

Garrett wondered if her heart was finally healing. And if perhaps there might be room in it for a man with a blackened reputation. Somewhere.

He seriously doubted it. Even if she surmounted her grief over Michael's death, he had no right to go back on their bargain. Their marriage was one of convenience—for the sake of Michael's child, he reminded himself. Though lately it had been more a marriage of inconvenience.

And what of his suspicions that Calvin and Elizabeth were somehow scheming together against him? That her only goal in marrying Michael, and him, was the ownership of Rowland Plantation?

Garrett slammed his fist into his palm. No matter what he did, she couldn't despise him half as much as he did this place, with its painful memories—the disintegration of a family due to war and a difference in opinions.

Memories of a young man cut adrift by a tyrannical father and a weak-willed mother unable to stand up to her husband assaulted Garrett. Memories of Michael, who had loved Rowland Plantation better than he. Who had sided with their father rather than risk his sire's displeasure and the possible loss of his birthright.

He especially recalled the beating his father had delivered the night he voiced his Union sympathies. He'd broken his arm blocking a vicious blow to the head, and afterward had been forced to wear his injured arm in a sling. That had curtailed his decision to run away from home for six grueling weeks....

Yet here he was, fighting to keep the plantation alive for Michael's unborn heir.

And coveting Michael's widow with a burning desire that made everything else pale into insignificance.

How ironic for a man who had left behind his heritage, Garrett thought. A man who had fought and gambled and caroused with women without becoming emotionally embroiled. Who had led a rough and carefree life, and who rarely looked back at the past with anything other than scorn. A man who had never coveted home and family, now had everything.

A home.

A child on the way.

And a wife.

Once he had resented Elizabeth with all his heart and soul for drawing him back to New Orleans and for fanning the tiny flame of family honor that he had believed extinguished. She'd usurped his precious freedom.

Where had the resentment gone? he wondered as he watched her brush a damp tendril from her lip and recalled the kiss they had shared on the steamer. His intent had been to punish her for the scene with Calvin in the steamer's dining salon, whether she was at fault or not.

He had pulled her into his embrace only to find all thoughts of punishment banished by the satiny texture of her lips against his.

And when she had leaned into his embrace and opened her lips to him, and pressed her supple body against his...

"What the devil was she trying to do?" he asked out loud.

Did she not realize how close he had come to throwing her down on one of the narrow twin beds?

Later, at the Jacksons' home, he had stood outside in the garden and watched her through the bay window. She had sat in a rocker in the parlor, holding a vial of violet water, laughing. He had been moved to see her innocently lighthearted and entirely enchanting.

He had told himself an affectionate display in Baton Rouge would protect the Rowland heir from undue gossip. He had assumed that in front of his friends it would be safe to indulge himself and purge his system by kissing her a second time. He'd told himself that before an audience of his peers, he need not fear a repetition of the desire he had experienced on the steamer.

He had lied to himself—he had kissed her because he could not resist the temptation. And it had done nothing to curb his need. And everything to whet his appetite for more.

Garrett watched as she reached up to unbutton the bodice of her indigo gown. It was a deliciously distracting habit she had acquired of late. Though he could not see it from this distance, he imagined the swell of her breasts above her chemise. He had committed to memory what he had seen that day in the library. The day Calvin presented her with the mourning brooch.

He even saw the tempting swell in his dreams. Creamy white. Smooth. Inviting. That was the main reason he now slept in the guest bedchamber. Because he dared not take the chance of rolling over and gathering her into his arms. Because, for a man who prided himself on his self-control, he seemed to be sadly lacking in it lately.

Shifting position, Garrett watched Liz frown and swat at her skirt. She settled back into her routine of digging up tufts of grass for a moment, then rocked back on her heels to slap at the skirt again. A mosquito, Garrett surmised, unable to stifle the chuckle bubbling up in his throat. The humidity was high, and they were bad today.

Determined to rid herself of the pesky insect, she rose, only to settle on the bench. Glancing around, as if to ascertain that no one was scrutinizing her, she raised her skirts to her knees and scratched at her shapely calf with the trowel.

The chuckle died away, to be replaced by a growl of desire as he recalled the flirtatious incident at the Jacksons, the way she had fluttered her lashes at him and dropped her voice to a low, seductive murmur. Garrett felt his body temperature rise. Had she seen him looking down at her from the window? Was she flirting with him again, as she had been doing that day? He could not be sure, but he could not move away from the glass, either.

Mesmerized and appalled at the same time, Garrett watched her stretch one leg down the length of the bench, turning it this way and that—to examine the welts, he presumed. Even from this distance, he could tell she possessed exquisitely long legs. Trim ankles. Delicate feet.

She glanced overhead, squinting toward the sun. As if something had suddenly occurred to her, she turned sideways on the bench and stretched both legs out, bunching her skirts midway to her thighs.

Garrett realized he was watching her with bated breath, anxiously contemplating what her next move might be. He was not disappointed.

Unbuttoning her bodice a little more, she spread the material wide, exposing the delicate lace of her chemise. She stretched her arms out behind her. Tossed her head back. Arched her back. And closed her eyes, as if she actually enjoyed basking in the sunshine.

She reminded him of a celestial being, uninhibited and alluring, that he had seen on a handpainted Grecian urn in a gambling establishment in New Orleans.

Garrett swallowed. Hard. He felt abused, resentful and titillated, all at the same time.

No wonder Michael had ended up bewitched by her. The same thing was happening to him.

Enough was enough! he decided. It was time to end it, once and for all.

Garrett pivoted from the window.

He was going to go down to the garden and do what he should have done long, long ago!

The fragrance of roses assaulted Liz. Full-blown and robust. An attar out of proportion to the bud-laden vines she'd been training to climb a fan-shaped trellis.

She glanced up, through the haze of the steamy Louisiana morning, to see Garrett standing like a magnificent statue beneath the chinaberry trees that overshadowed the gargoyled bird bath. His shirt was open at the neck, his sleeves were rolled to his elbows, and his hair was tousled, as if he'd been raking his fingers through it.

Garrett had been acting strangely, even for him, ever since their return from Baton Rouge. Brooding. Uncommunicative. In her heart she'd recognized the faint *tick-tick* of the time bomb that rested between them as he went his way and she went hers.

Therefore, it was a pleasant shock to find him seeking out her company. With a tentative smile curving her lips, she rose from the bench to greet him.

His expression thunderous, he said, "Don't move."

The smile died on her lips, and Liz froze in midmotion.

"What?" she asked.

"I said *don't move,*" he repeated.

With disbelieving eyes, she watched him slowly extract the ivory-handled knife from the sheath at his side. Her gaze flew to his face. The look in his eyes sent a chill up her spine that was like an eager flame skittering along a fuse. They shone clear, calm, and menacing.

Liz blinked. "What in the world are you do—"

"Be quiet," Garrett commanded. With grim determination, he flipped the knife in the air and caught it like a pro by the pointed blade.

"You can't mean to do this," she protested, preparing to run, as instinct dictated she must. But the hem of her gown was caught in the thorny branches at the base of the rose bush.

"Dead reckoning," he told her, aiming the lethal weapon at her head.

"Can't we talk about this?" she rasped, chastising herself for not heeding the warning signs. She'd known it was only a matter of time before the ticking bomb detonated.

"Too late," he murmured.

An ominous silence followed. Even the woodpecker searching for insect larvae in the tomb's wooden gables stopped his incessant tapping.

Liz watched in horror as Garrett raised the gleaming blade in the air and, with a whiplashlike flick of his wrist, released it. The knife sailed past her face, barely missing her nose. She heard it land with a heavy thump somewhere behind her.

Fear welled in the pit of her stomach and spiraled, gathering itself like a whirlwind. It inducted every nerve ending in her body as it gained momentum, blotting out every sensation except itself.

Gulping convulsively, Liz dropped the trowel she'd been using to aerate the soil, ripped the indigo gown from the clutches of the rosebush and scrambled to her feet. She forsook the beaten path and zigzagged through the garden, away from Garrett, toward the plantation house and Mrs. Crawford's kitchen.

"Elizabeth!" she heard him yell.

She stumbled, scraping her hand on the rough bark of a camphor tree she used to steady herself.

"What's gotten into you? For God's sake, *stop*," he called.

Clutching her ankle-length skirts in both hands, Liz kept right on running, through the garden, beyond the tomb, past the yard pump, to the doorway of the free-standing kitchen. Winded, Liz peered inside. Pans of aromatic *beignets* cooled on the butcher-block table. But Mrs. Crawford was nowhere in sight.

Her thoughts as tangled and disorderly as the Cher-okee rose vines, Liz continued to search out Mrs. Crawford, driven by pure instinct.

Alerted by the sound of Garrett's pounding foot-steps, she sprinted from the kitchen in hopes of gaining the house before he caught up with her. But her legs felt like clay, her heart like a lead weight. The air was as thick as honey and it resisted the passage of her body and slowed her steps.

Liz realized she had experienced this nightmare of some faceless something intent on murder before. And she couldn't race far enough or fast enough to escape the inevitable.

But this was no dream. And her assailant wasn't faceless.

Or nameless.

"Elizabeth!" Garrett thundered, in a voice that curdled her blood in her veins.

Liz ignored him. With perspiration trickling down her sides and molding the fabric of her bodice to her trembling body, Liz sprinted up the back steps.

"Leave me alone, Garrett!" she cried.

Liz glanced over her shoulder to find him not five feet behind her. She dropped her skirts to clutch at the stitch in her side and bolted down the central hallway toward the stairs.

Directly behind her now, Garrett reached out and caught roughly at her elbow. She heard her sleeve rip as she wrestled from his grasp.

"Get away from me!" Leaning heavily on the handrail, Liz ascended the stairs two steps at a time. She had almost reached the second-floor landing when a tread that had been solid earlier that morning suddenly gave way.

Liz toppled backward. Straight into Garrett Rowland's waiting arms.

She went wild, clawing at Garrett's face with her short nails.

He captured both her hands in one of his.

"Stop struggling. You'll hurt yourself," he growled.

His words were ludicrous, though his concern sounded genuine.

"As opposed to you doing it for me?"

"Have you gone daft again?" he asked. His arms tightened around her, pinning her to his muscular chest. "I'm not going to harm you."

"Yes, you are," Liz insisted.

"Preposterous!"

"If it walks like a duck and quacks like a duck, chances are it's a duck."

His incredulous expression was almost comical. "What?"

"You just tried to skewer me with your knife—that's what."

"You're distraught."

"What if I *am* overreacting? In my situation, what woman wouldn't?" Liz asked, trying to buy herself some time. Wondering if she was strong enough to tip him off balance and push him down the stairs.

"You mean a woman married to a man with my reputation," he said darkly.

I mean it's not every day someone is attacked by a man from the past. "Yes."

"Listen to me. I'm not your enemy. I only came down to the garden to talk to you."

"And decided on the spur of the moment it might be fun to draw a little blood."

"Not yours," he said wryly.

Liz raised a brow at him. "That's not how it looked to me."

"Only because the canebrake rattler was behind you, where you couldn't see it. Poised and ready to strike, I might add."

Liz stared at Garrett in amazement. "Are you trying to tell me you were aiming at a snake?"

Garrett nodded. "They normally keep to the shelter of the sugarcane thickets. I can't imagine why one would be coiled out in the open like that."

"I don't believe you," Liz said recklessly.

She saw something flicker in his eyes. Distress? Caused by her distrust of his motives? Surely not.

"Why would I lie to you?" he asked.

She shrugged brazenly, trying to bluff her way through this confrontation, as she had so many others. "Because you're tired of being married."

"If that was the case, I could have stood by and let the snake sink its fangs into you."

"Are they poisonous?" she asked, though she already knew the answer.

"Fatal."

"Did you kill it?"

"Rest assured, if I aimed at it, it is dead."

The word *if* was the key word, Liz thought.

Garrett must have read the skepticism in her eyes, for he asked impatiently, "Must I bring the carcass to you to prove there was a rattler in the garden?"

"Since I didn't hear it, seeing is believing," Liz said, realizing that the worst thing about the whole suspicious incident was that she was falling in love with Garrett—a prime suspect in a potential murder case. It came to her in a blinding, almost debilitating flash. One that baffled her even as she acknowledged it. Funny—she'd never thought of herself as having masochistic tendencies.

"Have it your way, Elizabeth," Garrett exclaimed.

Suddenly she was freed from his embrace, but not of the pain that shot through her heel and up her leg. She sagged back against him, surprising herself as much as she did him.

"You're injured after all! The snake didn't—"

"No. It's my foot. I think I've broken it. It hurts like hell...."

Garrett let the profanity slide without comment, glancing at the stair tread, askew on its riser, instead. "How did that happen?"

"You tell me. The step was fine this morning, when I came down to work in the garden."

"Are you accusing me of throwing a knife at you and then chasing you this way so you could fall down the stairs and break your neck?"

Liz nodded.

The snake temporarily forgotten, he scowled at her. "Don't be absurd. What if Mrs. Crawford had tripped on the stairs instead of you? Besides, if you incurred an injury it would thwart my purpose, Elizabeth."

"And that's a healthy child," Liz finished for him.

"Exactly."

Liz realized he was correct. If he allowed anything to happen before the baby's birth, he would have defeated his purpose in marrying her. He wasn't concerned about her.

She felt a profound sense of disappointment. And she still didn't know what he intended to do with her after the birth.

"And now, to that end..." he said.

In one swift motion, Garrett swept Liz off her feet, stepped over the tread and headed for the bedchamber.

Unable to resist the mad impulse, Liz asked, "Garrett, what would you do if you found out I wasn't pregnant after all?"

She felt him take a misstep, but he quickly recovered himself. "I honestly don't know, Elizabeth," he said dully, as if the thought had never occurred to him until now. "But I seriously doubt it would be a pretty sight."

Suddenly apprehensive again, Liz asked, "What have you done with Mrs. Crawford?"

A sable brow arched over one eye. "What do *you* think I did with her?" he asked.

"No telling."

"That's one of the things I've come to admire in you, Elizabeth—your bravado," Garrett said.

For once, Liz was rendered speechless.

"Never fear, Mrs. Crawford is still very much alive," he said. "I sent her on an errand. She should return within the hour. In the meantime, let's have a look at that foot."

Garrett deposited Liz unceremoniously on the bed.

Marshaling her wits like a shield of armor, she braced herself to resist him.

But his wandering hands felt too gentle, too soothing, too contradictory to what she'd expected, for her to resist.

He deftly removed her slippers, smoothing his fingers along the arch of her injured foot and around her ankle. A look of intense concentration registered on his face.

"Does that hurt?" he said. He pressed here and there at random.

Liz fought the wince rushing to her lips when he manually wiggled her toes. "Only when I laugh."

He glanced up sharply. Almost warily.

"Then don't laugh," he said solemnly.

Liz glimpsed something in his eyes that startled her. A vulnerability that he quickly masked with an almost imperceptible lowering of his lids. The moment passed so quickly, she almost thought she'd imagined it.

Finally, he said, "I don't think your foot's broken."

"How can you tell?" she asked.

"It's swelling, but not badly. And the skin isn't turning blue. Breaks usually cause discoloration."

She assumed he'd learned that during the War.

"If only we had some ice to pack it in," he continued.

"But we don't," she said. *Because you don't have an ice-maker, and it isn't winter.*

He looked thoughtful for a moment. "The next best thing is to elevate it."

Garrett plumped up the feather pillows on the bed and, gingerly cupping her heel, stuffed them in a mountain beneath her foot.

Critically eyeing her foot, she thought, *An ace bandage wouldn't hurt, either.*

As if reading her mind, Garrett said, "We'll watch it for a few hours to make certain I need not ride for Dr. Breninger. When Mrs. Crawford returns, I'll have her find something to wrap it in to keep down the swelling."

An uneasy silence settled between them. Finally Liz said, "I should thank you for...uh...rescuing me from the snake. And for checking out my foot."

"Checking out—" he began, then paused, as if mentally shaking himself. "I suppose you should," he amended.

"You act as if my thanks would be a first," Liz said, adjusting her foot more comfortably on the pillows.

"As a matter of fact, it would," he said, just as Mrs. Crawford appeared in the doorway.

"Whatever in the world—?" the housekeeper asked from the doorway.

Garrett glanced over his shoulder. "Mrs. Rowland has had a little accident. Do you have something in the house we can use for bandages?"

"Certainly." Mrs. Crawford hurried away, returning with a roll of material that looked surprisingly like an ace bandage.

Garrett deftly wrapped her foot, causing her heart to scamper while his fingers burned her skin everywhere he touched.

When he finally turned to Mrs. Crawford, Liz gave a silent sigh of relief.

"Did you deliver my message?" he asked the housekeeper.

"Yes, sir. The gentleman said he and his friends look forward to your arrival."

Liz glanced at Garrett. "You're going somewhere?"

Without responding to her question, Garrett said to the housekeeper, "Perhaps you'd like to go down and fix us a bit of lunch. I believe I smelled fresh-baked *beignets* when I passed the kitchen."

"Yes sir, you did." Mrs. Crawford looked relieved to be released from her duties as bandage holder.

Garrett followed her to the doorway and stepped out into the hallway. They conversed quietly for a moment. The housekeeper nodded. And then Garrett returned to Liz's bedside.

"You haven't answered my question," she said, wondering why the fact that he'd made plans without asking her disturbed her.

"There is a house party at Destrehan Plantation."

Liz knew the name well. Located near New Orleans International Airport, a part of the Live Oak Society and listed on the National Register of Historic Places, Drestrehan Plantation was one of the oldest estates in the lower Mississippi Valley. *In her time.*

"And?"

"The men plan to indulge in a game of hazard later this evening, after the ladies retire for the night."

"That's where you sent Mrs. Crawford—over to Drestrehan with a reply to the invitation."

He nodded.

"Of course, you accepted."

"I could hardly afford to do otherwise. The stakes will be quite high."

"I understand," she said. Garrett had ridden into New Orleans earlier in the week to pay some of the bills stacked on his desk in the library. She imagined he'd agreed to participate in the dice game in hopes of recouping some of his losses.

"You think you'll win a bundle tonight, don't you?" she asked.

Liz watched Garrett fight the smile that played across his lips.

"I hope to, as you so aptly put it, 'win a bundle.' But you never know. Sometimes fate plays havoc with the best-laid schemes."

Garrett wasn't telling her anything she hadn't experienced firsthand, Liz thought, visualizing the uncooperative tomb. For some reason, she'd expected it to work like a sci-fi transporter room. But some vital element was missing. She should have realized after being trapped inside that it didn't work on cue. Perhaps it happened only during storms. . . .

"Should you need anything while I am away, Mrs. Crawford has agreed to spend the night in the spare room off the kitchen. And, by the by, don't wait dinner for me. I may be gone until the wee hours."

When Mrs. Crawford returned bearing a tray laden with food, Liz and Garrett shared their first meal since the breakfast on the steamer. It was pleasant. They spoke of mundane things. She drank hot chocolate laced with ginger, which the housekeeper insisted was "good for calming the heart," while he sipped coffee. She ate two *beignets* slathered with whipped butter and honey, a serving of gumbo with rice, and a wedge of cheese. By the end of the meal, she felt so relaxed she could hardly hold her eyes open.

When Liz awoke a few hours later, the house was dark and quiet, and the room filled with the scent of roses which fell with the delicacy of a pink silk curtain over her face. She fought the curtain, acknowledging the conviction that Elizabeth Rowland was dead.

Had she dreamed it? Or had some poignant voice whispered it in her ear?

Restless and slightly befuddled, she slid from the bed, barely thinking of her foot as she padded to the window and brushed back the lace in search of fresh air.

Her eyelids felt heavy, and her mouth dry. And to top it off, she couldn't remember falling asleep.

Boy, did Mrs. Crawford's ginger pack a wallop!

Assuming the daylight hours had passed while she snoozed, Liz sucked in a great gulp of the cool evening air, trying to get her bearings. It was then that she noticed the ghostly lights weaving through the garden, only to stop at the tomb. Then backtrack and return to the tomb once again.

For a moment, she thought she was imagining things. No, there it was again! A distinct flicker.

Her eyes narrowed as she gazed out through the darkness.

What was it? It couldn't be fireflies. It was far too big for that. Candles? No, too bright. Too steady.

"What's going on here?" Liz asked out loud. Excitement assailed her as she wondered if this could be a supernatural signal from the tomb . . . her ticket home.

Apprehensive, yet feeling compelled to investigate, Liz made her way down the stairs, carefully, so as not to awaken Garret, should he be in the house. She crept past the open door of the kitchen's spare room, where Mrs. Crawford was snoring away as if there was no tomorrow. Liz paused at a bucket of water and took a drink. She splashed the remainder of the refreshing liquid on her face.

Then continued on, beyond the chinaberry trees.

Out into the gray-green shadows of the silent garden. . . .

CHAPTER TWELVE

Liz discovered Garrett seated in the gazebo with his arm braced back against the railings in a territorial fashion. Watching. Waiting patiently. As if he'd expected her to eventually find her way to him.

Her steps slowed.

Twilight spilled in pools around him, splashing on the greening plants and the gazebo's peeling paint and silhouetting them in a glow of molten silver. Liz wondered at his connection with the lights.

"I thought you were going to be gone until the wee hours," she said softly, surprised at how thready her voice sounded.

Garrett scanned her crumpled indigo gown. She, in turn, noticed that he'd tossed his coat over the railing beneath his hand, that his shirt was unbuttoned to the waist and displayed a patch of darkly curling hair, and that his sheath and knife were missing from his waist.

"It *is* the wee hours, Elizabeth," he said after a moment. A devilish grin curved his lips.

"Oh," she responded.

Liz studied the five-o'clock shadow hollowing Garrett's check and emphasizing his scar, then glanced up at the sky—bruised purple and yellow and crimson by the ensuing dawn. She'd slept through the afternoon, beyond full night and into the next day. How? Via drugs? she wondered. Perhaps a dose of laudanum to relax her muscles, administered in her food by Garrett when she wasn't looking, because he knew she would refuse to take it otherwise? She'd seen his sleight of hand before, when he'd slipped the Jackson children coins.

"You slept in your clothes," he said.

"I suppose I did." She glanced down at her skirt, with its torn hem, as if his observation were news to her. "I don't even remember falling asleep."

Liz expected Garrett to make some sort of reference to the fact that she'd been dead to the world for such an abnormally long time. Instead, he said, "You shouldn't be on that foot."

"You were right. It isn't broken. It feels fine now. Really." She should be afraid of him, she knew, but, surprisingly enough, she wasn't.

"I'm glad to hear it," he said.

"How did it go at Destrehan Plantation?" she asked, trying to recapture the lost hours.

"My, but you're in an inquisitive mood," he commented.

"Is that anything unusual?"

His good humor obviously restored by the night of gambling, Garrett laughed. "No, not unusual as of late."

Jolted by the thought that he was beginning to recognize the differences between her and Elizabeth, and wondering how much longer she would be required to remain in the past before the tomb revealed its puzzling properties of time travel again, Liz stuttered, "S-so... how about that dice game?" She wanted to get to the flickering lights, but she couldn't cut Garrett off without arousing suspicion.

His unsettling gaze remained on her face. "How do you think things went?"

They were conversing innocuously. Talking around something. She knew it and Garrett knew it. Yet they continued with their inconsequential banter.

"Considering your smug expression, I'd hazard a guess you cleaned them out," Liz said, feeling flirtatious, uneasy and impatient all at the same time.

"You're a saucy wench, but then, I'm not telling you anything you don't already know."

"And you're riding high on success."

"To be sure," Garrett remarked.

Liz glanced toward his waist once again. "By the way, where is your knife? I've never seen you without it."

He patted his side. "That's a very good question. I was wondering the same thing. After lunch, I looked for it. It had vanished into thin air, along with the snake. You wouldn't know where either is, would you?" he asked.

"I wouldn't waste my time asking about the knife if I knew where it was," she said indignantly. "As for the snake..."

Garrett studied her face intently, as if really seeing her for the first time. She was acutely aware of the brute strength emanating from the man. And yet this time a yearning that started as a mere flutter in her stomach, accelerated to a catch in her throat and spread as a tingling across her skin surpassed her fear of him.

"It's curious, but you know what?" he asked.

Liz shook her head, attempting to deal with her body's betrayal as she realized that the light was coming and going less frequently now. She wondered if she should confess her time-travel experience to Garrett, suggest that he accompany her into the future.

Then again, perhaps he couldn't travel to the future as she had to the past.

"I think I'm inclined to believe you concerning the knife."

"I suppose I could say the same about you and the purported snake."

"It must be the witchery of this garden," Garrett said. He panned the area around the gazebo, his gaze falling on the Cherokee roses. "You've done wonders here—Michael would be pleased. I wouldn't have thought it possible, considering the way it looked a week ago. It almost makes a man forget to keep his guard up."

His pose seemed too relaxed for the Garrett she'd come to know. Had he been drinking fine whiskey with the other men at Destrehan Plantation? Or was he being ultra-cautious while he fished for solutions to questions she couldn't or wouldn't answer.

"I've told you before, I..." Liz began, realizing the light had finally vanished, and probably taken with it her opportunity to return to the future.

"I know—you have a green thumb."

Liz could have cried, but she held back. It would come again. It had to! she told herself. And the next time she'd be ready for it.

Trying to sound as normal as possible under the circumstances, she said, "More importantly, I love plants. I... rarely admit this, but I talk to them."

He frowned. "Talk to them?"

She had his undivided attention now, which wasn't exactly what she'd been aiming for.

"They respond to it," she said. "It seems to make them happy."

"How do you know? Do they answer you?"

It was a strange conversation to be having at twilight, in the middle of a garden. But, what the hey...

"I can tell by the way they grow," Liz said. "They like music, too."

"The violin, perhaps?"

His smile mocked her.

Liz stiffened.

"That, among other things," she said. She put in a jazz CD some days. Classical, easy listening or country and western, others. It depended on her disposition.

"Do they enjoy fairy lights, as well, Elizabeth?"

The question soared at Liz from out of the clear blue, startling her.

"Do they look forward to your walks through the garden with a light at night as you signal someone?" he continued.

So, Garrett had seen the lights. They weren't just a figment of her wild-and-woolly imagination.

"I don't know what to say," Liz said, fighting to steady the ebb and flow of her emotions. One minute she felt so close to Garrett. The next...

He folded his arms across his muscular chest. "I bet you don't."

"You've got this all wrong. I wasn't the one with the light."

"No? Who, then?" he asked sharply.

Liz hesitated. Garrett would think she was crazy if she told him what she really thought.

"Go ahead," he prompted. "Confess something else to me. Something I'm dying to hear." His words were biting. And yet she suspected there were underlying reasons for it. Good ones.

Liz glanced at her nails to buy herself some time before she replied, "I think it might be a ghost."

Mouth agape, Garrett stared at her. Then he threw back his head and laughed until tears came to his eyes.

"It's not *that* funny," Liz said sullenly.

He hid his face in his hands, and for a moment his features were obscured. Then he took a deep breath and eased his head so far back his face was almost horizontal. Liz couldn't keep her eyes from straying to the strong column of his throat, wondering why she had an insane desire to run her fingers from his chin to his navel. And lower. And then follow it with the same sort of nibbling kisses he'd used on her in Baton Rouge.

Garrett was right. The garden was filled with witchery.

Or else the sensual fantasy was some kind of residual effect of the laudanum, Liz thought, watching as Garrett combed his fingers through his hair. He straightened, then stood.

"A ghost," he exclaimed with a muttered oath, "haunting Rowland Plantation? You expect me to believe that? What do you take me for?"

Believe me, I don't like this any more than you do. "I know it sounds kooky, but I'm only trying to give you a fair answer."

"Kooky?"

Liz wondered if she'd ever learn to mind her tongue.

"Offbeat. Crazy," she explained.

"You're right about that. Tell me this—who is this apparition? Or, more importantly, who was it before now... when it lived and breathed like you and me?"

Elizabeth, Liz mused. She believed either someone was getting kicks from playing psychological games or Elizabeth's ghost was trying to contact her, to guide her to the murderer. But she couldn't tell Garrett any of that. Because *she* was supposed to be Elizabeth.

"I'm not sure," Liz said finally.

"That's cruel—to taunt me with the prospect of my brother's ghost, when you know we never made peace between us." Then, as if another thought had occurred to him, he added, "You won't find him here. He's gone, Elizabeth."

Liz shook her head quickly. "I didn't say I thought it was Michael, and I wasn't looking for him when I came to the garden. I'm not sure what I expected to find, but it wasn't—"

"Me," Garrett finished quickly.

"No, it wasn't you."

"Shall I tell you what I suspect?" he asked.

Sensing his anxiety, Liz nodded. "Feel free."

"I fancy the lights are nothing more than a telltale sign of your moonlit trysts with Calvin," he said, almost wearily.

"That's why you came to the garden, isn't it? Expecting to catch us red-handed?"

She could allay his accusations by telling Garrett here and now that she wasn't Elizabeth. That she was just a conscientious observer dropped into the nineteenth century by the hand of fate. But it was no longer true. She was involved. Because, as outlandish as it seemed, she loved Garrett Rowland. The blinding flash had stayed with her, and now she saw it for the truth.

"You're wrong, Garrett. It's not what you think."

"Explain it, then."

"I can't. Not right now."

"I see. You refuse to implicate Calvin."

"I didn't say that."

"You didn't have to."

He'd never seemed so savagely contained. So dangerous. Not even in Calvin's company.

Garrett paced across the gazebo to stare out toward the tomb, then turned and retraced his steps.

"You're trying to drive me mad, aren't you?" he asked. "The haphazard manner in which you dress— Look at the way you're dressed now, with your bodice partially buttoned! The sparkle in your eyes. The eerie lights in the garden. Everything is calculated to that end."

Liz realized she was witnessing a real case of shattered nerves. It seemed their roles had reversed in the weeks since her arrival. At first, it had been Garrett encouraging her to calm down. Garrett, who seemed so strong and reasonable and sure of himself. But now...

Seeking some harmony and some balance, Liz said, "Come back to the house. Get some sleep. You're stressing out, Garrett."

"Stressing out? What do you mean, stressing out? If that's your way of telling me I've come to the end of my rope, then you're correct. I have. So...what now, Elizabeth?"

Liz involuntarily shivered. "You're frightening me, Garrett."

"Why? Because I'm once again charging you of conspiring with your cousin against me? Because I suspect you both of wishing to be well rid of me? Because I'm slowly losing control?" He paused, his eyes glittering with self-loathing. "Or because I'm not losing control fast enough to suit you and your fair-haired compatriot?"

His tortured expression transformed Liz's shiver into a sympathetic quivering that started somewhere in the regions of her heart. She couldn't stand to see him this way. In such...

anguish. And all because of her. She felt torn, because
the future's draw was lessening in relationship to her
feelings for Garrett. She still wasn't sure of him. She
couldn't afford to let her emotions color her rational
side. And yet...

In a calm, and she hoped, soothing voice, she said,
"You're frightening me because you're staring at me the
same way you did at the Jacksons' house."

Cocking a regal brow, Garrett relaxed somewhat at
the mention of the Jackson family.

Relieved that her ploy had worked, Liz continued in
the same vein, for she had glimpsed a gentler Garrett
through the Jacksons' eyes, and she hoped to reclaim
that side of him now.

"You were standing out in the herb garden with
Charles, gazing in through the bay window toward me.
I wondered if you were angry with me. Wondered what
I'd done to make you look at me that way."

"You laughed," he said simply.

She was totally unprepared for his response. "I
what?"

"Your face was alight with laughter. Your eyes were
soft and warm. Your lips full and rosy from the hot
tea," he said slowly, as if weighing the impact of each
word. "I'd never seen you laugh. It was a tiny, insignificant thing that burgeoned all out of proportion. It
nearly stopped my heart. God! How I wanted you! The
ache nearly choked me. I could only listen to Charles
and nod dumbly. And...stare."

Liz gulped. It was the first time she had ever heard
Garrett falter over anything. She could feel her heart
melting. "I don't know what to say."

"Later, I thought to indulge myself. A kiss here. A
kiss there. What could it hurt, with my friends looking

on? How wrong I was. I've thought of nothing else
since Baton Rouge. Do you have any idea what that
kind of desire feels like? How overwhelming? How ir-
rational?"

Liz surprised herself by saying, "Yes, I do. I'm feeling it right now."

Garrett towered over her, darkly handsome and decidedly agitated—with himself or with her for the audacity of her admission, Liz couldn't be sure.

"Do you know what you're saying?" he asked
gruffly.

She couldn't back down now. "Uh-huh."

"You cannot. I'm not Michael, Elizabeth," he
ground out.

"I realize that."

"I'm not tender...or gentle...or easily led down the
garden path you've devised. I won't court you with
flowers. Or woo you with loving smiles and sweet
words."

*You already have, with the poetic way you phrase
your sentences.* "You don't have to say this."

"Oh, but I must." He paused. "More importantly, I
won't tolerate your cousin in our lives."

"I'm not asking for that."

"What are you asking for then?"

She spoke before she could stop herself. "Your
heart—"

"Carved up and laid out on—and I quote—a 'silver
platter,'" he finished for her.

The pain in Garrett's voice stabbed at Liz. It dug
deeper and twisted more efficiently than any knife
could. Being in love was terrifying, because it coerced
one into spontaneous feelings. You couldn't turn off the
emotion. It wasn't sensible. Or cautious. Or even sane.

The thought carried through as Liz said, "You think of me as a threat to your sanity." *As you are to mine.*

"I think of you as a very desirable woman who expects more than I can give." The words seemed torn from his larynx by invisible hands.

With a sweet sensation building inside her, Liz realized Garrett would not let himself commit to her, and yet she wanted him to take her in his arms. She wondered what she would do if he asked to be invited back into her bed.

Their thoughts were running hand in hand, for he asked abruptly, "Would you invite me into the master bedchamber right now, this moment, if I asked?"

She dared not answer him, for fear of changing his world beyond recognition, and in the process somehow deleting her own future. She thought of her job at the library, her shotgun duplex, her life in the twentieth century. They suddenly seemed immaterial as she heard herself reply, "In a heartbeat."

"Then, by God, I'm asking."

This time, it was impossible to make a dispassionate decision. Going against every grain of common sense she possessed, Liz said, "Yes, Garrett."

"I've warned you, I'm not Michael," he said, giving her an out even as he reached for her hand. It was the most gallant thing she had ever seen Garrett Rowland, or any other man, for that matter, do.

It seemed both of them feared being a substitute for someone else, Liz thought. Only she wasn't Elizabeth. And she'd never known Michael.

Only Garrett.

"I know that. That's one of the main reasons I...want to." Oh, how she *wanted* to. Regardless of the consequences. Her fears. His fears. The incompatibility of their worlds. The incredible strangeness of the situation.

Liz realized with a start that she had found an even more compelling obsession than her need to discover the door back to her own time. She must put to rest her doubts concerning Garrett by uncovering history's dark secrets, for love bereft of trust was merely a shadow stretching from the darker side of human emotion. She hoped that by unraveling the past and coming to grips with the truth she could save Garrett from years of despair and unhappiness.

"So be it," Garrett rasped.

He entwined his fingers with hers, bridging the gap between them as he led her from the garden, toward the plantation house and up the balustraded stairs, toward the sanctity of the red-and-black-flocked bedchamber.

Liz allowed Garrett to escort her there without a struggle. Knowing in the meandering corridors of her mind that surrendering herself to him might be the biggest and most dangerous mistake of her life.

CHAPTER THIRTEEN

Irreparable damage. That's what this is going to cause, Liz told herself. She shouldn't do it. Shouldn't tilt her head to receive Garrett's kiss as he tugged her against him. But she did so anyway. With enthusiasm.

His kiss was entirely in contradiction to his outward persona. Gentle, when he always seemed so hard. Tentative, when he always seemed so sure of himself.

He spoke to her with his kisses, told her of his need. And when the kisses deepened, she clung to him more tightly. Encouraging him.

"Starved," he murmured against her lips.

There was only one thing Liz knew to do with a hungry man—feed him.

She unbuttoned the bodice of the indigo gown to the waist, pushing the gown off her shoulders to expose the swell of her breasts above the shift's lace trim. Her own need was so fierce, her body shook.

She heard Garret's indrawn breath as he trailed warm, wet kisses down her cheek and throat. He roamed lower, and when he reached the sensitive area just below her collarbone he said, "The consequences be damned."

He inserted his hands beneath the indigo gown, brushing his strong, work-roughened fingertips across the sheer fabric of her shift as he peeled the bodice over her hands. It fell to her waist with a soft whisper.

"Beautiful," he rasped.

A small smile curved her lips.

"You're not half-bad yourself," she said.

As if unable to stop himself, he cupped her breasts. Smoothing. Kneading. Teasing.

Liz reveled in his touch.

"You said you wouldn't woo me. If this...isn't wooing...I don't know what it is."

His jaw tense, his eyes dark, bottomless pools of blue, he paused. "I didn't see this coming. In the beginning, it was simply a matter of pride. I started out to prove something to myself. That I was strong enough to pick up the shattered pieces of this family. That I could be the triumphant one," he said. "But now...I've come to...care about what happens to you."

She realized what it cost him to admit he cared for her. She could have said something sarcastic about Michael's purported baby. But she didn't. It would only spoil the magic of the moment. And that was the last thing Liz wanted to do.

His eyes flickered with desire, stoking the fire within her and vanquishing any protests she might have made. She banished the uncertainties to the deepest recesses of her mind and momentarily dispelled any fear of the past, any longing for the future. Their time was now and Garrett had become too important to her for her to waste it.

He glanced toward the light streaming in through the lace curtains. "I know it's full daylight, but God, how I want you," he growled.

She was afraid to make love with Garrett, yet she found herself more afraid *not* to. His eyes were promising her things she'd never known. And might never know again, if she didn't reach out and make a grab at the golden ring. Possessed by love, she closed her eyes, leaning against the solidity of his hard, lean body.

"I'm not afraid of the daylight," Liz said. "I'm not afraid of anything right now, with you here."

She unlaced the ribbons of her shift, slipping her arms from the straps and baring her body to the waist, confirming what she'd just said. Liz stood proudly before him, the epitome of the twentieth-century woman—without shyness, comfortable with her decision about their physical union, accepting of her innate sensuality. Willing to give as good as she got.

Garrett became unnervingly silent—so still he might have been carved from granite. Except for his eyes, which traveled over her indolently.

Her heartbeat accelerated as she waited with bated breath for him to say something.

Finally, unable to stand the suspense a moment longer, she said enticingly, "Show me how much you want me. Make me *feel* it, Garrett. I've grown tired of guessing." She reached for the crisscrossing laces of his shirt and fumbled with the knot at his throat.

She felt him suck in his breath.

"Minx. I've never met a lady as bold as you," Garrett said, brushing away her hands. His expression of pain mixed with pleasure as he worked the knot undone himself told Liz he'd decided to allow the chips to fall where they may.

He impatiently swept his shirt over his head, tossing it onto the floor as he swept her into his embrace.

"I fear your boldness will be my undoing," he said.

The fine hair on his chest teased at her breasts. Her nipples puckered as if in anticipation as he bent his head to nibble at each one in turn. She moaned, entirely unprepared for the punishing tenderness his mouth inflicted as he laved her breasts with his tongue into twin peaks of longing.

He's opened up to you so much... offered you succor in a world that fate has turned topsy-turvy. How can you do this to him? her conscience nagged. *How can you pretend to be someone you're not?*

Liz tried to ignore the daunting questions, tried to lose herself in Garrett's passionate ministrations. In the end, her conscience won out. It simply wasn't fair to deceive him any longer.

It took all the strength of will she could muster to lean away from him.

"Garrett, we have to stop... for just a second." *I hope.* "I have something important I have to tell you."

"Important or not, it can wait awhile," he murmured.

Could it? For the first time in ages, she wanted someone to hold her, caress her, make her his. But he wanted... Elizabeth. At least he thought he did. It was time to set him straight and clear her conscience.

"We've got to talk. There's something you have to know about me. I'm a big phony."

"Phony?"

"A fake."

"Big, yes. Fake—never," he said. Laughter lurked in his voice. Unable to resist the contact, Liz reached up to trace his dimples with her fingertips, exploring their hollows, giving herself time while she sought the words to explain that she'd traveled to him down through the decades to fill the void left by Elizabeth. That she didn't know how or why, and that she could vanish from his life without forewarning, as easily as she'd appeared.

"I'm not kidding," she said.

He grabbed her hands. "Neither am I. You're a beguiling woman." He peered deeply into her eyes. "But then, you know that already, don't you?" he said. And with quiet resolve he released her hands and twined his fingers through her hair. Cupping her head, he pulled her toward him and covered her mouth with his, deliberately cutting off her confession with an interminable kiss that carried them across the room and to the bed.

She tasted the male essence of him—spiced brandy, ginger tobacco and blatant desire.

"I want you to know something," she said.

"Don't—"

"You have to let me say this much. I care about you, too, Garrett," she said as they sank into the feather mattress together. "Not . . . Michael, you."

His face darkened. "You would have to mention Michael."

"Only because I thought you might have him in the back of your mind."

He stretched out beside her. "Michael is the last thing on my mind right now," he said, his hardness pressed intimately against her hip. His hands played sensually along the tender flesh of her inner arm, doing tempting things to her insides as he emphasized the validity of his comment.

Resolved that their talk would indeed have to wait, Liz shimmied out of Elizabeth's indigo gown and kicked it impatiently from the foot of the bed.

Due to the heat, she wore nothing under her shift. Garrett soon discovered this—much to his astonishment, Liz decided. She supposed he'd been expecting something more substantial. Now, as he pushed her shift up to her waist, there remained no barrier between them except the band of white cotton gathered at her waist.

"God above," he sighed, planting a kiss on her strawberry birthmark as his hand strayed to caress the blond mound cradled between her legs.

Thinking aloud, Liz whispered against his lips, "Katie, bar the door."

"What?"

"Nothing. Don't stop," she said anxiously, clinging to him.

"Never," he replied, his voice raw with desire.

He kissed her until she felt breathless. Moist, and bruised, and wanting. Until she didn't care if she ever breathed again, as long as he finished what they'd started.

In an unconscious attempt to communicate her feelings to him, her hand fluttered to the waistband of his pants. She felt his stomach muscles tense as she relentlessly measured his need through the constricting broadcloth.

"You'll be the death of me yet," he groaned.

"I hope not. I have much better plans for you than that. Languid, delicious plans," she said, in a barely audible voice. She continued the thought with a kiss that started at his chin, lingered on his chest and ended in the region of his navel.

Almost...

"Like this," she said, pressing lower along his abdomen. "And this." She reached for the fastening on his pants and felt his shiver of pleasure.

"And...this."

Frustrated, she pushed his pants down to his knees, catching them with her toes to strip them off, along with his undergarments. His clothes landed with a soft sigh on top of her gown as Garrett rolled to cover her body with his. She slipped one arm around his neck, splayed her fingers of her other hand through his crisp, dark hair and hugged him tightly to her.

She trailed her hands lower, to his waist. And then lower still, to the curve of his buttocks and his hair-roughened thighs. Stroking. Caressing. Appreciating the firm, shapely contours of him.

As if they'd waited an eternity for this moment, impatience gripped him. Their eyes met.

"I can't stand this much longer," he said hoarsely.

She didn't have to ask what he meant. She felt the same way. The waiting, the anticipation, was driving her wild.

"Then don't," Liz said softly.

Garrett's lips found hers as he entered her with a sure, quick thrust that brought her arching against him.

Again.

And again.

And again.

Until a shower of ephemeral light burst in her head. Bright white, and ultimately satisfying.

Sleek with perspiration, drenched in the rhythmic convulsions that racked her body, Liz sensed Garrett's shuddering release. A release borne on the wings of her own devastating climax.

Afterward, basking in the throes of bittersweet contentment, they lay in each other's arms, sated, his hand moving casually, possessively over her torso.

"Mmm. That was wonderful . . . *is* wonderful," she said, thinking that a massage after sex was a marvelous idea. Sometimes, doing things backward had its advantages.

Garrett moved from the small of her back to her hips, up along her rib cage, then over and down. Liz didn't think anything of it—until he reached her stomach.

He paused, saying in surprise, "It's still flat, Elizabeth."

And my breasts aren't tender. And my hormones aren't playing Russian roulette with my equilibrium. Because I'm not pregnant. At least, not that I know of. Yet.

The sweet inner serenity brought on by their love-making evaporated. "Yeah, I know," she said. Liz dashed at the tears welling in her eyes.

His comment about her stomach instantly forgotten, Garrett asked in concern, "What's wrong? Did I hurt you?"

Yes and no. Yes, he'd hurt her by calling her Elizabeth. And no, because she'd been the one to hurt him by not forcing the issue and insisting he listen to her first. Before they went too far too fast.

"You didn't hurt me. You gave me great and lasting pleasure," she said.

"Then what is it? Women don't cry for no reason."

"Sometimes they do, but not in this case. Before we got carried away, I tried to talk to you." Liz took a huge gulp of air and rushed on before she lost her nerve. "I've been trying to explain that I've been lying to you, Garrett. I'm not the woman you think I am."

"I agree. You're more. Much, much more. I'm only sorry it took me this long to find out what I've been missing."

"You aren't *listening*," she said. The stress of the situation showed in her voice.

"Yes, I am," Garrett said hastily. Liz saw the flash of apprehension in his eyes. She decided to disregard it.

"I've lied about my memory, because I was afraid."

"What have I done to you?" he asked.

"Nothing.... No, as I said, wonderful things. Things I probably don't deserve."

"You're over—"

"I'm not overwrought, Garrett. Not delirious. Or crazy. I'm baring my soul to you. And there's no easy way to break the news to you except to blurt it out. I'm not Elizabeth. I'm not pregnant with Michael's baby. We aren't...married."

"What are you saying?"

Liz faltered, battling to find her way beyond the incredulous expression on his face. "I'm a twentieth-century woman, Garrett. A volunteer tour guide who went down to the gates of the historic homesite on a lazy Sunday afternoon, dressed in period costume, to lock up a back gate, and somehow wound up in your arms. I only look like Elizabeth."

He exploded. "You can't be serious!"

"I can be and I am. I prefer to be called Liz, but my full name is Elizabeth Adair Hayden. Born September twenty-fifth, nineteen hundred and sixty-eight."

He shook his head. "I don't believe I'm hearing this. You must be out of your mind!"

"*Believe it,* Garrett. I'm a research librarian by trade, who doesn't particularly care for hot tea, who enjoys cultivating flowers, and lives alone in a shotgun duplex in New Orleans's Garden District. I feed stray cats, though I've never owned a cat of my own. And I love Chinese food, particularly chicken chow mein chock-full of bamboo shoots and water chestnuts."

"You have a fantastic imagination."

"I do, but there's no need to use it, because I'm not making this up. It happened, as sure as I'm lying here beside you."

"So... if what you're saying is true, then where is Elizabeth?" Garrett asked bluntly.

"I'm not sure—dead, I think."

"For God's sake, Elizabeth! You've come up with some pretty strange things in your time, but this takes the biscuit. I've never heard anything so ridiculous."

"What will it take to force you to believe me, Garrett?" Liz asked in frustration.

"That's a good question. I wish I had an answer for it."

"Isn't my strange turn of phrase, my lack of memory, the pear-shaped birthmark on my hip, proof enough for you? You said you'd never seen one before. You didn't notice it when you and Elizabeth..." Liz paused, unable to finish the thought aloud. "You didn't see it, because *she* didn't have one. I do."

Wavering, Garrett ground out, "Even if I could, I'm not sure I want to believe you."

"You have to try. For my sake, as well as for yours. We have to be prepared for whatever happens. I'm not Scarlett O'Hara. I can't think about this tomorrow."

"Who is Scarlett O'Hara?"

"A fictional character in an American masterpiece—written long after your time, and well before mine. She was good at putting things off. I'm not. If I don't get this out of my system, expose it to the light of day, I have a funny feeling I might burst at the seams."

"Elizabeth—" he began, in his most soothing voice.

"Please, don't call me Elizabeth again," she said, the weariness in her voice touching him in areas he'd considered inaccessible. "My name is Liz—Liz Hayden!"

* * *

If he believed her, it meant he could lose her, Garrett thought. And he couldn't bear the thought of being without her.

Garrett leaned forward, once again silencing her the only way he knew how—with a kiss. He was badly shaken, and for the moment he wanted to keep all the truths, her truths and his truths, at bay.

"At the moment, I don't care who you are—Scarlett O'Hara, Elizabeth or Liz. I long to make love with you again," he said without preamble. His heart thudded in his chest as he anticipated her response.

"I hate it when you wax poetic," she said, in a strangled voice. Her tone mirrored his own qualms concerning her sanity....
and his.

Dare he trust her? Dare he not?

Gazing into her capricious whiskey brown eyes, he decided to risk it all. To take the gamble that she might be telling him the honest-to-God truth, as incredible as it sounded.

He wanted to immerse himself in her intoxicating woman's scent. In the silken feel of her skin. In the honey-sweet taste of her delicate lips. To experience once again her capacity for passion and her gift for sure and certain gratification.

As his kisses deepened, she tried to turn her face away. He held her head in place.

"Don't turn away from me," he said, hating himself for the pleading note in his voice. Becoming more inextricably involved with her—whoever she was—was the last thing he needed in his life right now. And the only thing he truly desired.

Garrett felt her relax against him, degree by degree. Until he couldn't tell where he ended and she began.

"I won't shut you out, Garrett. Not now. Not ever. Not as long as you need me," she promised, moving softly against him, touching his heart as no other woman ever had. Assuaging all the hurt, all the pain, all the myriad indifferences, he'd known over the past few years.

She peppered his taut body with warm, succulent kisses, instinctively touching on all his most vulnerable spots. Sending tremors to the very tips of his limbs, taxing his control.

She made him forget everything except the tantalizing feel of her lithe body against his, and his precarious balance on the precipice of fulfillment. They were forging a physical bond between them, a bond that he doubted could ever be broken.

By time . . . or otherwise.

Suddenly, nothing mattered as much as her breathless gasps, which matched the quickness of his own. He tried to pace himself. He was succeeding, admirably, as a gentleman should.

And then she straddled him, wrapping herself around him.

The self-control he prided himself on disintegrated around them as she shared with him the small measure of peace he so desperately sought and could so ill afford.

Liz rested, wide-eyed, beside Garrett, listening to his even breathing. She suspected he was sleeping more deeply now than he'd slept in months.

She changed position to test her theory, removing her leg from across his thigh and taking her hand and head away from his chest. Garrett disengaged himself from her arms and rolled onto his side without waking, lost in dreams that made him smile in his sleep as he hugged a pillow to his chest.

Her mind awhirl with unanswered questions, Liz sighed. This was the opportunity she'd been waiting for. The chance to accomplish the things that needed doing.

Careful not to disturb him, she scooted from his side, easing from the bed and drawing the net shut around him. She quietly gathered up her gown and headed for the wash basin for a quick sponge bath, glancing over her shoulder periodically to assure herself he still slept undisturbed. Liz thought that he was gorgeous in all his naked male splendor.

Toilette completed, she donned the shift and gown, thrust her feet into Elizabeth's slippers and tiptoed into the hallway, gently closing the heavy door behind her.

Liz pressed her ear against the polished wood. She could hear Garrett's softly muffled snores through the door.

Good!

With a deep sigh, she hurried down the hall, pausing on the landing to gaze through the fan light at the darkening horizon. A storm was brewing across the river. She only hoped its distant rumble didn't awaken Garrett before she completed her mission.

Liz sprinted down the remaining steps into the central hallway, glancing through the library's open doorway.

She'd seen a coatrack in the corner, hadn't she? Perhaps it wouldn't be a bad idea to stop and collect a cape—in the event the rain started before she returned to the house.

Liz tripped into the library, choosing a lightweight worsted from the selection dangling on the clawlike hangers. She tied the cape around her neck and flipped it over her shoulder.

She pivoted in preparation for flight, only to have her attention arrested by the oil portrait fixed above the mantel. Elizabeth's gaze seemed to pursue her as she passed beneath it.

Liz scurried from the room, closing the pocket doors behind her and fighting the eerie sensation that Elizabeth still watched her as she exited the house through the back door.

A bleary-eyed Mrs. Crawford glanced up from her daily baking as Liz passed the open kitchen. The housekeeper waved. Liz returned the greeting without stopping, following the path through the garden to the tomb. She spared the Rowland family vault only a cursory inspection as she continued on toward the water.

Liz skirted the levee and the floating dock, trailing the river downstream, deeper into the tangled green-brown wilderness that bordered the churning water. She scanned the receded banks for signs of her striped muslin costume, with its nylon zippers and precise machine stitching, her tennis shoes, with their Made in the U.S.A. acetate labels sewed on the tongues. And her footie socks. Modern items that would be proof positive to Garrett she was indeed a time traveler.

CHAPTER FOURTEEN

Liz thought she heard the trembling warble of a human voice. Or was it the fitful wind that was blowing a fine mist in across the Mississippi? She wasn't sure. Suddenly she had a premonition that made her skin crawl.

Following its lead, Liz inhaled. The foul odor permeating the hot, static air told her with almost certain accuracy where she would find Elizabeth.

With an acute sense of unease, Liz craned her neck and squinted toward a tangled thicket several yards inland from the river. She spied a piece of striped muslin torn from her tour-guide's costume dangling from a twig. As if planted there by a ghostly hand, it fluttered in the breeze like a banner, beckoning her to step forward for a closer inspection.

Holding her nose, she forced herself to do so.

Liz reached out tentatively to tug at the muslin. The fabric clung stubbornly. Tugging harder, she inadvertently separated the thicket's branches and saw what she had hoped for and dreaded at the same time. As if extended in supplication, an open hand stretched up through the tangle of brush and leaves. A hand wearing on its skeletal appendage the Rowland family heirloom wedding band that Garrett had earlier accused her of losing.

Elizabeth!

Startled, Liz abruptly released the muslin, allowing the foliage to fall back into place. She slowly backed away from the thicket, wondering what she should do next.

Before she could come to a decision, the scent of Cherokee roses suddenly welled up so powerfully around her that she could taste them. The cloying floral blanket enveloped her, temporarily covering death's rank odor.

Liz didn't have to hear the stealthy footfalls or the rustle of heat-dried grasses to know she'd been followed. It seemed weird that she'd never smelled the roses in Garrett's company, Liz thought. Then again, maybe not. Perhaps this was what Elizabeth had been trying to do all along—protect her from her murderer. Warn her when he was near, as he was now.

"So, finally, the jig is up," said the man strolling nonchalantly up the river bank toward her.

The smoothly spoken words chilled Liz. She pivoted to face Elizabeth's worst enemy—Calvin Trexler.

"For you or for me, Calvin?" Liz asked, marveling that she'd somehow missed the forest for the trees. How could history have been so negligent with the facts?

"Alas, it would seem so for us both," he said.

His insolent gaze raked her body. "You are almost the exact likeness of Elizabeth. I must say I was quite relieved a moment ago to finally discover you and my cousin were not one and the same. I have to give Garrett credit there."

"What makes you think Garrett is involved in this?"

"He has to be involved. Garrett is not so dense that he could live under the same roof with you and not recognize the difference between you and the woman he married."

That's what you think. "How did you learn I was impersonating Elizabeth?"

"I did not know for absolute certain until a moment ago."

"What do you mean?"

"I have been searching for Elizabeth, as well."

"It was you in the garden with the lantern."

"I first suspected the deception when you spoke of your loss of memory. But the garden finally gave you away to me for a certainty."

"I don't understand," Liz said, desperate to keep him talking long enough to devise a game plan.

"My cousin Elizabeth could not tell a snapdragon from a buttercup. It was Michael who built the gazebo, planned the garden, planted and nurtured it. He was the one with the acute affinity for flowers—not Elizabeth. I have been racking my brain to figure out how there could be two of you, or, barring that, how Elizabeth came back to life after I stood on the riverbank and watched her drown."

Liz glanced toward the thicket where she'd made her horrendous discovery, then back to Calvin, astonished that such unadulterated evil could be contained in such a handsome package. Calvin's chivalrous facade hid a diabolical monster, his fine eyes camouflaged a decidedly sinister and depthless soul. Calvin Trexler was the culprit history had overlooked—perhaps because he knew how to cover his tracks so well.

"You killed her," Liz said dully as the pieces of the mysterious puzzle finally fell into place. Flooding during the storm must have washed her body inland.

Calvin's laughter echoed through the trees. "Don't look so stricken, sweetheart. I assure you, it was an accident."

Taken aback by his casual endearment, Liz said, "I'm not your sweetheart."

"No, of course you're not," he agreed.

"How did it happen, Calvin? How did Elizabeth die?" *And why do you seem to have so little remorse.*

"It's a rather involved story."

"I like long stories." *They give me time to think.* "Besides, I'm a good listener," Liz added bravely. "Try me."

"Elizabeth and I had a bargain."

It seemed Elizabeth had bargains with everyone. Evidently they caused her nothing but trouble.

"It goes a long way back, to just after the War. Michael Rowland was a captain in my regiment. We became good friends. Through my association with him, I visited Rowland Plantation while on leave for Christmas. I witnessed the respect bestowed on him as heir to the estate. From that day forward, I wanted to own it."

"Did Michael know that?"

"Michael was too absorbed in getting the estate back on its feet to notice. I built an empire after the War on financial speculation. When the time was right, I shared my dream of owning Rowland Plantation with Elizabeth."

"Why Rowland Plantation? You probably could have bought any one of a hundred plantations after the War."

"You are correct, of course, but Elizabeth did not see it that way. Her father, my uncle, died at Gettysburg. His part of the business in New Orleans was passed on to me as the only male heir. Elizabeth had no money, and no social standing, as the daughter of a tradesman. She needed security."

"So you introduced her to Michael."

"Not exactly. She stumbled into him on my front doorstep one day."

"And cast out lures to him."

"She found him appealing. Though it did not exactly suit my plans, at first I thought it an excellent notion that they become better acquainted. No man could help himself where Elizabeth was concerned. One thing led to another. Suffice to say, they married almost immediately."

"With you financing the wedding," she said hazarding a guess.

"I gladly supplied the dowry."

"Hoping to gain control of the estate through her."

"You are an intelligent woman."

"Intelligent enough to know that your plans backfired."

"Then what?"

"Elizabeth reneged on the bargain. She fell in love."

"It seemed the scheme was still salvageable when Providence interceded and Michael died from yellow fever. Elizabeth was Michael's beneficiary. I immediately asked her to marry me," he said, and Liz realized he'd been more than a little in love with Elizabeth himself.

"And she refused."

"She told me she was 'repulsed by the idea of intermarriage with a first cousin.'"

"But you weren't."

"Damn her! She wanted a husband, a home, a family—established roots for her child. But more than anything else, she wished to retain the Rowland name. It was a quaint notion, but hardly realistic, considering how far in debt she was. She had been living off my income since her father's death. In conjunction with the wedding, her account came to a tidy sum. Elizabeth *owed* me!''

That's why she'd found no clothes to speak of in Elizabeth's trunk. No jewels to account for the stack of bills on Garrett's desk. She'd sold them to try to pay Calvin back. In an attempt to get him off her back so that she could have her baby in peace.

"I had always been able to manipulate her before introducing her to Michael. I hoped after his death she would be more agreeable, but she grew more and more distraught. More uncontrollable than ever. Eventually Garrett, looking like a younger version of Michael, arrived on the scene and whisked Elizabeth off her feet."

"Did he?" Liz asked absently, her mind on escape.

"He has a way with women," he said dryly.

Somehow, she had to gain Calvin's confidence. To bargain with him, too, just as Elizabeth had. Or, barring that, to escape him.

Determined to keep him talking until she figured out which way to run, she said, "Finding a way to keep the Rowland surname, she chose Garrett over you."

Liz immediately realized she'd said the wrong thing, for he paused, glaring at her as if everything was her fault.

"I followed the honeymooners to Rowland Plantation, pleading with Elizabeth to divorce Garrett. But she, weak-willed kitten that she had always been with me, was suddenly no longer so weak. In fact, she had become a tigress, downright belligerent, and nearly as pigheaded as Garrett in her determination to protect Michael's offspring. From me! Her own flesh and blood! Needless to say, we argued."

"Near the tomb," Liz guessed.

"Inside it. She placed fresh flowers on Michael's coffin each and every day. I followed her to the vault after dinner, while Garrett was in the library, absorbed with the account ledgers. I tried to reason with her. She refused to listen to me. We struggled. She fell, striking her head on the corner of Michael's coffin. I put my ear to her chest. She didn't seem to be breathing. I assumed she was dead."

"Fearing Garrett's reaction, you panicked," Liz said encouragingly.

"Though he had permitted me to visit Elizabeth periodically, I knew he hated me and he would have liked nothing better than to see me rot in prison. I had to get rid of the evidence . . . so I tossed Elizabeth's body into the river."

"Only she was still alive."

"The water revived her." The agony reflected in his eyes recounted the horror of it. "She called my name over and over, each time her head bobbed to the surface. Begging me to do something, to save her."

Liz winced at the vivid description, wondering what Elizabeth had been thinking during her last moments. Of the baby? Or Michael? Perhaps, unable to cope without him, she'd experienced a certain sense of relief that she would soon be joining him. Or maybe she'd cursed Calvin for destroying her baby's chance at life.

Determined to cajole him into confessing to Elizabeth's murder, Liz said, "And yet you stood by and watched her drown."

His eyes grew suddenly cold and glassy, his voice defiant. "She knew I cannot swim."

"It was you all the time, wasn't it?" Liz asked abruptly.

A cunning grin crossed his lips. "Whatever are you talking about now?"

"Don't play games with me. You know exactly what I'm referring to. You deliberately set the fire in the wastepaper can," she said, trying to hide her nervous tension as she awaited his answer.

Thus prompted, the latent truths seemed to splash from his lips like spray from a fountain. "No. I can honestly say that incident was no more deliberate than Elizabeth's death."

His recounting of the facts dispelled all fear that Garrett was responsible for the legacy of murder that darkened the steps of the Rowland Plantation.

"You left the note for me."

"I borrowed a sheet of the mourning stationery from Elizabeth's desk. I wanted to converse with you alone."

Liz had wrongly assumed that the bold handwriting slashing the black-bordered page belonged to Garrett. She would have expected Calvin's to be more effeminate. How diligently he had worked to hide his true character from the world.

"Mrs. Crawford is not the most astute housekeeper I've ever seen. It was incredibly simple to deposit the unsigned note on the salver on the hall table as I left the house."

"And she delivered it back upstairs to me."

"Naturally."

"Thinking it was from Garrett."

"Servants never think of things like that, one way or another. It was simply a note, to be delivered to the mistress of the house. Plain and simple."

"Why the fire?"

"Elizabeth kept a journal. She wrote *everything* in it. I could not chance the possibility of someone finding it."

"You mean Garrett."

Nodding, Calvin said, "So I burned it."

Liz listened attentively as the somber mystery unfolded, recalling the crumpled vellum sheets curling to ashes beneath the fire's onslaught. The smoke. Her hysteria.

"You were the presence I felt in the bedroom when I woke up. It was you that locked me in with the smoke."

He shrugged. "A harmless prank. Seeing how frightened you were, I am afraid I simply could not resist teasing you."

"Teasing me? You scared the hell out of me!"

"Tsk, tsk. Such language for a lady."

Liz had an almost irresistible urge to tell Calvin to can it. That he hadn't heard anything yet. That her father had been in the navy in his younger days and she knew words that would make his head spin. Instead, she said, "I don't like smoke."

"I know. It was the first indication I had that you were an impostor. That Garrett had not somehow fished you from the river after I threw you…Elizabeth…in. My cousin would not have feared a little thing like smoke."

Your cousin never saw her family consumed in a house fire. "That's why you looked so startled when Garrett came charging into the house with me in his arms."

"Soaking wet. Yes, you gave me quite a turn."

Keep him talking. It's your only chance, Liz told herself.

"What about that day I was trapped in the tomb? Did you engineer that?"

"Your reaction to the fire planted the seed for that incident. I walked up when your back was turned, positioned my fingers just so, and—"

"Pushed," Liz said, despising the offhanded manner in which he recounted his despicable deeds. "I knew I hadn't imagined the hand between my shoulder blades."

"I must compliment you on your endurance. I fear I would have started screaming my head off for help long before you succumbed to the temptation."

"And the canebrake rattler? Was that your doing, too?"

"Although I'd like to take credit, that was the snake's idea."

"The stairs?"

"A mere afterthought."

Liz suspected he'd simply been high on the knowledge that he could flit in and out of the house at will, and yet go unnoticed.

"Such a devious mind," she muttered.

"I shall take that as a compliment."

"I assume you're the one who slipped something into my chocolate at lunch."

"You intend to count the incidents off one by one?"

"I do." *Explanations were the reason she was here.*

"Knowing that the ginger would hide the flavor of the laudanum, I placed a dram or two in the chocolate pot when Mrs. Crawford's attention was elsewhere. I thought it would be intriguing to see both you and Garrett simultaneously incapacitated by my hand. But Garrett drank coffee instead. Later, Mrs. Crawford finished the chocolate you'd left."

No wonder the housekeeper had been sleeping so hard when she passed by the kitchen. Calvin had accidentally drugged her, as well.

"Actually, it worked out quite nicely. With Mrs. Crawford out of the way, you sound asleep and Garrett off to Destrehan, I had a grand opportunity to search the garden for clues to Elizabeth's whereabouts," he continued.

"So, you're confessing to everything," Liz said, wishing desperately for a tape recorder. It would make things so much easier.

"Facts are facts."

As long as history doesn't distort them. "Why did you do it? What could you hope to achieve with your pranks? Did you intend to drive your cousin back into your arms, where you imagined she belonged, by making her frightened of Garrett?"

"What difference can it make now?"

All the difference in the world—to me. "I want to know."

"Poor, love-smitten Elizabeth once told me passion justifies anything," he said ruthlessly. "Now, I believe she was correct. I have a passion for this plantation. Therefore, my actions are justified," he said, his twisted smile matching his twisted mind.

"You tried to dominate her after her marriage to Michael."

"She dominated me most of my life . . . right up until the War. And she would have continued to do so, if I had not come home a different man."

Marveling at his rationale, Liz eyed him warily. He was dangerous. The avarice growing inside his brain had eaten away at his compassion like a malignant tumor.

Thunder shook the ground, and Liz glanced up into the gray and forbidding sky. A storm brewed on the horizon. Almost as if the elements were in sympathy with her, they promised rain at any moment.

"You're sick, Calvin. You need help."

"I think in the future it is best if I work alone," he commented.

"I didn't mean *I* could help you. I meant you need professional advice." Psychotherapy. Or at least the nineteenth-century equivalent of it.

Calvin extracted his pocket watch from his waist-coat, opened the case and glanced, not at the time, but at the miniature within. Liz had seen him do it so many times in their brief acquaintance. She realized belatedly that Elizabeth's picture must act as a sort of talisman for him.

"I cannot allow you to leave this thicket," he said finally, solemnly. "Not alive." He replaced the watch in his waistcoat pocket and flipped aside the tail of his coat to withdraw Garrett's knife from his belt.

With a sharp exhalation of breath, Liz asked, "Where did you get that?"

"Where do you think?"

"From the garden. You took the knife and the snake and—"

"Not the snake," he said blandly. He took a step toward her. And then another. "An owl took care of that," he said, reaching with deceptive tenderness to brush a stray curl from her damp forehead.

Liz jerked away.

Dropping his hand to his side, Calvin chided her. "Am I such a villain that you cannot bear for me to touch you?"

Bent on more important matters, Liz ignored the perverse comment, thinking that her response to it would only incense him further.

"What do you plan to do with Garrett's knife?" she asked.

"Why, the logical thing, now that I have finally lured you away from him . . . or, more accurately, now that *Elizabeth* has. Would not she be appalled to know that in death she is cooperating with me better than in life?"

Maybe she does. Maybe that's why she can't rest.

"We must put an end to this, you know. I realized the moment I saw the knife I had my solution. Garrett is not a bad sort, but he is in my way. If you . . . expired . . . upon the blade of his knife . . ."

Now she knew what he'd meant by his reference to using the snake's misfortune to his advantage. It was all her fault. That day in the gazebo, when he'd given her the brooch, she'd confided in Calvin. She'd made him privy to her thoughts and fears when she'd told him she felt Garrett was trying to kill her. She'd even mentioned the ivory-handled knife.

A poignant thought came to her unbidden. "What about Garrett? What happens to him after I'm gone?" she asked, continuing to buy time.

"A trivial matter. I will simply explain to the sheriff that I walked in on a lovers' quarrel. Garrett will be implicated in Elizabeth's murder. And, *voilà*, my problems will be solved. I can purchase the plantation outright when it goes on the block."

Calvin was so calculating, so sure of himself. Her fear sickened Liz to the point that she felt she might actually throw up. She was dealing with a bona fide nut! Not only that, his plan must have worked somehow in the past. Otherwise, legend wouldn't have deemed him the good guy, and Garrett the bad.

Liz marveled at the way history had failed the Rowland family, how the future had distorted the truth until it was unrecognizable. And at the lies that had slithered down through the centuries unhindered and uncontested. Calvin had set Garrett up. Made *him* look like the bad guy, to her and to the outside world. His deviousness astounded her.

Clutching her queasy stomach, Liz began, "Perhaps we could come to some viable solution here, short of—"

"Murder," he finished for her, and Liz could see he wasn't about to relent. "There is no *viable* solution. You have provoked the worst from me by throwing in your lot with Garrett Rowland. That was Elizabeth's mistake. And yours. Neither one of you were . . . are . . . trustworthy," he said with a mirthless chuckle.

His words snatched at Liz's composure. She'd screwed up big-time. But she still had a chance, she reminded herself. She knew self-defense. If only he didn't seem so detached. So deadly.

Now that she knew the whole truth, fear overwhelmed her. She grappled with it.

She'd wanted to unravel the past. Now it was all laid out in a neat row, and she wasn't sure what to do with it. She didn't even know how to go about contacting the authorities. There were no phones. No police cruisers. No hostage-crisis squads.

Realizing that appealing to Calvin's saner side was useless, she forced a calmness into her voice—something the rest of her was far from feeling.

"I'm trustworthy," she said.

"No, you are not."

She had to do something! But what? Liz wondered desperately.

There was only one way to escape him. One place he dared not follow her. The river.

She'd rather contend with her wet, heavy clothes than with Calvin. It might be a vain endeavor, but at least she would go down fighting, Liz decided.

Clouds obliterated the sun, turning the water black as Liz set her chin defiantly and inched toward the banks of the Mississippi, careful not to make any overt movement that might alert him to her intentions.

He stalked her, and it soon dawned on Liz there was something different about Calvin's gait. He wasn't leaning on his gold-knobbed cane.

"You aren't limping," she said in surprise. "You're not lame after all."

He flashed her a cunning smile.

"The War left me with a vague limp on rainy days. I played upon it because an infirmity made matters easier," he said in a condescending tone. "Who would suppose a cripple could do the things I have done?"

"Who indeed?" Liz glanced behind her to see how much farther she must go before she reached safety.

It was a terrible mistake. Calvin's face contorted with rage, and he seized her wrist with a demonic strength that cut off her thoughts as efficiently as his fingers did the blood flowing to her hand.

"Little fool! Do not imagine you can escape me!" he grated harshly.

"I plan to do my best."

"A pity. You were such a pretty little thing, too. So like dear Elizabeth in appearance," he said. In the wink of an eye, he'd wrestled her arm behind her back and pressed the knife blade to her throat.

Her mind screaming all the things she could not say aloud, Liz prayed for a miracle as lightning brightened the bleak summer sky.

"I'm afraid I can't condone your dishonorable intentions, Calvin," an achingly familiar voice said.

Adrenaline pumping, Liz looked toward the riverbank. Garrett seemed to step from the refreshing gust of wind that rushed up to meet her off the surface of the water, and she was rewarded with one of his rare warm smiles as he strode toward them. Mrs. Crawford must have pointed him in the right direction—bless the ineffectual old dear!

Garrett's lips were set in a grim line, and his eyes were twin pools of purpose. His fists rested relaxed at his side, though his body seemed taut and ready for action. Liz noted the way his sable hair tumbled across his brow in soft waves. She longed to run her fingers through it. He'd never looked so good. So strong. So capable of running interference between her and Calvin.

Thank goodness!

"I had hoped this to be short and sweet," Calvin said to Garrett, so casually the three of them might have been sharing afternoon tea.

Garrett drawled, "I never have had a very high opinion of your cocksure demeanor, Calvin. No wonder you're only allowed to travel on the outer fringes of polite society."

As Garrett continued, Liz realized he was trying to rattle Calvin, to mentally gain the upper hand and as quickly as possible.

"I suspect that's the main reason you covet Rowland Plantation," he continued. "Not for love, but for the

power you think it will bring you . . . the respectabil-
ity."

Calvin's eyes narrowed to mere slits. "How long have
you been listening to our conversation?"

"Long enough to know your diabolical scheme will
never work."

"Oh, but I assure you it will," Calvin said, pressing
the ivory-handled blade more deeply into Liz's tender
flesh.

She tried not to jump at the keenness of the edge
against her windpipe.

Garrett took a deep breath and stepped purposefully
forward.

Calvin scowled at him. "Watch yourself, Garrett.
Not too close. You would not want this knife to . . . slip,
now would you?"

"You're mad, Trexler!"

"You are damned right I am! This plantation should
have been mine. If only Elizabeth had cooperated with
me. She must pay, Garrett."

"She already has—with her life," Garrett said
gravely.

"Can you not see? *That is not enough!* I want it
all . . . and I intend to have it. One way or the other."

"No matter that an innocent gets hurt in the process."

"She is not an innocent. And neither are you," Calvin argued above a drumlike roll of thunder.

An eerie hush fell over the thicket. The lull before the
approaching storm, Liz thought, realizing that no matter what Garrett said, Calvin would not be distracted
from his objective. Especially now that Garrett had finally acknowledged that she was not Elizabeth Rowland.

CHAPTER FIFTEEN

Garrett stared dubiously at his ivory-handled knife, gripped in Calvin's fingers.

"I do not think you are in any position to threaten me," Calvin said, and Liz wondered why she had never noticed before how short his chin was compared to Garrett's, how thin his lips, how close-set his eyes—all of which accentuated the weaknesses in his character.

How could she have ever perceived Calvin as her savior, when all the time Garrett had deserved the accolades?

"As I told you once before, I don't make idle threats," Garrett responded.

Liz watched the play of expressions on Garrett's face as a savage spark ignited his bluer-than-blue eyes. She welcomed the intense eye contact that warned her to brace herself, that he was about to do something drastic.

"It seems we have a standoff then," Calvin said.

Garrett ground out, "Not quite."

The day took on a surreal quality as, with his usual panache, Garrett gathered himself and dived at Calvin. He knocked the lesser man off balance as he shoved Liz out of harm's way.

The men grappled like winded boxers hugging each other for support, while Liz watched the knife flash between them as Calvin made repeated attempts to raise it against Garrett. Each time, Garrett managed to deflect its impact.

With a superhuman strength born of madness, Calvin thrust Garrett away. He backed off a moment, only to change his tactics.

He lowered his head like an enraged bull preparing to charge and lunged at Garrett, butting him in the stomach. The blow knocked Garrett to his knees. He reached out with both hands, snatched at Calvin's knees and hauled Calvin with him to the ground.

Then they were rolling together, twenty feet down the bank, toward the river. They stopped at the edge of the water. Liz squinted in their direction, her nerves as taut as bango strings as she watched one man go slack, and then the other shudder and rise to his feet.

"Now, sweetheart, it is your turn," Calvin said, a self-satisfied expression brightening his sallow countenance.

Her hand flew to her lips. "Nooooo!" Liz knew she should run, but she couldn't leave Garrett. He needed her, now more than ever.

"I am afraid your habit of playing me for a fool is at an end," Calvin said, gazing steadily toward Liz, then beyond her—toward something in the distance.

His face suddenly turned a dull, pasty white, and his eyes took on a glazed, faraway look.

"Do not come near me!" he cried, throwing up his arms as if to shield his face.

The hairs on the back of her neck bristling, Liz peeked over her shoulder. She saw only the thicket, and Elizabeth's wedding ring glinting through the leaves. Nothing more.

"By heaven, I said no!" Calvin screeched. He brandished the knife as if fending off an invisible foe, and

Liz could only assume he'd finally descended into the depths of complete insanity.

"You see them, do you not?" he asked Liz urgently.

She ignored Calvin, determined to get to Garrett.

"Them," he said, pointing with the knife toward the thicket.

"There's no one there, Calvin," she said, as calmly as she could, working her way around him.

Wide-eyed, he argued, "Yes there is!"

"Thin air, Calvin," Liz said, moving closer to Garrett with each step Calvin took toward the churning river.

"No. It is them, I tell you. Can you not *see* them?"

Even as Liz shook her head, the air was suddenly drenched with the overpoweringly sweet fragrance of Cherokee roses.

"Do not come near me! I...I... Do not touch me!" he shouted frantically. A look of abject horror in his eyes, Calvin stepped backward, past Garrett, down the bank to the river. "I am warning you! I will do something dreadful!"

Frozen in place, Liz watched in fascination as Calvin stumbled off the bank and splashed into the mighty Mississippi. He floundered in the water as the current dragged him out over his head.

Calvin bobbed twice, struggling with something only he could see, and then vanished completely. As if ghostly hands held him underneath the surface of the water, Liz thought.

"What in the hell happened?" Garrett asked, shattering the spell.

Liz watched him struggle to his feet, dusting off the dry grasses that clung to his pants. She scrambled the rest of the way down the bank to him. The sky shuddered with electrical current as Liz tumbled into Garrett's embrace without reservation. She felt the pulse in her temple pounding against his lips as he hugged her close.

Liz sighed. "I'm not sure—it all happened so fast. It was crazy. One minute he was coming toward me, and the next—"

"I know. I saw it too," Garrett said.

"Could it have been Elizabeth?"

"I don't know. I had the strangest sensation. It was almost as if—" He broke off a moment, then continued. "I could have sworn I heard Michael's voice."

"Maybe it was him all along, instead of Elizabeth. Trying to warn me. To protect me from her killer," she said softly.

They both stared out across the water.

"I don't suppose we'll ever know for sure," she added.

"Are you going to be all right?" he asked finally, with an odd breathlessness.

"I am now," she said as she slipped her arms around his back and hugged him tightly, feeling the moistness almost immediately. At first she thought it was perspiration generated by the fight. But she soon realized it was far too tacky for that.

Liz disengaged her arms and turned Garrett so that she could view the spot between his shoulder blades. The gauzy material of his aubergine shirt was saturated with blood.

"God in heaven, I should have known it! What has Calvin done to you? Why didn't you say something?" she cried, staring at the multiple slashes in his shirt.

Nothing made sense. And then everything did.

As the storm heaved around them, Liz made a conscious effort to modulate her voice. "We have to get you to the house, Garrett."

"I'm not sure I can make it," he said with a grim smile.

Frantic now, Liz adjusted her shoulder beneath Garrett's while he draped his arm around her neck. "Here, lean on me. I'll carry you if I have to," she said.

They made it as far as the gazebo before Garrett's strength gave out entirely. Liz's exhaustion ran a close second.

"I...have to...stop. To...rest," he rasped. The sound reminded Liz of bubbles blown through a straw into a soda glass.

"Don't stop now," she pleaded. "We're almost there. Just a little bit farther, I promise. You can make it. I know you can," she said, flashing him an encouraging smile. But as she watched his face, her smile fragmented into a million jagged shards of doubt.

"No," he said. It was then that Liz noticed the blood seeping from the corner of his mouth.

Her first thoughts were that his ribs were broken and he had punctured a lung. She dabbed at the crimson blood with a fingertip.

"Maybe we should rest a minute after all," she said. She tried to control the tremor in her voice but she could not. Desperation barreled through her like a runaway freight train.

Together, they eased down on the seat in the gazebo. He grabbed her hand and pulled her tightly against his side.

"There's something I have to tell you," he said. His voice came now as no more than a wheezing rattle in his throat, and Liz found herself leaning toward him to comprehend his words.

"Save your breath," she said, her own voice catching on a sob as tears gathered in her eyes.

"I must..." He struggled, clutching convulsively at her hand as his face paled to an ashen gray that terrified Liz.

"*Please* don't try to talk now," Liz said, breathing each agonizing breath with him. "We have all the time in the world to—" *Past, present, and future.*

He grimaced and his fingers tightened upon hers. "You must...hear it...from my lips...before it's too...late. I've come to the conclusion...we're inextricably linked. And I...love you, Liz Hayden...with all my heart."

Sniffing, she fought back the tears.

"What do...you have to...say to that?" he asked with a weak smile, a bit of the old devilment shining through his pain.

"Soul mates," Liz mused out loud. She'd never believed in it before. She did now. "I've never heard anything so terrific," she whispered above her tears.

"That's not what...I'm asking you," he said.

She knew what he wanted. Now that she'd broken through the wall of indifference Garrett used to protect himself, he expected reciprocation on her part. She simply couldn't bring herself to say it. It was as if expectation of her response were the only thing holding him here with her. And she wasn't ready to let him go— would never be ready.

"Say it," he rasped, entwining his fingers with hers and squeezing her hand almost cruelly.

"Oh, Garrett," she said softly. Subconsciously consigning his face, his eyes, his touch, to memory.

"Say it." He fought to form the words coherently, yet ended by merely mouthing them. But Liz understood.

"I love you, too... and I always will," she said finally, committing herself to him emotionally, as she had earlier committed herself physically. Because she knew she was losing him.

With a serene smile gracing his lips, he reached up and brushed a tear from her cheek with the back of his hand.

"For... always," he managed.

The air fell still. As if nature were blessing them with a moment of silence in honor of their love. And then the life force flowed from him, Garrett's eyes fluttering closed as he slumped against her.

Liz blanched. "Garrett?"

She shook him gently. He didn't respond.

"Garrett!" She shook him more roughly, willing him to answer her. Still he failed to respond.

"Oh, dear God, no!" she exclaimed, refusing to believe he'd been mortally wounded. "Garrett!" The tears fell freely now, streaming down her face to stain his deep purple shirt.

"Please," she pleaded loudly, her voice bordering on anger. And then, more softly, she coaxed, "Please. Open your eyes, darling. *Open your eyes.*"

Garrett's eyes remained closed, his lashes fanning his cheeks as if he merely slept.

Liz slowly lowered a trembling hand to his chest. She felt no telltale rise and fall. Desperate, she placed her ear to his heart. She could detect no beat.

Liz's world reeled as her heart plummeted to her knees and a stone-cold sensation settled in her chest. She heard a strange keening. It took her a moment to realize it was her own voice.

Easing Garrett gently down across the seat, Liz staggered to her feet. She had to get help, reach the house and send Mrs. Crawford to New Orleans for Dr. Breninger! If only there were a telephone, an ambulance, paramedics. But there was no immediate help. Nothing!

The differences in their worlds had never seemed so graphic.

Her heartbeat accelerated like a jackhammer thrumming in her breast as determination set in.

''I'll find help somewhere,'' she promised aloud. She wrenched her cloak from her shoulders and covered Garrett's chest with the flowing material, refusing to believe the obvious. Refusing to let him go.

Adrenaline pumping, Liz hurtled down the gazebo steps, stumbling through the garden, past the blossoming rosebushes bursting with color and the cheerful chinaberry trees, the Spanish daggers and the evergreen holly. Gathering her skirts, she bunched the indigo fabric above her knees and ran until her breath rushed from her lips in short gasps and her cheeks burned with the heat of the blood coursing through them.

Until a violent streak of lightning cleaved the dark sky, illuminating it with an almost spectral incandescence that nearly blinded Liz.

By that time, shock had carried her as far as the Rowland family vault.

Forced to take a breather, she sheltered beneath the engraved arch, gazing out across the oak alley toward the plantation house. She had to get help for Garrett!

As if in answer, the weather worsened.

Like a dog with its fangs bared, stinging raindrops drove her deeper beneath the shelter, toward the tomb's doorjamb. Shaken, she steepled her fingertips against the cool marble door to steady herself and gazed out into a world hazed by the gray sheets of water cascading from the sky like a waterfall.

She instantly realized she'd made a grave error. Touching the door felt the way she imagined sticking a metal-handled screwdriver into an electric socket would. The white-hot energy surged through her fingertips, up her arms and throughout her body, setting her senses afire. The sensation terrified Liz with its familiarity.

"You can't do this! It isn't fair! I won't let you," she railed as an angry lightning bolt zigzagged directly above the tomb. The walls of the vault trembled.

Liz wildly defied fate, willing herself to remain in the past with Garrett. Resisting the future with a strength born of desperation.

But she was no match for fate's superior willpower. Inch by inch, her strength drained from her body. The past grew dimmer. And, with the dimness, her hold on the past weakened.

Liz defiantly tilted her chin toward the somber sky. Her eyes blazed with raw determination. "I won't go! You can't make me!" she wailed.

But her cries were useless.

She felt herself being torn from the past as easily as a petal might be plucked from a blossom. The gray world blurred like the muted colors of an impressionist painting. Everything became progressively more indistinct, even as Liz struggled to hang on to the past's clarity.

"*Please,*" she whispered. She slid to her knees in prayerful supplication. "I...don't...want...to... lose...him."

For a spit second, Liz thought she heard a woman sobbing as if her heart would break. It was a keening sound that superseded the rain pelting the tomb's roof like marbles spilling from a grab bag.

And then the voice was swallowed by a moment of silence, softened only by the subtle fragrance of roses.

EPILOGUE

Dazed, Liz huddled beneath the wisteria-shadowed inscription spanning the tomb's warped doorway and gazed out across the rainwashed landscape, toward her umbrella, snagged on the power lines bordering the service road, the oak sprawled across the iron gate and, finally, the quarter-mile alley that led to the rear entrance of Rowland Plantation.

She'd felt strong, vibrant and determined only moments ago.

Now, weak with shock and painfully alone, Liz wandered from the family vault in search of a garden, a gazebo, and a man who no longer existed. Garrett Rowland—last descendant of the Rowland dynasty, black sheep, libertine and professional riverboat gambler—had sacrificed his life for her freedom.

It was a harsh realization, the irony of which was not wasted on Liz. She'd never known such despair and heartache.

Why had time cast her into the past? She'd done no one any good, not really. Oh, she'd solved the age-old mystery of Elizabeth Rowland's murder, but in doing so she'd lost Garrett.

Liz hugged herself while tears streamed unheeded down her cheeks. How could fate be so damned cruel? So thankless? How was she supposed to cope without the man she loved? She could still feel the indelible touch of his lips against her temple, see the question in his eyes as he committed himself to her and waited for her to reciprocate.

Garrett had left an imprint on her spirit that nothing and no one could erase, Liz thought, pausing in the middle of the alley to listen.

She heard something. A voice. A man's voice, to be exact, calling her name. She couldn't be sure, but it sounded like—

Suddenly filled with renewed energy, Liz sprinted toward the indistinct figure striding from the plantation house to meet her. As he drew nearer, she slowed, too terrified to breath, to think, to hope against hope that she wasn't dreaming.

"Liz Hayden?" he asked tentatively, in the deep, rich voice she'd come to appreciate.

Her breath tripped over a joyous sob as her world vividly refocused itself.

Not wanting to look him dead in the eye and be disappointed, Liz started with his leather running shoes and worked her way up. Past his muscular thighs, encased in snug-fitting faded jeans, to the aubergine silk shirt open at the throat, and the broadcloth sports coat slung carelessly over his shoulder. Her gaze scanned higher. His hair was sable and wavy and neatly styled in a contemporary fashion. She noted that he wore wire-rimmed glasses, though she could see the sparkle of his heart-stopping cerulean eyes through the lenses.

He represented the most scrumptious sight she'd ever seen. Liz drank him in like sweet, cool water on a long, hot day.

"How did you get here?" she rasped finally, trying to sort out the miracle in her mind.

With a puzzled frown, he said, "By car. I'm Garth Randall, the new curator. I just arrived from Baton Rouge. I stopped to take a peek at the estate while things were quiet. The other tour guides seemed worried—they said you went to lock up and must have gotten caught in a pretty severe storm. I volunteered to search the grounds for you."

Still slightly muddled, Liz heard only bits and pieces of his explanation. Garth sounded so much like Garrett. And they had the same last initial. Coincidence? Or déjà vu? Or had fate, at the eleventh hour, decided to be merciful?

"Are you all right?" he asked.

"I'm...uh...I think so," she managed. Her tongue felt like a glob of peanut butter stuck to the roof of her mouth. "I know it sounds...crazy, but I have the strangest feeling I know you from...somewhere," she stammered.

He gazed at her lips. Her hair. Pensively studied her eyes. Then he smiled wryly, and Liz saw the question coming by the endearing arch of his brow even before he asked, "Have we met before?"

Liz felt her insides melt. "Once," she whispered huskily.

He frowned. "Do you mind telling me when? I can't seem to remember."

It was a line she'd used often enough in the past, Liz thought. She actually laughed out loud.

"It was a long, long time ago," she said with a bittersweet smile. Decades ago.

"I knew it," he said on a softly released sigh. "For a second there, when you were walking down the oak alley toward me, it was like..." He struggled for an appropriate description. "I'm not sure I know how to put this."

"Like a sort of spiritual recognition," Liz supplied.

"Yes. And when you laughed just now, the words *soul mates* popped into my head. What do you have to say to that?"

Breath catching in her throat, Liz responded, "I've never heard anything so terrific."

The past had been torn from her. Yet, through it, she'd discovered her destiny.

Garth paused for an instant, a heartbeat, the measure of a sigh. Then he spread his arms wide.

Liz glided into his embrace as naturally as a homing pigeon returning to its nest. He draped his coat around her shoulders, and then, slowly but surely, wrapped his arms tightly around her.

"I don't know how to explain the way I'm feeling right now," he whispered against her ear.

"There's plenty of time for explanations," she said as the sun broke through the clouds, chasing away the shadows. "All the time in the world."

* * * * *

SILHOUETTE Shadows®

Join award-winning author Rachel Lee as

CONARD COUNTY explores the dark side of love....

Rachel Lee will tingle your senses in August when she visits the dark side of love in her latest Conard County title, **THUNDER MOUNTAIN, SS #37.**

For years, Gray Cloud had guarded his beloved Thunder Mountain, protecting its secrets and mystical powers from human exploitation. Then came Mercy Kendrick.... But someone—or something—wanted her dead. Alone with the tempestuous forces of nature, Mercy turned to Gray Cloud, only to find a storm of a very different kind raging in his eyes. Look for their terrifying tale, only from Silhouette Shadows.

Fifty red-blooded, white-hot, true-blue hunks
from every State in the Union!

Look for MEN MADE IN AMERICA! Written by some of
our most popular authors, these stories feature fifty of
the strongest, sexiest men, each from a different state in
the union!

Two titles available every other month at your favorite
retail outlet.

In May, look for:

KISS YESTERDAY GOODBYE by Leigh Michaels (Iowa)
A TIME TO KEEP by Curtiss Ann Matlock (Kansas)

In June, look for:

ONE PALE, FAWN GLOVE by Linda Shaw (Kentucky)
BAYOU MIDNIGHT by Emilie Richards (Louisiana)

You won't be able to resist MEN MADE IN AMERICA!

Stories that capture living and loving beneath the Big Sky, where legends live on...and the mystery is just beginning.

Watch for the sizzling debut of
MONTANA MAVERICKS in August with

ROGUE STALLION

by Diana Palmer

A powerful tale of simmering desire and mystery!

And don't miss a minute of the loving as the mystery continues with:

THE WIDOW AND THE RODEO MAN
by Jackie Merritt (September)
SLEEPING WITH THE ENEMY
by Myrna Temte (October)
THE ONCE AND FUTURE WIFE
by Laurie Paige (November)
THE RANCHER TAKES A WIFE
by Jackie Merritt (December)
and many more of your favorite authors!

Only from **Silhouette®**

where passion lives.

MAV1

Silhouette Books
is proud to present
our best authors, their best books...
and the best in your reading pleasure!

Throughout 1994, look for exciting books
by these top names in contemporary
romance:

DIANA PALMER
Enamored in August

HEATHER GRAHAM POZZESSERE
The Game of Love in August

FERN MICHAELS
Beyond Tomorrow in August

NORA ROBERTS
The Last Honest Woman in September

LINDA LAEL MILLER
Snowflakes on the Sea in September

**When it comes to passion,
we wrote the book.**

Silhouette®
™

Rugged and lean...and the best-looking,
sweetest-talking men to be found in the
entire Lone Star state!

In July 1994, Silhouette is very proud to bring you
Diana Palmer's first three LONG, TALL TEXANS.
CALHOUN, JUSTIN and TYLER—the three cowboys
who started the legend. Now they're back by popular
demand in one classic volume—and they're ready to
lasso your heart! Beautifully repackaged for this
special event, this collection is sure to be a
longtime keepsake!

"Diana Palmer makes a reader want to find a Texan
of her own to love!"   —*Affaire de Coeur*

**LONG, TALL TEXANS—the first three—
reunited in this special roundup!**

**Available in July,
wherever Silhouette books are sold.**

LTT